## *"Kiss me, Julienne, or let me kiss you."*

Nick ground out the words in a voice that held nothing back. He hungered with an intensity he'd never known before. Her combination of bold temptress with hints of shy innocence captivated him.

The first taste of her wet velvet mouth shot his blood south in a painful rush. Her kiss was inquisitive, a cautious exploration. He let her take the lead, though he ached to deepen their kiss, to drive his tongue into her mouth and test the limits of her passion.

She rewarded his restraint, darting her tongue across his bottom lip. A light touch, a taste really, but there was an intimacy that opened the floodgates. Suddenly her grip tightened and her mouth made demands of him that stole his breath.

Julienne tested his control, lit fires inside him that he knew wouldn't be doused until he experienced this woman naked with her hair tumbling all around them.

He eased back, staring intently into her eyes so there would be no question about his meaning.

"Can you imagine my hands on you, Julienne? Let me touch you. Let me pleasure you."

ROMANCE

# Blaze™

Dear Reader,

More often than not, my family and friends jet around the globe while I stay home to check the mailbox for postcards. But I do occasionally venture into the world. One trip I'm very familiar with is the one that leads north along the eastern seaboard. My sister Kimberly and I never thought twice about hopping in the car and heading to our childhood home in New York, and whenever we did, we'd always find some reason to detour through Savannah, Georgia, just to experience the charm and beauty of this grand Southern city.

Julienne Blake wants to experience something in Savannah, too—passion. With the help of self-hypnosis, she lets her hair down and takes a walk on the wild side, a walk that leads her straight into Nick Fairfax's arms. Nick signed on only to renovate Savannah's erotic theater, but one night on the empty stage with this naughty girl convinces him he'll never be content until he knows all her secrets.

Blaze is the place to explore red-hot romance, and I'm excited to write for a series that excels in steamy happily-ever-afters. I hope *About That Night...* brings you to happily-ever-after, too. Let me know. Drop me a line in care of Harlequin Books, 225 Duncan Mill Road, Don Mills, Ontario M3B 3K9, Canada, or visit my Web site at www.jeanielondon.com.

Very truly yours,

*Jeanie London*

P.S.—Don't forget to check out www.tryblaze.com!

## Books by Jeanie London

HARLEQUIN BLAZE
28—SECRET GAMES
42—ONE-NIGHT MAN

# ABOUT THAT NIGHT...

*Jeanie London*

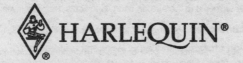

TORONTO • NEW YORK • LONDON
AMSTERDAM • PARIS • SYDNEY • HAMBURG
STOCKHOLM • ATHENS • TOKYO • MILAN • MADRID
PRAGUE • WARSAW • BUDAPEST • AUCKLAND

To Ann Josephson, for your skill,
your friendship and all those spicy brainstorming sessions
that never fail to make our husbands blush.

And special thanks to Cheryl Mansfield, for sharing your
architectural expertise and writer's sight.

ISBN 0-373-79057-0

ABOUT THAT NIGHT...

Copyright © 2002 by Jeanie LeGendre.

Visit us at www.eHarlequin.com

**Printed in U.S.A.**

# *Prologue*

*Twenty-one days ago.*

*NAUGHTY GIRLS feel good about feeling naughty.*

Julienne Blake silently read the phrase from the open book, then again, before rallying the courage to say it aloud.

"Naughty girls feel good about feeling naughty." The words rolled off her tongue, unfamiliar and shockingly bold in her quiet living room. On the walls hung photographs of her youth spent traveling with her bachelor great uncle to renovate historically significant buildings all over the world.

Thankfully, Uncle Thad wasn't in the room to hear her read the words again. Despite being seriously out of his element, he'd tried his level best to rear his orphaned great-niece as a good girl after awakening one morning to find her on his doorstep.

"Naughty girls feel good about feeling naughty."

There, she had it. Her voice sounded natural, relaxed. A feat that had required a significant amount of practice, given that Julienne had spent her entire adult life studiously avoiding concepts like *feeling good* and *feeling naughty*. These weren't concepts any good girl should dwell on, not when there were other, more productive uses for her time, like focusing on an education and a career.

Julienne had been the ultimate good girl, a fact she'd been proud of—until six months ago when a broken engagement had made her question whether there was more to life than living up to other people's expectations and always doing the right thing. Especially after her ex-fiancé had placed the blame for their breakup on her, complaining she lacked fire and passion.

Snapping the book shut, she set *The Naughty Handbook of Naughty Girl Sex* on the end table and leaned back in her favorite chair, a leather recliner where she normally spent nights pouring over her students' papers. Closing her eyes, she let the message filter through her.

*Naughty girls feel good about feeling naughty.*

Julienne planned to feel naughty and feel good about it. She'd just turned thirty, a turning point for finally realizing she should enjoy life. After spending five years with Ethan…she still couldn't believe she'd spent five years with Ethan simply because it had seemed like the right thing to do.

*Come on, girl. Whoever said a woman had to finish college, establish herself in a career and then settle down to get married? When do you get to have fun?*

The voice in her head asked valid questions. Although she'd spent a lot of time soul-searching since the breakup, Julienne didn't have any answers. Not even an answer for why life without Ethan seemed as tepid as life with him had been.

"Why are you sitting here in the dark, Julienne?" Uncle Thad asked. "Are you feeling all right?"

Julienne opened her eyes to find her uncle silhouetted beneath the archway that led to the hall. Snatching *The Naughty Handbook* from the end table, she flipped the cover down on her lap and gazed at him, an always-welcomed sight. His red apple cheeks and neat white beard lent him a rather Santa Clausish air that always made her think of Christmas. Perhaps because he'd come into her life just like

Santa Claus down a chimney, generously devoting his golden years to rearing her.

"I'm fine, thanks," she assured him. "Just a little tired."

"You should get to bed then." He strode into the room and sat in the recliner opposite hers, apparently not noticing her book. "Unless you're up for a documentary on the History Channel. The show will feature that Philadelphia courthouse Dr. Fairfax renovated a few years back. Since he's coming to town soon to start work on the Risqué Theatre, I thought I'd watch the program. Starts in a few minutes."

Julienne usually enjoyed watching programs that featured the work of this well-known preservation architect. With citations from more than three dozen historic organizations and an appointment to the President's Advisory Council for Historic Preservation, Dr. Nicholas Fairfax was the noted authority in her area of expertise.

But tonight the very idea of TV seemed so symbolic of her staid lifestyle that not even watching the much-admired Nicholas Fairfax could silence Ethan's unkind comments about fire and passion echoing in her head.

*It's always the same thing, Julienne. If I didn't suggest get-togethers with our university colleagues, you'd have us at home every night watching urban renewal shows with your uncle.*

Though she hadn't been that gung ho about Ethan's recreation of choice—especially since get-togethers with their colleagues usually degenerated into long-winded debates on the merits of hypnotherapy in today's societal climate—she couldn't argue his point.

Here it was Saturday night and instead of visiting with friends or enjoying one of the many entertainments Savannah offered, she sat at home, contemplating a night *watching* a very handsome preservation architect prop up rotting joists on TV.

Sheesh. It had taken her weeks to come up with a radical solution to her good-girl problem, a solution she couldn't implement with her uncle sitting a mere foot away.

Flipping down the recliner footrest, Julienne tucked her book under her arm. "I'll pass on the documentary tonight, and take your suggestion about getting a good night's sleep." She stood, circled his chair and kissed her uncle's cheek. "See you in the morning."

"Sleep well, my dear." Smiling absently, he reached for the remote control on the end table.

Julienne headed upstairs, hoping she could find a balance between the "good" girl Uncle Thad had raised, and the woman who needed to know she possessed at least a spark of fire. She didn't always have to do things the right way. Ethan had been *right* and look where he'd gotten her.

A professor of hypnotherapy at the University of Savannah, Dr. Ethan Whiteside had been stable. He'd also been upwardly mobile, financially secure and attractive. But he hadn't been very aware or supportive of her needs.

After graduating with her doctorate in historical preservation at the unusually ripe young age of twenty-five, Julienne had wanted to go into the field and work on a rehabilitation project to flex her hard-earned skills. She'd been reared in the field with Uncle Thad, right up until he'd retired to an academic position at the university in time for her to start college. She loved to travel and going into the field again before marriage had sounded like a good...okay, a *fun* thing to do.

But Ethan had wanted a wife on staff at the university to fulfill his dream of being part of an academic power couple. He'd insisted she be groomed to take Uncle Thad's place at retirement. Julienne had acquiesced. She told herself she should spend as much time as possible with her aging uncle—which she had, and that she couldn't expect to have things go her way all the time—which they hadn't.

Although she loved her job and found satisfaction teaching her students, she couldn't overlook that her relationship with Ethan had always been focused on *his* desires and *his* goals. For some reason she still couldn't quite put her finger on, she'd accepted that. After all, no relationship could be perfect.

*It doesn't have to be perfect, girl, but it should be fulfilling,* that voice in her head said. *You haven't been living, you've been existing. Time to shake things up.*

Julienne headed into her bedroom and quietly closed the door behind her. She planned to start having fun. She was through with existing, done with living up to other people's expectations. No more tepid emotions. And absolutely no more tepid sex ever again.

Time to shake off apathy and enjoy life.

Glancing in the mirror above her dresser, she noticed pale cheeks where her blush had faded away, the once-neat French braid so at odds with the naughty girl image in her head.

"You can do this," she told her reflection. "You can put aside your good-girl notions. You can take charge of your life and explore your sensuality."

Curiously enough, the ex-fiancé and hypnotherapist, had unwittingly provided the key to shedding her inhibitions with a nifty form of conditioning called self-hypnosis.

*Hypnotherapy can be a powerful tool, Julienne. It uses autosuggestion, imagery and imagination to improve different aspects of your personality. I can show you a few techniques.*

She didn't want Ethan to show her any techniques, nor did she desire his help in deciding which aspects of her personality needed improving. And if she hadn't gotten the general idea about hypnotherapy after listening to him talk about his work for the past five years, she had access to the university library and all his treatises on the subject.

"Naughty girls feel good about feeling naughty," she chanted her key phrase, smiling when the words slipped from her lips without making her blush.

She breathed deeply and tried again. "Naughty girls feel good about feeling naughty."

Twenty-one days of mastering suggestibility techniques, of chanting key phrases, of visualizing herself as a naughty girl, would create a lasting subconscious impression that she could be the type of woman who could catch a hot-blooded man's attention.

And when she'd convinced herself she did have a spark of passion inside...Julienne knew the perfect hot-blooded man to test her skills on.

# 1

*Today*

After taking a deep breath to steel her nerves for what was possibly the most outrageous—and potentially disastrous—decision she'd ever made, Julienne pushed through the etched-glass front door of Casa de Ramón, plunging herself into a frenetic world of bright lights, whirring blow dryers and pungent chemical smells.

Chic Art Deco furnishings incorporated the hydraulic chairs, rows of shampoo bowls and otherworldly hood dryers in an upscale salon that brought to mind images of grooming beautiful people who didn't mind looking at themselves in walls and walls of mirrors.

Julienne hoped she could cultivate that particular skill, because when she caught sight of herself walking into the reception area, French-braided hair and dove-gray business suit unassuming amid the surrounding grandeur, she could only pray Ramón was up for a challenge.

*Come on, girl. Think beautiful. Naughty girls come in all shapes and sizes.*

"Jules, sweetheart." Owner and stylist extraordinaire, Ramón, hurried down the aisle between the stylists' booths, long black overcoat whipping out behind him like Batman's cape. "I saw you on my book and I'm marked off for hours. Tell me, tell me. What are we doing today?"

Clients peered up from beneath wet bangs and foil strips

that made their heads resemble shiny antennae. Now that she had everyone's undivided attention…

*Naughty girls enjoy being noticed.*

"We're doing something different today," she said, not quite as enthusiastically as someone who enjoyed being noticed might say it, but reasonably self-possessed all the same.

"Not the usual 'just put a new line in the bottom but don't take off much length'?" Ramón didn't give her a chance to reply as he waved at the receptionist, a beautiful young girl who sat behind a desk, completely unflustered by her boss's theatrics. "Don't put any calls through. And for God's sake don't let anyone back to bother us. I don't care if Elvis himself shows up crooning. Jules and I have business."

With that he latched a long-fingered hand around her upper arm and practically frog-marched her back to his semi-private station past the rows of booths where his stylists waved, smiled and eyed her with interest.

"What is it, Jules? You finally want some shape in this mop? Or curl?"

Julienne allowed herself to be guided into the hydraulic chair and spun to face another unforgiving mirror with such speed her already fluttering stomach gave a decided lurch.

"No curl."

"Color?" A tall, lean man, Ramón bent over her and peered myopically at her reflection in the mirror. "Don't tell me you found a gray."

"No. You don't see any, do you?"

He surveyed the top of her head. "No grays. So why are you finally letting me do something to bring out the beauty of this exquisite color God gave you?"

*Naughty girls look the part.*

"I just want something different."

"Be more specific, please."

"I'm not exactly sure what," she admitted. "That's why I'm placing myself in your capable hands. I want a new look."

Julienne expected exultation, or enthusiasm at the very least. After all, Ramón had been after her for the entire five years of their acquaintance to do something…*anything* with her hair.

But he only eyed her skeptically above the slices of black eyeglass frames resting low on his nose.

"How new?"

"*New*-new. Just not anything too short or too crazy."

He circled her slowly, assessing, reminding her of Uncle Thad whenever he stepped inside an old building to assess the construction of walls and decorative moldings for restoration.

"What prompted this sudden need for a new you?"

"I just turned thirty."

"Okay, a milestone birthday. What else?"

"What do you mean 'what else'?"

He frowned.

"I'm just ready for a change." She wasn't about to tell him the truth.

"Does this sudden inspiration have anything to do with Dr. Whiteside?"

"Ramón, what kind of question is that?"

"A personal one I need an answer to, before I'll touch my scissors to this mop you've been growing forever." He sniffed haughtily. "Once I cut into the length, it'll take decades to grow back out if you don't like it. I don't have the patience to listen to you sob the whole time."

"Oh."

She could understand caution. She'd lived a whole life filled with it. And she really had no reason to be uncomfortable about fessing up to Ramón. He'd been styling her hair ever since Ethan had insisted she make an appointment with *his* stylist. Besides...

*Naughty girls feel good about feeling naughty.*

"Okay." She took a deep breath. "Ethan does factor in a little. We called off our engagement six months ago and I'm ready to move on with my life. I'm ready to head in a new direction."

Curiosity finally sparked in Ramón's expression, and he leaned forward to rest his elbows on the back of the chair, his face so close she could smell the spicy scent of his aftershave mingling with powerful traces of permanent wave solution from an earlier client. "A new direction, hmm? How new?"

"*New*-new. I plan to enjoy myself."

*There, you said it and you didn't even blush. See, girl, twenty-one days of self-hypnosis are paying off.*

"You're booked in for the whole day," Ramón said. "You want more than just a new hairstyle, don't you?"

She nodded.

"Facial, makeup and image consultation? The works?"

She nodded again.

Ramón bolted upright as if he'd been shot from a gun, making Julienne jump in the chair.

"Celeste, round up the troops," he bellowed toward the front of the salon. "Jules'll be leaving here a new woman."

*A new woman! That's exactly what you want to be. Now sit back and enjoy the transformation.*

Julienne didn't have a chance to sit back and enjoy anything before being herded into a dressing room, instructed to strip out of her suit and don a black salon overcoat.

The troops arrived. Kathy the skincare specialist and makeup artist. Stephanie with the body spa. Judith, the salon's colorist, though Ramón assured her he'd be doing her color himself. She already knew Katriona, the six-foot-two manicurist, who dripped gold spandex and flaunted her cake makeup and razor-stubbled cheeks proudly.

"Well, hey, sister," she said. "What's this Ramón said about real nails? Tell me you're finally giving up that modish farmhand look you've been sporting since the dawn of time."

To Katriona *real* nails meant acrylic and lots of it, along with sparkly gems, traffic-stopping colors and gold jewelry that resembled Barbie-doll sized nose rings.

"Just something feminine for tonight. I can't wear them too long or I won't be able to work. I've got my interns taking samples at a one hundred and thirty-six-year-old church this week."

"Fascinating, I'm sure," Katriona said in a decidedly bored drawl. "But what's happening tonight? Something more lively than scraping paint chips off rotting floorboards, I hope."

"The closing performance at the Risqué Theatre."

"The Risqué?" Ramón asked, his fingers coming to a sudden halt in her braid. "You're joking."

"No," she said, unsure why he was so surprised. "The Risqué Theatre is a building of architectural and historical significance. I've been there lots of times."

"With your uncle?"

The subject matter performed at the Risqué was on the racy side for her sweet, but whole-other-generation uncle. "Ah, no."

"I know you didn't go with Dr. Whiteside." Ramón frowned. "I can't imagine him stepping foot inside the place no matter how architecturally or historically significant it is. The Risqué is an *erotic* theater, Jules. I've seen performances there that made my hair curl."

A feat in itself, given that as far as she could tell his

perfectly coiffed hair looked as smooth as a pin. While Julienne had never attended any hair-curling performances herself, she'd seen some very provocative ones. "Well, um, I usually go by myself."

Ramón relinquished his grip on her braid and motioned to his crew with a smug smile. "Jules, sweetheart, that man was the root of all your troubles. I am so happy you've finally broken free. Once we get you a new look, we're going to have to work on getting you a new guy."

Julienne had a new guy in mind, but she didn't intend to share that with Ramón and company. Which was just as well since Ramón began conferring with his crew again in a rush of instructions that made her head spin.

They circled her. They freed her almost waist-length hair from its braid. They held swatches to her cheeks and discussed color choices. They generally consulted on her new look.

Ramón reassured her with a smile but Julienne mentally chanted her key phrases and breathed like she'd sprinted a quick mile by the time they'd arrived back at his station. He issued orders like a drill sergeant to an assistant, who opened tubes of haircolor and mixed various thick pastes in bowls.

"I'm going to do a little highlighting and lowlighting to frame your face."

She wasn't sure what lowlighting was, but she knew highlighting well enough to ask, "You're not making me blond, are you?"

"Perish the thought." He rolled his eyes. "You're a natural auburn, Jules. Way too red to ever lift you through all the brass. And I don't do brassy blondes, thank you. Think subtle strands of deeper and lighter red woven around your face. Think naturally enhancing this incredible color. Think everyone who sees you will ask what genius did your hair and you'll give her one of my cards." He winked and reached for a thin sheet of foil. "I'll make sure Celeste sends you home with a stack."

Julienne laughed, all nervousness about her hair fading away, but in its wake came an unsettling thought. "Ramón, does Ethan still get his hair cut here?"

"Mmm, hmm," he replied around the long-tailed comb he currently clamped between pursed lips.

Julienne took that to mean yes. "You'd never... I mean, you wouldn't repeat anything we discussed—"

He flipped the comb out of his mouth and speared it into her hair with a ruthlessness that made her wince. "I'm quieter than your confessor. Trust me. Just because I take the man's money doesn't mean I like him. It's business, and he's a good tipper, especially at Christmas. Did you know he books his next appointment before he even walks out the door?"

"Organization was always one of his strengths."

"I'm all for a little chaos myself, but I'm glad he referred you to me. I'm tremendously fond of you, and Uncle Thad. I knew one day you'd come to your senses...."

Julienne wasn't exactly sure dabbling in self-hypnosis and letting Ramón renovate her from the ground up could be classified as sensible, but she'd spent the past twenty-one days preparing to put her plan into action. Tonight was the big night, her debut as a woman daring, beautiful and confident enough to catch a hot-blooded man's attention.

*The Naughty Handbook* called it starting off with a bang, jumping feetfirst into her future as a woman who enjoyed her sensuality and made no apologies for it. A healthy sexual appetite was a natural, healthy thing.

*Naughty girls have the courage to explore their desires.*

But no matter how often she chanted key phrases and practiced suggestibility techniques, Julienne knew she could never *start off with a bang* by flirting with a total stranger. Uncle Thad was a very noble gentleman from another era and Julienne had lived with him since she'd been barely six years old. He'd raised her to be a moral, upstanding, *good* girl, and while she appreciated his efforts in shaping the woman she'd become, she had some work to do putting *good* into perspective.

She'd flirt tonight, but within comfortable parameters. Nicholas Fairfax wasn't a stranger. Not exactly. Though she'd never met the man, she'd read every article and treatise he'd ever written. She'd studied his work so much that she could identify his subtle, yet aggressive technique on any building at a glance. She knew his credentials as a nationally recognized expert in the historic preservation field, every board he'd ever served on—and he'd served on many—and every lecture he'd ever given.

But she hadn't known a thing about his personal life until his appointment last year to the President's Advisory Council, a federal agency that oversaw and advised on all national historic preservation matters.

His presidential appointment had placed him under the media's scrutiny and she'd learned that the founder of the renowned Architectural Design Firm, one of the largest preservation organizations on the West Coast, was not only a brilliant and ambitious architect, but an incredibly virile man.

If she could believe one-tenth of what the papers reported, the man she'd revered for his architectural brilliance was a naughty boy personified. And lucky for her, this naughty boy had accepted the commission to renovate the Risqué Theatre and would arrive for the closing performance tonight.

To her knowledge—and Julienne believed herself very knowledgeable about Nicholas Fairfax's work—he'd never renovated any buildings in Savannah, which meant his black book might not be all filled up when he got off the plane.

She wanted her phone number to be his first entry.

Julienne knew she'd never catch a naughty boy's attention looking the way she did now. Not that there was anything wrong with her looks. She'd always been very grateful for her natural, easily maintained appearance. But she'd never exactly been a fashion plate. Once she and Uncle Thad had settled in Savannah, she'd led the life of a busy student and an academic. She'd always leaned toward the conservative and hadn't had the impetus to change.

Until now.

She clung to that thought through the color and shampoo process, a facial, a manicure and pedicure.

But when the first strands of hair to hit the floor were well over a foot long, Julienne's anticipation veered sharply toward worry. "You won't make it too short, will you?"

"Of course not." Ramón exhaled sharply with impatience, spinning her chair so she faced away from the mirrors. "Don't wig on me now, Jules, because you'll look ridiculous if I stop. I'm only layering your hair to put some shape around your face. You won't miss what I take off, trust me."

*Relax, girl. He's brilliant and you know it, otherwise you wouldn't be sitting in his chair.*

Julienne tried not to cringe as the next chunk of hair hit the floor with a wet plop. She closed her eyes to shut out the stimuli of the busy salon. After all, her one-length hair had never been as much a styling preference as it had been a necessity.

Working in the field with Uncle Thad had taken them to some pretty remote parts of the globe, where regularly scheduled haircuts hadn't been available. More often than not, *schools* hadn't been available and as a result, her uncle and his crew had tutored her until she'd entered college. She'd only worn her hair one length because the style had been easy to pull back into a presentable ponytail. A comfortable style and since Julienne was officially done with comfortable...

"What kind of product do you have at home?" Ramón asked.

"I buy whatever you tell me to buy." *Eager-to-please Julienne.* But no more. Opening her eyes, she resisted the urge to turn her head and peek in the mirrors.

"Shampoo, finishing rinse and an ends' conditioner. That's not enough. You need gel, mousse and spray now that you have shape, sweetheart. Celeste," he called out and the tolerant receptionist hurried through the salon to join them. "Put a care package together for Jules. Basic styling products. Oh, and throw in some of the hair glitter, too. Pearlescent."

"Pearlescent hair glitter?" Julienne asked.

"*New*-new, remember?" Shooing Celeste off, he poured a glob of what she presumed to be styling gel into his palm. "If you're inhabiting places like the Risqué, you'll need hair glitter, trust me. Now tell me what you're wearing tonight."

"I figured I'd decide after I saw the new me."

"Tell me about the choices."

As Ramón styled, Julienne told him about her formal-length black sheath and green velvet taffeta.

"I don't like those," he yelled over the roar of the blow dryer, motioning her to lean forward and put her head between her legs while he flipped the—gratefully—still considerable mass of hair over her head. "What else do you have?"

"A caviar-beaded skirt set."

"What color?"

"Black."

He snorted. ''I thought you said you'd attended perform-ances at the Risqué before. Sounds like all you do is go to funerals.''

Julienne might have scowled if she'd stood a chance of being seen, but as she was buried beneath damp hair with the blood rushing to her head, she could only correct him. ''Black is a classic color for formal functions, not the only color I own. I have a pale-pink sequined ball gown I wore to a New Year's party, but I think it would be too much for tonight.''

The blow dryer abruptly cut off and suddenly the curtain of hair parted to reveal Ramón peering at her upside down.

''Can you make time to visit Leona's Boutique next door? She'll have something that won't make you look like Cin-derella on her way to the ball.''

Julienne nodded. Cinderella in a ball gown was *not* a look to start her off with a bang. The time had apparently come to expand her wardrobe.

*Naughty girls dress the part.*

She'd read that in *The Naughty Handbook,* too, and tried to imagine what types of styles would be suitable for the new her, but as she hadn't actually seen the new her yet…

''I'm a bloody genius.''

Ramón spun her chair around to face the mirrors with a triumphant laugh, and for a split second, Julienne didn't recognize the woman staring back.

A cloud of hair, *incredible* hair, floated around her face, tumbled down her shoulders and reached halfway down her back in a mane of tousled waves. The subtle color change gave her hair a sunlight glint, which cast her skin with a creamy glow that couldn't possibly be natural. And her face. Suddenly her cheekbones seemed less austere, her features not quite so sharp. She looked somehow softer…and a whole lot sexier with all that hair waving around her face.

"You are a bloody genius," was all she could say.

He actually bowed with a grand sweep of his arm. "Remember that when Celeste gives you my bill. But the best is…" he lifted some of the fringy pieces around her face to reveal her scalp. "The foil technique I used means your regrowth will be so natural you'll barely notice."

Julienne supposed she'd be suitably grateful a month or two from now, but at the moment she couldn't think that far ahead. Not when her hair, *her* hair, looked so…wild.

"Did you curl it?"

Ramón shook his head. "Didn't need to. Once I cut into the bulk your natural wave sprang up. Who knew?"

Julienne didn't and wasn't about to complain. Not when each glance in the mirror caused her to do a double take.

*Looking good, girl.*

She held that thought through Kathy's makeup application and the short walk to Leona's Boutique.

"None of Leona's things are off the rack," Katriona whispered when Ramón rushed through the boutique calling for the owner. "She only deals with New York designers. We'll find something for you to wear tonight."

Julienne refused to think about what the minimum payment on her credit card would be next month.

*What are you working for anyway? Life's short. Live.*

And live she would. Even if it meant shrugging off a lifetime of reasonable budgeting. Her smile came easily as a svelte older woman appeared and Ramón performed the introductions.

Leona was a sharp-eyed woman who pegged her correct size with one glance. Leona's Boutique was the type of upscale up-to-the-minute fashion establishment Julienne had simply never considered shopping in before.

With everything from elaborate formal wear to accompanying undergarments in colors like *innocently white, per-*

*fectly nude* and *temptress black,* Leona's Boutique catered to women in the mood to indulge themselves.

Julienne allowed herself to be herded into yet another dressing room, and gave in to the excitement of silk shantung skirt sets with plunging scoop necks, sequined sheaths with bare-tie backs and tube dresses that reached the floor in a sweep of clingy satin.

And leather, lots and lots of leather in a rainbow of shades, which seemed to be what everyone thought she should wear to the Risqué tonight.

Julienne pirouetted in the full-length tri-mirror yet again, the red leather slip dress clinging to her body in a way that would have made her blush twenty-one days ago. Right now she only trembled with excitement and blessed Uncle Thad for sharing his low-cost solution to exercising in the field— running. An exercise that kept her toned.

"Yow. Do that again." Ramón circled his hand in the air, motioning her around once more. "Look at that hair move, sweetheart. God, I'm good."

"Yes, Ramón, you are. Thank you so much for renovating me with such brilliance and enthusiasm today." Meeting his gaze reflected in the mirror, she smiled.

"The enthusiasm's on the house, but I'm charging you for every drop of brilliance," he said dryly, but when he stepped onto the raised platform to kiss her cheek, Julienne knew he'd been pleased by her praise.

"No problem. I still can't believe this is me." She pirouetted again, hair flying around her and earning his smile. "Look at all this skin. I'll freeze tonight."

"Leona, shawl, jacket, duster, *something.* Goose bumps aren't sexy."

Katriona reappeared. "All that hair should keep you warm."

She was right. Julienne's hair looked almost hedonistic in

sheer volume, in the heavy, untamed way it fringed around her face then tumbled over her bare shoulders. And the dress. The leather hugged her from bodice to thigh—accentuating curves she hadn't realized she'd had—before the leather fanned out to the floor, leaving her knee and calf bared through a sexy slit.

Katriona surveyed her critically. "Needs more cleavage."

"Cleavage?" Julienne glanced into the mirror again, very pleased with the effect of the leather molding and shaping her breasts into noticeable fullness.

*The Naughty Handbook* had certainly been right about one thing—sexy clothes definitely affected attitude. This body-hugging red leather transformed her into a stranger.

"Leona," Katriona said to the owner, who had just stepped through the dressing room door. "Jules needs a Miracle Bra to turn her 34-B into something memorable."

"I've got just the thing." Handing Ramón a short bolero jacket designed from matching red leather, Leona disappeared from the dressing room only to reappear again a few minutes later with an armful of undergarments Julienne had only seen before on the pages of a Victoria's Secret catalogue. "That's more than a Miracle Bra."

The older woman smiled. "Corset bra with garters, a thong and silk stockings to match that exquisite dress."

"Oh." Seemed a bit extravagant when she had no intention of letting anyone see beneath her new sexy leather dress—not tonight at any rate. Tonight was for flirting and catching the attention of a very hot-blooded man.

Then again, *The Naughty Handbook* said that naughty girls dressed the part, both in public and private, and she couldn't wear those sexy undies without feeling sexy. To prove the point, she held the erotic corset in front of her.

"That'll do the trick. Trust me, sister." Katriona spun sideways and struck a pose that emphasized the amazing shape of her own silicone bustline, molded in gold spandex. "It'll lift and separate those puppies. You'll kill tonight."

"Go try them on." Ramón motioned her toward the booth. "Let's get the whole effect."

Julienne lifted her hair to allow Leona to unzip the red leather creation, then hurried inside the small, plush interior of the dressing booth. Peeling the dress away, she stepped into the lace corset, shimmied it up her body. The lace hugged her snugly, made her aware of the way the underwires forced her breasts high, the way the wispy lace caressed her skin.

The matching thong was no more than a scrap of bright fabric around her hips, decadent beneath the garter straps dangling toward her thighs, awaiting the stockings she'd tossed carelessly onto the upholstered bench.

Catching a glimpse of her bare bottom and the strip of red silk disappearing between her cheeks, Julienne trembled in an unfamiliar wave of feminine satisfaction.

*Well, well, look at you, girl. You're downright sexy in your new finery.*

Twirling in a slow circle, she absorbed the sight of lace molding her curves, familiar, yet provocatively unfamiliar.

*Naughty girls feel sexy.*

Julienne looked the part. She felt the part.

Taking a deep excited breath, she smiled into the mirror. "Nicholas Fairfax, here I come."

# 2

*That night*

NICK FAIRFAX tugged up the knees of his tuxedo slacks and knelt to inspect the cornerstone of the Risqué Theatre. The sidewalk below him was cracked and uneven, the result of too many years of eroding soil and landscaping that had overgrown the boundaries of its original design.

This property needed work, both inside and out, and as the project architect for the theater's renovation, he would see it restored to its former glory during his stay in Savannah.

Splaying his palm over the Roman numerals indicating the first stone had been laid in 1865, he closed his eyes and quietly pledged the promise he made before beginning every new project. "I'll do my best."

By nature Nick wasn't a superstitious man, yet he felt obliged to declare his intentions before contributing his vision to that of architects from other generations, a passing-the-torch ritual he'd begun when his newly founded company, the Architectural Design Firm or ADF as it had become known, had accepted its first project.

Now, ten years later, ADF had grown into one of the largest historic preservation architectural firms on the West Coast. He enjoyed a success that was as much a result of hard work as good fortune and Nick preferred not to overlook the basics of that success. Or lose sight of the responsibility he undertook when starting work on any historical building.

"I haven't seen you go wrong yet," Dale Emerson, ADF's senior project manager, said. "And we've been rebuilding these babies together for a long time."

Nick appreciated the sentiment, knew Dale took their work just as seriously, which had earned him his place as Nick's right-hand man. Getting to his feet, he raised an eyebrow. "The Risqué Theatre is a bit richer than our usual fare."

"Don't tell me all those naked bodies in the pargeting are giving you cold feet, buddy?"

Nick laughed. Renovating the ornamental plasterwork on the Risqué Theatre's ceiling hadn't bothered him while reading Dale's property analysis—though he'd suspected the original designer had worked with a relentless hard-on all through construction. After seeing the Risqué Theatre in all its glory, Nick realized he'd probably be empathizing with the guy before long.

"Come on, let's go inside." He wouldn't dwell on the unique obstacles this project presented, not with the monumental task that lay ahead. "The Arts Council is paying big bucks for ADF's services. Schmoozing will go a long way to keep them smiling while they cut the checks."

They walked past the box office. Though well after Labor Day, the Georgia night enveloped them with a sultry breeze, temperate though still cool enough not to break a sweat. The theater loomed above, a neoclassical structure constructed after the Civil War as part of a massive reconstruction effort to incorporate the crushed Confederacy into a newly united America.

Savannah had escaped Atlanta's fiery fate during Sherman's March to the Sea, and as such had seemed the logical place to focus efforts to begin the nation's healing process.

The Risqué Theatre had been one such effort, a place to celebrate culture and art at a time when the city's morale had been low and people's faith shaken. Culture and art hadn't seemed especially important while coping with husbands and sons lost in the bitter struggle to preserve the Southern way of life. Not when many faced the difficult task of rebuilding homes, careers and lives from the ashes of defeat.

A dark period in the nation's history, the goal had been to rebuild America into a nation stronger and more united than ever before. Savannah's insightful politicians of the time had caught their city's attention by targeting men's—and women's—fundamental interest in sex.

Nick had researched the history of the theater back to its conception, a task he both enjoyed and found integral to starting a project of this magnitude. The Risqué Theatre was a part of history and he was obligated and honor bound to maintain not only the structure, but to preserve the essence of the time period that made this and every historical project unique.

He'd worked on a variety of buildings through the years—churches, museums, private mansions—but the Risqué Theatre presented a new challenge of retaining the distinctive flavor of a building that had provided a home to an eclectic variety of theatrical venues through the years. From vaudeville, burlesques and gangster films, to modern film noir, performance art and improvisation, the Risqué Theatre had been home to them all.

"Whoa, buddy." Dale peered up at the ceiling moldings once inside the theater, at naked cherubs who grinned maniacally while pointing golden love arrows at them from every direction. "The thought of spending the next few months fixing every erection in this place is killing me.

Damn good thing the media has stopped sniffing around your love life.''

"Why's that?"

"Because you were a real pain in the ass when you gave up dating to avoid the press. I can't imagine tackling this place if you were living the celibate life. I'd quit right now."

Nick frowned. A close friend and valued employee, Dale Emerson might clean up well in his expensive tux, but his background was firmly rooted in construction, where men worked with men and spoke their minds freely.

"What choice did I have? You know how the media zeroed in on me after I accepted the presidential appointment. That sort of notoriety isn't fair to any woman. If I didn't give them news to report, I knew they'd replace me as playboy of the month."

"Try playboy of the year." Dale rolled his eyes. "I told you to think hard about accepting that appointment."

Nick handed the tickets to a uniformed usher and said dryly, "I didn't see a choice about that, either. Besides, the presidential appointment gives ADF prestige and credibility, which has been good for business. And it gives me a chance to get out of the office and into the field more often."

"Yeah, yeah, gotcha. The only thing more important than your sex life is ADF. But I still say we weren't without prestige and credibility, whether you're on-site or not." Dale glanced around the foyer, where the crowd already gathered, though they'd arrived early. He let out a low whistle. "Looks even more risqué than when I conducted the site analysis. Would you look at that."

Nick glanced at a column supporting the semicircular arch above a sloping spiral staircase. At first glance the sculpture appeared to be no more than an intricately worked column, but upon closer inspection the plasterwork depicted a life-size bodycast of a nude couple joined at the genitals.

Sex was everywhere at the Risqué Theatre, in the architecture, on the stage, in the walls that displayed playbills of naked bodies and edgy artwork from decades of erotic performances. If Nick had anything to say about it, sex would be in his immediate future, too.

Dale shot him an amused glance. "Buddy, we're in for a treat if all Southern belles look like her."

Nick followed Dale's gaze to an opening in the crowd where a woman stood amazingly alone, a woman who made every drop of blood in his veins plummet south.

"You're not kidding." This Southern belle was a vision straight out of a wet dream with her long slim curves swathed in a red leather dress designed to make men crave sex. Supple leather clung to every sleek curve of a body equally designed to inspire thoughts of tangled limbs and sweaty skin.

She wasn't exactly tall, rather lanky and very feminine with long dancer's legs and creamy skin that swelled over her bodice and made his breath catch hard.

And her hair. Nick had never seen hair like hers, deep-auburn hair that made him yearn to do a lot more than run his fingers through it. Rather he wanted to run his naked body through it. Falling far below the sassy short jacket she wore, her hair shimmered beneath the lights and inspired images of that mass of wanton waves playing peek-a-boo with lots of bare skin.

"Why don't you introduce yourself?" Nick managed to grind out, wishing like hell he'd caught sight of this red devil first. If she and his senior project manager became an item, he'd be hard pressed to curtail all the fantasies he'd be having about her.

"Life just isn't fair, is it?" Dale stared like that red

leather had been magnetized. "But she's more your speed, buddy. Expensive champagne, fancy restaurants and suites in five-star hotels. Too high ticket for grabbing a six-pack and taking a spin in my classic Mustang."

Nick thought Dale sold himself short, but couldn't bring himself to disagree. Not when it meant his senior project manager would take himself out of the running. This red devil exuded class if ever he'd seen it, and he had. Loads of times. She exuded class, and expensive seduction, and provocative, mind-blowing sex.

Watching her sweep that magnificent hair back from her shoulder and move along with the crowd, Nick decided Dale was wrong. Life was fair. Very fair. Otherwise he might be somewhere else in the world, instead of in this theater with a growing hard-on before the show had even started.

PROFESSIONALLY DIMMED lighting and a ceiling that replicated a black velvet night filled with twinkling stars made even Julienne's not-so-great orchestra seat seem like a gateway to a magical world. The American variety stage show that would close the Risqué for the first time in its illustrious history celebrated the evolution of the theater's unusual performances.

A turn-of-the-century strip show brought to life the exotic dance entertainment of Gypsy Rose Lee before segueing into more family-oriented vaudeville—though there wasn't much family-oriented about this sketch, with off-color jokes and women tap dancing in fringed costumes that shimmied over lean muscles and lots of bared skin.

The theatrical years passed. A short gangster film yielded to a segment that was an adaptation of the theater-in-the-round so popular in the fifties and sixties. The actors actually filed off the stage, milling around the musicians in the orchestra pit, all of whom good-naturedly continued playing despite actors miming various sex acts all around them and their instruments.

Beautifully choreographed and skillfully executed, the sight had Julienne stripping off her jacket and wondering why she'd ever worried about getting cold. Then again, her rising body temperature may have more to do with the man sitting in the loge than the performance.

He sat in the very front row of the balcony to the left of the stage with a dark-haired gentleman and several people she recognized from the newspapers as board members of the city arts council that currently operated the theater.

Julienne had seen pictures of Nicholas Fairfax before, but no picture came close to the man himself, even at this distance. Though she really only had a view of him from the shoulders up, his blond hair, tanned skin and chiseled features spanned the distance with an intensity that kicked up her body temperature another few degrees.

As gorgeous as his work was brilliant, the man's inky black brows contrasted sharply with his blond hair, a look that she'd forever associate with California in her mind. With features chiseled and masculine in a polished, beachy sort of way, he wore an intent expression, which made her wonder what he thought about the actors milling through the orchestra pit, naked for all intents and purposes in their flesh-toned liquid latex. Was he as turned on as she by the thrusting hips, gyrating bodies and jiggling *parts?*

She was definitely turned on. The now-moist thong had wedged itself between her legs, making her squirm to relieve the pressure, or maybe to create more friction. Julienne wasn't sure which. She only knew she was more aware of her body than ever before, a combination of her new clothes, the erotic performances and the fantasy man sitting out of reach above her.

Scanning the program for some clue to when the performance would end, she found her answer in a jolting rock beat from the seventies. The "Living Theater" performance, which meant she only had to survive the eighties and nineties before heading to the bar for a cooling sip of champagne to relieve her overheated body.

*Naughty girls feel naughty.*

She'd have to say one thing for *The Naughty Handbook* and self-hypnosis—they were a powerful combination. Thinking about sex left her hovering on the edge of a sexual excitement that had skyrocketed through the performance. She couldn't ever remember being so affected by any show she'd ever seen at the Risqué. Was this what Ramón had meant by a "hair-curling" performance?

If anything would curl her hair, the actors beckoning their audience onstage to join them in a liberating striptease might just do it. Even under the influence of self-hypnosis, she couldn't even consider accepting such a provocative invitation.

Then again, Julienne didn't have to, because a pair of strong hands physically ejected her from her seat. She was on her feet and heading down the aisle before realizing what was happening.

"Ramón? Katriona." Digging in her heels, she made a stand. "What are you doing here? What are you *doing?*" She tried to shrug off the hand Ramón had fastened around her arm.

He wouldn't let go. "Half these actors are my clients, sweetheart, and you're my latest creation. I want to show you off." He tried to tug her toward the stage as they were blocking the aisle, causing a traffic jam of spectators who were intent upon getting on that stage to liberate or be liberated.

She resisted. "I can't, Ramón. Let me go."

Katriona may have dressed in an exquisite white chiffon

that accentuated both her height and regal bustline, but that didn't negate the fact that she'd entered this world as the opposite sex, growing to be somewhere around six foot two with shoulders as wide as a linebacker's. *Her* hands on Julienne's back propelled her into motion again, no questions asked.

All the sexual heat that had just been rushing through Julienne dissolved into a mingled mess of adrenaline and embarrassment as she was herded onto the stage.

*Naughty girls go for it.*

And Julienne planned to, all right. She was going right for her seat before this crowd of stripping, bare-assed maniacs started liberating her. She spun around...she may have been going for her seat, but she accidentally got a handful of some actor's crotch, a tidy handful if she were to judge.

The actor gave her a grateful kiss on the cheek before leaving Julienne standing stock-still, blushing so furiously she must be as red as her dress.

Time to add a new key phrase to her self-hypnosis sessions—*naughty girls don't lose their cool.*

Deep breath. *Don't look out at the audience.* Another deep breath. *Move.* Then she started gyrating to the music, blending in with the crazed crowd, all the while making her way back to the stairs that circled the orchestra pit and led off the stage. And thanking all the angels in heaven that even if anyone she knew sat in the audience, they'd never recognize the *new* her.

How Julienne survived the eighties and the nineties was a mystery, because she couldn't remember a thing about the final acts or the finale. In fact, her cheeks still burned when she left her seat for the lobby. And of course, she was trying so hard to avoid Ramón and Katriona, before they dragged her backstage to meet the man whose *parts* she'd grabbed, that she barreled right into someone.

Whipcord lean arms reached out to steady her, anchored her against a very tall, very physically fit man. One quick intake of breath later, a breath tinged with a deliciously spicy male scent, and Julienne lifted her gaze to the blackest, most potent eyes she'd ever seen.

It took only a moment, a fluttering heartbeat, for her to realize those black-velvet eyes were framed by very tanned skin, blond hair and a chiseled jaw she'd have known anywhere, even if she hadn't spent the past two hours covertly staring at him.

Nicholas Fairfax.

She must have looked shell-shocked because those potent eyes crinkled with amusement and he grinned, a charming grin that lit up his face and cast the lobby and the crowd around them into obscurity.

"I should apologize," he said in a rich, cultured voice that sent a shiver right to her toes. "But as I'm holding you in my arms, I can't say I'm sorry I ran into you."

Unless he'd intentionally stepped in front of her, she'd technically run into him, but he was very gallant to accept responsibility for their collision.

*Naughty girls don't lose their cool.*

The key phrase echoed in her memory when she needed it most, and Julienne laughed, she actually *laughed,* a throaty, sexy sound she didn't even recognize as coming from her mouth.

"I'm not sorry, either. Actually, I was aiming for you, just to see if you'd catch me."

*You go, girl.*

His black eyes flashed. She might be breaking new ground by flirting, but clearly Nicholas Fairfax was in his element. His grip tightened, just enough to put her off-balance so she relied on him to hold her upright, just enough to feel the impressive reaction of his groin against her stomach.

More *parts*. Only these parts sent a blush into her cheeks, made her gaze up to the grinning cupids overhead in a vain attempt to hide her reaction.

He apparently noticed, because he asked, ''Are you interested in architecture?''

She nodded.

''This place is about to undergo a major restoration.''

She met that potent black gaze again, couldn't quite believe how his glance, *a glance* for heaven's sake, sizzled through her like a power surge. ''That's why I'm here tonight. I wanted to see it one last time.''

''Afraid you won't recognize the place?'' Then he smiled, a blinding sort of smile that radiated so much testosterone she could barely catch her breath.

Stepping back, he broke the connection between them, allowed her to regain her balance. But he didn't let go of her hand. He brought it to his lips instead, a gentlemanly gesture that drew all her attention to the place where his warm skin touched hers. ''I promise that won't be the case, beautiful, because I'm heading the design team. Nick Fairfax.''

Julienne blinked as he brushed his mouth across her skin. Had Nicholas Fairfax—*Nick*—brilliant restoration architect and naughty boy extraordinaire, just called her beautiful?

The glint in his sultry eyes answered that question positively but before she could absorb such an amazing thought or push an introduction past her lips, she heard a familiar, and very unwelcome, voice yell, ''Jules.''

Turning toward the sound, she found Ramón and Katriona weaving through the crowd toward them. In barely the time it took her to inhale a steadying breath, Julienne saw Ramón's gaze pivot to the hand Nick Fairfax still held against his lips. Katriona didn't appear to notice; in fact, she eyed the man himself with such a hungry expression Julienne guessed she'd like nothing better than to gobble Nick up in one bite.

"Jules." He brushed his lips across her skin again, before releasing her. "My pleasure."

"Nick," she managed to reply, before Ramón and Katriona were upon them and she made polite introductions.

"I've read all about you," Ramón told Nick, but not before casting her a surreptitious wink that reminded her of their earlier conversation about finding a new guy. Apparently Ramón thought Nick Fairfax could be an acceptable contender. "Take my card. You'll need a stylist while you're in town. Send your employees in, too. My staff will take good care of everyone."

Julienne rolled her eyes, still feeling a bit dazed by the chemistry between her and this utterly exquisite architect who towered above her, though she wasn't exactly short in her heels.

But Nick took Ramón's solicitations in stride. "If you've played a part in this beautiful lady's appearance, I'll book an appointment and recommend you to my team, no problem." His gaze trailed from her hair to her toes, and she couldn't miss the approval flashing in his dark eyes.

"I can't take all the credit," Ramón said magnanimously. "Jules is a joy to work on."

Katriona inclined her regal head, clearly about to add her two cents, but Ramón clamped a hand on her arm and stopped her before she opened her mouth.

"Would you look at the time? Come on, Kat." With a vice grip on her chiffon-clad arm, he launched Katriona into the crowd, no mean feat given her size. Then he glanced back and said, "Jules, don't forget your appointment tomorrow."

Julienne stared. Appointment? Since when was Casa de Ramón open on Sundays? When Ramón glared at her over his eyeglass rims, she realized he wanted her to call.

"I won't forget," she shot back, earning Ramón's smile before he and Katriona disappeared into the crowd.

After tucking the business card into his pocket, Nick fixed her an examining look. "Did you come with them?"

"No."

"I don't see a date. I've been watching you since I arrived."

"You have?" Okay, not the most confident of replies, but it seemed to amuse Nick, judging by the grin suddenly playing at the corners of his mouth.

"I have. And I particularly enjoyed your performance during the living theater. You made a very graceful exit."

That earlier blush returned to haunt her and she hoped he didn't notice in the dim lobby lighting. But the heat in her cheeks also served to knock some sense into her.

*Naughty girls feel good about feeling naughty.*

"No date. I'm all by myself tonight."

"Not anymore." Nick extended his hand in a very gentlemanly gesture of invitation. "If you'll allow me, there's a party downstairs and I'd like you to be my guest."

# 3

NICK WAITED for Jules's reaction. Then there it was, a slight melting of those clear gray eyes, a sudden softening of her mouth. When she slipped cool fingers into his, he breathed again.

"I'd be delighted," she said in a sultry voice that made his nerve endings rise to attention, along with other parts of his anatomy that had no business behaving as though they'd been ignored of late.

Tucking her hand securely in the crook of his arm, Nick led her through the lobby down to the basement and dressing rooms where the Arts Council currently hosted a closing night party for the actors, musicians, theater patrons and other attendees from the arts, cultural and historical societies.

What was it about this woman that made him feel as if every nerve in his body was live with max voltage? Was he simply reacting to a very beautiful woman?

From her shimmery hair, the color of claret from the vineyards around his home in Northern California, to her intriguing combination of bold words and shy blushes, he noticed everything about her, wanted to know even more. He planned to spend his night discovering exactly who this beauty was.

He couldn't believe his good fortune earlier when he'd recognized her heading onto the stage. His good fortune hadn't been hers, though, because from his seat he could see her face and recognized that she hadn't been thrilled to be onstage.

But she'd handled her exit very well, gifting him with an incredible show of swaying curves and wild hair as she danced her way off the stage again, inspiring all sorts of fantasies about her dancing across that stage just for him.

Nick hadn't been the only one affected. Dale had hung out of their box, vowing to give up beer and joyrides for good. Nick had told him not to bother. He'd had his chance for a shot at this red devil. He wouldn't get another.

The closing night party hosted an eclectic mix of actors in outrageous costumes—or barely any costumes at all— and the more conservative members of the city's various boards. He and Dale were the only ADF staff currently in Savannah as his design team wrapped up various tasks from their last project and would arrive throughout the next week.

Seizing two flutes of champagne from a passing waiter, he cornered Jules across the room from Dale, who schmoozed with several matrons from the Arts Council near the buffet, earning his high-figure salary by representing ADF when its principal was otherwise engaged.

"So tell me, beautiful." He let his fingers linger on hers when he handed her the glass. "What brings such a lovely lady to an erotic theater alone?"

She shrugged, just a slight lifting of her shoulders that seemed at once both feminine and noncommittal. "There aren't too many men who appreciate the historic significance of this theater and I wanted to see it one last time so I can marvel at your skill when the renovation's done."

Nick couldn't decide what turned him on more, her interest in his architectural abilities or her confidence in them. "So the history of the place appeals to you. What about the architecture and the performance?"

"If I were to put them in order of importance, I'd actually

have to say the renovation would be first on my list, then the history and finally the theater. What's onstage doesn't seem to matter much. The real magic is being here.''

Nick eyed her over the rim of his glass, could detect nothing but genuine interest in her rapt expression. Was she just flirting with him? He'd known more than his share of women who'd professed an interest in architecture, only to be bored stupid whenever he'd mixed business with pleasure and combined a weekend away with a site analysis.

He was a man of limited interests and architecture topped his list and encompassed his life, which probably explained why dating best suited his life in the field.

''So the architecture brought you here tonight. That's my good fortune.'' Clinking the rim of his glass to hers, he ignored the imploring look Dale shot him from across the room. ''But the performance didn't excite you at all?''

''Excite.'' The word formed on her lips in a breathy whisper. ''What an interesting choice of words, Nick. Yes, the architecture brought me here, but I'd have to be dead not to have been...*excited* by that performance. I'm alive.''

''I noticed.''

''And what about you? Did the performance excite you?''

There it was again, that breathy puff of sound that glided over those champagne-moistened lips and turned his thoughts to kissing. Stolen teasing kisses. Deep-throated hungry kisses. Wet demanding kisses.

''No reflection on the actors or the play, but the show didn't do half of what you're doing for me right now.''

He expected some reaction to his admission, surprise or pleasure, but quickly realized Jules intended to play this game her way. Arching an auburn brow, she touched the rim of her glass to her mouth, sipped, then darted her pink tongue out to wipe away the remnants from her lower lip.

He followed the movement with his gaze, imagining how

that sweet liquid would taste warmed by those luscious lips. This woman was playing with fire and she knew it. Nick knew it, too. He enjoyed the chase as much as the next man...okay, probably more than most. But he prided himself on his control. So why was Jules having this damned intense effect on him? He'd blown off his schmoozing duties, which constituted work in his mind, to keep her all to himself.

Unfortunately, remaining isolated wasn't possible and before long the Arts Council president corralled them.

"There you are, Dr. Fairfax. I'm interested in hearing what you think of the Risqué Theatre now that you've seen it firsthand. I can't tell you how thrilled the board members are that you're supervising the project personally."

"Thank you, Mrs. Turner, I'd supervise all my senior teams if I could, but unfortunately I can only be in one place at a time. Your theater presented a challenge I couldn't resist."

He glanced down at the beautiful woman by his side, surprised at the frisson of excitement that coursed through his blood when she lifted her smoky gaze to his. "Mrs. Turner, this is my friend Jules," he said, never turning back to the matron as he completed the introduction, because Jules's beautiful face transformed into a polite social mask before his very eyes.

She extended her hand. "It's a pleasure. I greatly admire the work the council does. Your grant program has an impressive track record of benefiting artists and cultural renovation sites in the area."

"How delightful of you to notice." The president positively beamed and Nick drank his champagne, content to listen for whatever clues Jules's conversation might reveal.

She hadn't offered her full name or mentioned why the cultural affairs of Savannah interested her. Nick found himself strangely disappointed. And challenged to find out all he could about her.

"Tonight's performance was actually part of the grant program," Mrs. Turner said. "Local writers submitted proposals for closing night scripts. The variety show tribute to the theater's long and illustrious history overwhelmingly won the council's approval and the grant."

Jules looked thoughtful. "I thought the format was particularly appropriate, given that the sets for each vignette mirrored a historical transition in the theater's architectural evolution. Didn't you think so, Nick?"

"Absolutely," he replied, but the truth was he'd been so busy admiring Jules from the balcony that he hadn't noticed that the vignettes had reflected anything about the theater's architecture, except as a tribute to the different eras.

This was his first clue that Jules's interest in architecture was an honest one and since he wanted to know just how honest, he steered the conversation around to the detailed work needed to replace broken nosing and the crumbling cusps around the room.

Sure enough, Jules's gaze traveled straight to the molding on the stairs, then up to the nearby doorway, with a certainty only a familiarity with architecture would bring. Nick decided right then to get her away from this party to find out more about this exotically beautiful woman who shared a common interest.

But he'd no sooner shaken off the Arts Council president when Dale arrived. He planted himself squarely between them for an introduction, and Nick knew at once Dale intended to bust his chops by making a play for Jules.

This wouldn't be the first time Dale had challenged him. What Nick couldn't figure out is why he even bothered, since he usually came off worse for the effort.

"Jules, this is my senior project manager Dale Emerson."

"Well, hello, gorgeous." Dale sandwiched her hand between his big paws and held on for dear life.

"Nice to meet you," Jules replied and something about the surprise in her eyes made Nick suspect she wasn't as used to flirting as she pretended to be. A niggling suspicion, but one he made a mental note to look at more closely. His gut feelings usually served him well with the opposite sex, because he made a point of paying attention.

Retrieving more champagne from a passing waiter, he offered the flute to Dale, forcing him to relinquish his death grip on Jules's hand. Dale shot him a grimace that revealed he knew exactly what Nick was doing. But he forged ahead anyway.

"What did you think of the performance tonight, gorgeous?"

"I was just telling Nick I found it rather exciting."

Ah, that breathy little sound again. It set his blood on fire, and when she cast her sparkling gaze his way, reserving the sound just for him, he experienced a surge of pure male satisfaction.

"Jules was also telling me how clever she thought the different sets were tonight, because each mirrored the architectural evolution of the theater's renovations."

If Nick hadn't noticed the sets' unique designs, he knew Dale hadn't. Not that he'd have admitted the oversight. Dale didn't, either. Instead, he segued neatly right back to the only topic that seemed to interest him at the moment—the beautiful woman standing between them.

"Really? You're stunningly gorgeous and interested in architecture. What a perfect combination."

Jules only shrugged, another slight lifting of her shoulders that did amazing things to those creamy breasts swelling above red leather. "I've got an uncle in the business. He has shared his work with me most of my life."

Well, that explained her interest. An honest interest. An intelligent one, too.

"What's your uncle's specialty?" Nick asked.

"Materials conservation. He retired last year."

Dale shook his head. "Whew, wish we'd have known him before he retired. Right about the time we were doing the flood restoration on the Mark Twain Museum."

"What happened at the museum?" Jules asked.

"The project was such a beast that our material conservationist had a heart attack." Dale shook his head at the memory. "We had to finish up with a staff member we stole from a junior team."

"Fortunately he's okay and back to work now," Nick said.

"Only after we talked him out of retiring early and relocating to a beach in Florida."

Nick set his empty glass down on a nearby table. "Our good luck. Finding someone who knows his, or her, way around the chemical and physical complexities of building materials is always a challenge."

"Finding *anyone* to hire onto Nick's team is a challenge." Dale gave a low whistle. "This man's such a tyrant in the field no one wants to work for him."

Amusement sparkled in Jules's eyes. Though Nick knew Dale only ribbed him, he wasn't above defending himself in front of this lovely lady. "I'm not a tyrant, evidenced by the fact Frank came back to work."

"Trust me, I'll keep your uncle in mind," Dale said. "We stand a better chance of luring him out of retirement than of keeping Frank from the beach for long."

Jules laughed brightly. "Does Dale have hiring privileges? Shall I give my uncle a call? I'm not sure how he'd feel about working for a tyrant."

Nick scowled, a scowl that faded quickly beneath her

high-beam smile. He liked the way she reserved her smiles for him, dodging Dale's flirting without being cold, yet expressing she'd already decided who had her attention tonight.

Jules was a class act and he'd just hit his limit of listening to his integrity impugned while his friend tried to steal his girl. Plucking the flute from Jules's hand, he passed it to Dale.

"We're touring the theater. Jules would like to see the place before we work our magic. You schmooze."

"Tyrant." Dale spun on his heel and plunged back into the crowd leaving Nick staring after him and Jules giggling.

"I take it Dale's more than your employee," she said.

"A friend. A good one most of the time."

Taking her hand, he led her toward a waiter, where they picked up fresh champagne before heading through the doorway with the crumbling cusps. Resting his hand lightly on her hip, he directed her to precede him up the stairs.

As he watched the gentle sway of her leather-clad behind, Nick knew exactly where he would take her. The memory of her dancing across the stage still played vivid in his memory, and being alone there together would go a long way toward fueling his fantasies.

Jules followed willingly where he led and during their roundabout tour toward the dark stage, they discussed where he'd be staying during his visit in Savannah—ADF had rented his design crew townhouses in a fashionable community. He quizzed her for the details of the citywide debate about whether to gut-rehab the Risqué or renovate it. She regaled him with questions about how he planned to handle accessibility for the disabled, what historic materials he intended to retain and if he would attempt to qualify for tax-credit benefits.

While they talked one thing became very evident to Nick,

Jules knew her stuff. She also knew how to keep him talking about everything but her. A phenomenon he intended to end now.

Leading her onto the dark stage, he drew her down beside him on the rolling spiral staircase where an actress portraying Gypsy Rose Lee had descended during her striptease. She sat on the step above him, her incredible body contracting in a fluid fold of leather-clad curves, clearly not bothered about the effects of the stairs on her dress. He liked that she wasn't uptight or prissy.

"You've picked my brain about this theater for the past two hours and I've answered all your questions. Now I want you to tell me about you. What you do for a living. Where you live. Tell me all about the woman who asks such intelligent questions and comes to an erotic theater by herself."

Jules swirled warm champagne in her glass, considering. Then she lifted her gaze and gifted him with a smile. "Okay, my life in a nutshell. I'm in education and I've lived in Savannah since I started college. I already told you why I came to the Risqué tonight, but I came alone because I'm not seeing anyone."

"Are you dating?"

She shook her head, sending shiny auburn waves dancing along her shoulders. "I haven't been. I was engaged, but my fiancé and I ended our engagement about six months ago."

He wondered why but wouldn't ask such a personal question. He asked how long she'd been engaged instead.

"Five years."

"Well, beautiful, are you over him?" When she nodded, he saluted her with his glass. "Your ex's loss is my gain. So where did you live before college?"

"All over. We traveled a lot."

Probably military, he decided, which could account for her nonchalance at attending the theater alone and her ease in impromptu social situations. He'd known his fair share of women who wouldn't have been comfortable attending any formal event without at least bringing a friend. Speaking of... "What about your friends, Ramón and his...*girl-friend?*"

Jules laughed, a throaty sound that arrowed through his senses at close range. Her thigh was mere inches away, and he couldn't help but wonder how she'd react if he ran his hand along its sleek length, though he hadn't been invited yet.

"Katriona's not his girlfriend," Jules said. "She's his head manicurist at the salon. Technically, she's not even a she."

He winced. That much had been obvious. Nick hadn't missed the gigantic bustline, either, and the mechanics of her appearance were more than he wanted to know.

Jules laughed again, another burst of sultry sound that— gratefully—shattered the image of the manicurist and kicked in his pulse like a jackhammer.

"She does a lovely manicure, though." She held up a hand to emphasize her point and that was exactly the in he needed.

Taking her hand under the pretense of examining her manicure, Nick brushed a kiss across her knuckles. He heard her quick intake of breath and the moment became charged with the promise of sex.

"So what else do I need to know about you before we can explore this intense physical attraction between us?"

"I can't think of a thing." She sounded excited, exactly the reaction he'd hoped for. "Nothing interesting about my life, I'm afraid. I work a lot."

She was kidding, right? Jules knew the difference between a cornice and a corbel-table and she didn't think she was interesting? He'd lay odds he could disabuse her of that notion before they parted ways tonight. "I work a lot, too. Plays hell with my social life. Have to make time when I can."

"A good thing you seem to make new friends easily."

New friends? Given the way she'd just fielded his questions, he didn't know enough to call her a friend, but she obviously didn't want to share her personal life. Keeping it simple. He understood and respected that.

"I'd like to become better acquainted tonight."

Her clear gaze never left his as she set her glass on a step above her. The shadows played across her features, a striking study of dark and dusk that bleached all color into soft shades of muted grays.

She seemed almost tentative as she stretched her hand toward his face, and he had the impression again that Jules wasn't nearly so experienced at seducing strangers as she'd have him believe. Her fingers trembled as they brushed his skin, just a light caress of warm fingertips against his temple, a touch that was less sexy than...*reverent*.

Nick wasn't exactly sure what to make of the tender expression softening her beautiful face, but any thought he might have given the subject vanished beneath a savage backlash of reaction to her combination of tentative and tender.

"Kiss me, Jules, or let me kiss you," he ground out in a voice that held nothing back, though common sense urged him to take it slow.

But to his profound pleasure, her long hair suddenly swung forward, surrounding his face and shoulders in a thick curtain of cool silk that blocked all the shadows from the stage, cocooned them together, parted lips, hot breaths and an incredible attraction for two people who'd just met.

Keeping his hands where they were, one holding hers, thumb stroking the smooth skin of her palm, the other clutching the stem of the flute, he resisted dragging her mouth against his.

He hungered with an intensity he'd never known before, that combination of bold temptress with hints of shy innocent captivated him. Nick usually relied on his control, but it failed him big-time tonight. His breath came raw in his chest, the first taste of her wet velvet mouth shooting his blood south in a painful rush. Her hands held his face lightly, not really to hold him—she must know he wasn't going anywhere—but more to reassure herself that he was here, waiting, eager to be touched.

Her kiss was inquisitive at first, a cautious exploration of a man she didn't know. He let her take the lead, though he ached to deepen their kiss, to drive his tongue into her mouth and test the limits of her passion.

She rewarded his restraint as though she knew he held back and darted her tongue across his bottom lip. A light touch, a taste really, but an intimacy that opened the floodgates.

Suddenly her grip tightened and her tongue plunged into his mouth with a demand that stole his breath. Sliding one hand around her neck, he anchored her mouth against his and obliged her. Using his tongue to make her acquaintance, he discovered what made her issue those soft sighs that made him ache to drag her into his lap and grind his erection against her bottom.

Man, could she kiss and Nick was a man who appreciated kissing. He enjoyed making out, building the anticipation, tantalizing and torturing himself with each forward step, with each triumph that wore down a woman's defenses and made her ache for his touch as he ached for hers.

Jules tested his control, lit fires inside him that Nick knew wouldn't be doused until he experienced this woman naked with her hair tumbling all around them.

And still he held back, instinctively knowing she needed the control right now, their acquaintance was too new, too intense and he wouldn't risk frightening her off. With one hand hanging onto hers and the other absurdly clutching his champagne glass, he tangled tongues with this beauty, caught her sighs on his lips and marveled at the effect she had on him.

When she finally drew away and inhaled deeply, Nick's instinct kicked in, warning that this was his chance to move them to the next step.

"Dance with me." Setting his glass aside, he got to his feet, not giving her a chance to think, let alone refuse him. "Watching you dance tonight turned me on. I want to feel you in my arms."

"The orchestra is downstairs partying," she said breathlessly. "Or maybe not. It's gotten late."

The instant her foot touched the stage, he swung her into his arms. "I'll provide the music. I can't really sing, but I'm a helluva hummer."

Jules giggled, and his last glimpse as he bent his head low to her ear was of her eyes alight with laughter. Then he began humming some show tune that had stuck in his head from tonight's performance and she melted against him.

The dark auditorium faded away and Nick knew only the sound of his voice and Jules—her scent, her graceful movements and the way her body molded his. She fitted against all his pressure points as if her incredible body had been designed for his pleasure. He could rest his chin right on the top of her head. Her shoulder fit snugly beneath his arm. Her breasts pressed against his chest, full and perfect in their red leather prison, taunting him to offer escape. And by flexing his arm around her waist, he held her close, imprisoning his erection against her warm stomach.

He sighed. She sighed.

Two bodies in perfect accord, the fact they'd just met of little concern. This woman was meant to be in his arms at this moment. Nick knew on a primitive level, knew with every inhalation of her subtly spicy scent and the way that scent filtered through his senses, priming his libido, making him forget everything but how much he wanted her.

Eventually his humming gave way to the sounds of their breathing and the soft shuffle of their feet across the wood-beam stage floor. Any sense of time vanished beneath an insistent need to stroke his arousal against her, take advantage of the way she parted her thighs and gently rode his thigh as they danced.

Nick even forgot they were in a theater, a *public* theater where a hundred people partied in the basement directly below. Apparently Jules was also so caught up that she forgot, too, because when Dale's voice echoed through the empty auditorium, "Hey, buddy, are you in here?" she appeared as surprised as he.

Fortunately they were close enough to the wings to disappear offstage before Dale caught them. Drawing her behind the main curtain, he held her close, his pulse quickening with adrenaline matched by the sudden hammering of Jules's heartbeat—hard, even beats he felt right through his tux jacket.

"I think you lost track of time because the party's over." Dale's voice rang out, louder as he approached the stage. "Time to go home. The caterers are done cleaning and they're locking up. Madam President thinks you took off without saying goodbye, and she's miffed. Better have Betty send her some flowers tomorrow."

Silence. Nick wasn't leaving, not when he had Jules in his arms and this theater to himself.

"If you're still in here, I hope you can get back out again," Dale tried again. "If you don't show your face for coffee in the morning, I'll send out the posse."

The footsteps receded, then finally faded into silence.

"Can we get back out again?" Jules whispered.

Nick seized the opportunity to reassure her with a kiss. "I've got a key, beautiful. But I won't use it until I'm done making you sigh with pleasure."

# 4

*NAUGHTY GIRLS love to sigh with pleasure.*

Julienne mentally chanted that key phrase while her breath fluttered somewhere between her lungs and her nose. Nick held her anchored against him, his dark gaze searching, holding her rooted to the spot.

Could she do this? Could she really let this sexy man make her sigh with pleasure? She'd come to the Risqué tonight to test her skills, to attract his attention and flirt outrageously. Sure she'd thought about seduction, but within hours of becoming acquainted? Julienne hadn't considered that.

Could she really take the next step? Could she rise up on tiptoes and press her mouth to his in a delicious kissable yes? Or could she be even more bold and slip her hand between them to stroke that rock-hard erection pressing stubbornly against her?

Her body pleaded with her to say, "Yes. Yes." The moist throbbing between her legs had grown distracting, resolute, urged on by riding his hard thigh while they'd danced.

But a more rational part of her brain kept insisting, *Sleep with this man on the first night?* What would he think about her? Would he ever respect her?

*Naughty girls take advantage of the moment.* That inner voice cried. *Have a one-night stand. He'll respect a sexy memory, so make your sex scrumptious, for yourself and him.*

Her self-hypnosis seemed to be working. Julienne was pleased because when she slipped her hand between them, laid her palm full length against that awesome erection, the pleasure on Nick's face made her just dissolve into sensation that coiled through her veins and pumped her full of daring and adventure.

The Risqué would be theirs tonight. The empty audience beckoned, called out that the theater was empty—*allegedly empty, because they really couldn't be certain, could they?*—and inspired her to an audaciousness Julienne hadn't known she possessed.

She had one night to act out a fantasy. Her fantasy man was willing, so shouldn't she jump at this chance?

*Naughty girls love to sigh with pleasure.*

She'd sigh and make no apologies. She wouldn't think about tomorrow. Nick didn't know who she was, so why shouldn't she make the most of the moment?

*Watching you dance tonight turned me on.*

Inspiration struck and Julienne sprang away from him in a burst of unfamiliar excitement, could barely catch her breath when she met his questioning dark gaze.

"Will you hum for me again, Nick?"

He gave her an obliging smile. "Beautiful, I'll do *anything* for you. Just say the word."

This man was a naughty boy, a kindred soul—at least for the night. She scanned the set, where props from the futuristic finale still crowded the stage, and found what she was looking for instantly.

Taking Nick's hand, she led him across the stage. "Sit here."

His smile widened as he took in the love swing hanging from fly lines above—a contraption made of nylon straps and soft padded stirrups where actors had mimed a weightless sex act to depict a lusty high-tech future for the Risqué.

"Taking me for a ride, beautiful?" His voice was deep, the echoing quality of the auditorium making his whisper resound through the dark quiet, making it resonate through her.

"A ride I promise you won't forget."

Bold words spoken by a bold stranger. He was obviously willing to take her at her word, because he struck up a lively tune, eyes heavy lidded with expectation as he stripped off his jacket and vest, loosened his collar, then grabbed onto the balance bar and maneuvered his attractive backside onto the padded seat. Leaning back, he hooked his hands behind his head.

The moment of truth.

Julienne headed toward center stage. Inhaling deeply, once, then again, she envisioned people down in the orchestra pit, in the first rows of the audience, in the loge.

Using a technique she'd devised when overcoming her nerves in the classroom, she imagined her audience's faces—a man with inky black hair, a fresh-faced woman who looked a lot like Mary Ann from *Gilligan's Island*.

Then Julienne envisioned what they'd look like in the throes of orgasm. She saw the man squeeze his eyes tightly shut, his mouth parting with gusty breaths. She heard the woman's pleasured moans, imagined her sighing to the sounds of her lover's thrusts.

Then she pictured Nick, how he'd looked when she'd first kissed him, the chiseled angles of his handsome face sharpening with excitement, his deep eyes growing heavy with pleasure. The tune he hummed filled the stage, filled her senses, some vaguely familiar melody she couldn't place.

And she began to dance.

The music immediately glitched as her orchestra choked on a gasp, but resumed quickly. Julienne smiled. With her feet braced apart and her knees slightly bent, she moved to the sound, arms relaxed and head bent backward so the ends of her hair brushed her waist, lured his attention to the motion of her swaying hips.

She could feel his gaze upon her, wondered if he wanted her to turn around and face him. Working her movements upward, she included her waist, her breasts, and her shoulders in the dance. She swayed with a languorous rhythm, a steady motion that hypnotized her, aroused her senses until she felt each pass of her hair swoop softly against her waist, felt the lace of her corset graze nipples that gathered tight, felt the air caress the exposed skin above her bodice, skin that grew damp with her exertions, with arousal.

And still Nick hummed, though his tempo had picked up, a change she guessed hinted at his own escalating excitement.

She shared his excitement, too. This sexy man placed himself at the mercy of her whim, followed willingly where she led, eagerly accepted what she offered.

This feeling was power, a provocative sensation heightened by the vastness of the theater around them, dangerous for the darkness she couldn't penetrate. The feeling captured her, flushed her skin, urged her to indulge in this newfound need to titillate, and be titillated.

Slowly circling her head, first a tiny spiral that she widened slowly, Julienne shrugged the jacket from her shoulders, a slight movement she didn't think Nick could have noticed beneath the fall of her hair.

She breathed deeply, committing to this course, knowing that once she stepped down this path she'd be obligated to follow where it led. Turning back would only be a disappointment for her, and for him, though she knew Nick's emotional psyche wasn't riding on tonight's outcome.

Hers was. She needed to know she was capable of passion. Tonight was her chance to prove it. Pushing all doubts from her mind, she tugged the jacket down her arms with trembling fingers.

The music faltered, fading away and not resuming until after what sounded suspiciously like a growl.

Dropping the jacket, Julienne nudged it aside with the toe of her pump, never stopping her sinuous motions. She let her eyes drift closed and her arms float up. In lithe, airy measures, she lifted them above her head, caressing the air, giving Nick a glimpse of bare skin and the promise of more to come.

Twisting to the side, she arched her back so her leg peeked through the slit in her dress and was rewarded with another stutter in the music, which had grown higher in pitch, strained.

With a smile she rocked her hips back and forth in a suggestive motion as old as time, a motion that wrung a response from her own body, dampened the tiny silk string of her panties, made her breasts swell heavily. The long smooth motions of her dance heightened the sensation of leather against silk, of lace against skin.

*Naughty girls love to sigh with pleasure.*

Julienne had never been more aroused in her life, hadn't dreamed she could feel this way. And that amazing realization gave her the strength to coil her arms behind her and reach for the top of her zipper. One tug and red leather gaped open to reveal the lace corset below.

The music stopped completely and she waited, waited, but it didn't resume. She was left to dance alone to the sound of Nick's breathing and the beat of her own boldness. Arching her back, she lifted her breasts to the rafters, felt the lace ride upward along her torso, the garters tug the stockings up her thighs.

She let her dress drop to the floor.

"Ah, beautiful," Nick choked the words out on a groan, his passion echoing through the theater, resonating through her.

Stepping out of the puddle of red leather, she swung her hair back and shimmied around, needing to see his face, to gauge his reaction to the sight she must make, dancing in her very sexy underthings on a stage in an empty theater for a man who was practically a stranger.

She couldn't have imagined his expression if she'd tried. There was nothing tepid about his look, a look that declared there was nothing tepid about her. His look was lust, pure and simple.

He lusted for *her*.

Julienne's reaction had everything to do with knowing Nick wanted her, of witnessing the profound appreciation on his handsome face, a feeling of being so very beautiful to this man in this moment that each breath tasted sweeter.

She'd been praised throughout her youth for her intelligence and skill, lauded during her accelerated academic career, but this feeling, this feeling was all about being a beautiful, desirable woman who had a night of opportunity at hand with a hot-blooded man.

A *world* of opportunity, judging by the hunger she saw when Nick extended his hand, beckoned her nearer.

"Come here, Jules." His harsh whisper shot across the distance between them, filled her with the strength of his longing, made her tremble in response to such raw honesty. "I've been watching you move, watching you expose your beautiful body and I want to touch you. You look like sex."

His eyes, glazed and heavy-lidded, fixed on her, captured her with the potency of his words. "Can you imagine my hands on you, Jules? I want to slide them down your creamy neck and along your shoulders. I want to free your breasts and touch them. Can you imagine my mouth on your nipples?"

Julienne's stomach swooped in on itself at his hot words, a longing, desperate pull of sensation that made her gasp. "Yes."

"Then come here. Let me touch you. Let me pleasure you."

His blond hair was a pale shock in the darkness, his words bridging the distance between them, his words a promise that set her into motion with hip-swaying steps that fired his expression even hotter.

He caught her wrist, his fingers tightening around her like a vice as pulled her toward him. "Hop on. I'll help you."

For a moment, Julienne feared she might hurt him with her awkward efforts to climb onto his lap, but his legs were braced to hold them steady and his thighs were pure muscle. He never even flinched as he hoisted her into place. The swing bounced wildly, but Nick held her snugly against him, his laughter rumbling from deep in his chest.

He tipped his head back and blond hair fell away from his brow leaving his chiseled features boldly exposing his pleasure. "Hello, Jules."

The moment became charged, both surreal and wild as they bounced weightless in the swing, her thighs straddling him, the bulge of his erection nestled squarely against her sex, his face level with her breasts.

"Hello, Nick."

That's all Julienne had a chance to say, because he kept his promise. He wanted to touch her. And he did.

His fingertips grazed her cheeks, forced her gaze to his. "I want to make love to you. Will you let me?"

She wanted to come up with some bold reply, but the hunger in his face, the sound of his voice scattered her thoughts. All she could do was sigh her pleasure and drop a kiss onto his mouth.

*Yes.*

That was all the consent Nick needed. Thrusting his tongue into her mouth, he engaged her in a heated kiss, a kiss that shimmered through her body, touching every nerve ending along the way. He ran his hands along her jaw and down her throat, the strong strokes of a man used to taking what he wanted.

He wanted *her.*

And she loved the feeling of being wanted, of wanting, of tangling tongues with wild abandon, of exploring the hot recesses of his mouth with no apology, only a profound appreciation of this incredible chemistry they shared.

Dragging her fingers through his hair, she explored the cool texture, followed the lines that tapered toward his neck. She ran her hands over the fine silk of his dress shirt, learned the knotted muscles making up the expanse of his shoulders.

No wonder women adored him. With his charming smile and skilled hands... They traveled along her body, down her bare arms, along her back, her waist... The thong left her backside bared to his touch and his fingers sank into her cheeks, kneading, exploring her flesh in the palms of his hands.

She sighed. He groaned. Then he ground the bulge of his erection between her legs, that thick ridge riding the nub of her sex as if the silky scrap of her panties or his slacks weren't even there. And they might not have been for all the protection they offered. Dipping his fingers into the cleft of her backside, he followed the curve until his fingers curled into her moist sex.

Julienne shuddered, a full-bodied motion Nick couldn't

have missed, and she knew he hadn't when his mouth broke from hers to trail eagerly down her neck. Arching backward, she lifted her breasts to his face, gasping when he caught the lace edge of her corset and dragged it down with his teeth.

Her breasts were so precariously perched that one tug bared her to his gaze, a gaze that flickered with the most profound appreciation for the sight before him. When he bent his head, used his tongue to lave her nipples until they glistened, peaking to beg for more attention, Julienne let the last lingering remnants of shyness dissolve beneath the power of his touch.

*Naughty girls take advantage of the moment.*

Her sexual appetite was proving itself very healthy and she reveled in that knowledge, in the reality of this man's hunger for her, of her own arousal.

"You're beautiful, Jules," he whispered almost reverently, before his mouth clamped onto a nipple, drew it into his mouth with one hot pull.

The breath fluttered from her lungs and she could only grab his shoulders and hang on when he sucked her nipples, first one then the other, while his erection rode her sex and his fingers softly curled into the wet folds there.

If pleasuring her was a reward for her dance, Julienne decided she'd dance for this man anytime. Her body vibrated with sensation, the thrill of sex with an almost stranger, the empty theater distorting their impassioned sighs into decadent sounds that echoed through the dark quiet.

Possessed by an abandon she'd never known before, she needed to feel Nick inside her, filling all her moist places with that hot length. Slipping her hand between them, she splayed her fingers over his erection, rubbed that thick ridge until he moaned against her breasts. His flesh swelled in response to her touch, larger and impossibly larger, and she didn't stop until his fingers sank into her hips to hold her still as he rocked upward, all abandon and need.

Her own control came under fire at his lack of control, his fevered mouth at her breasts, plucking her nipples with sharp little tugs that had her fumbling at his zipper and carefully unleashing his maleness until she could wrap her fingers around its scorching thickness and issue a few tugs of her own.

Nick bucked hard, tossing his head back, his expression passion personified. His eyes were closed, his black brows drawn against his tanned skin, his features sharp, his mouth parted around ragged breaths. Julienne felt her sex clench at the sight.

Moving against him, she rode his erection as best she could with only the nylon stirrups to anchor her, her own juices making each stroke slick with the promise of what was yet to come....

Some dimly functioning part of Julienne's brain reminded her that she'd come to the Risqué tonight looking to flirt, not to have sex, which translated into a decided lack in the protection department. As daring as she'd become tonight, she wasn't willing to be *that* daring.

"Oh no, Nick," she said on the edge of a frustrated breath. "I didn't expect, I mean... I didn't bring protection."

"Got it covered, beautiful." His eyes popped open with an obvious effort, and he grinned. "I'll swing us toward the stairs and you grab my jacket."

Before she could compliment him on his common sense or even exhale in relief, he launched them into motion, carrying them backward as far as his legs would allow, then letting them glide forward. With a gasp, Julienne hooked an arm around his neck to hang on while they swung forward once, twice, then he leaned backward to gain momentum before... "Got it."

She dragged his jacket off the banister, sending his neat white vest to the floor in the process.

"All right, beautiful. Here, hand it to me."

As he fished inside to an inner pocket and retrieved his wallet, Julienne supposed a real-life naughty boy would carry condoms. Thankfully he was more proficient at this naughty stuff than she was, but then Julienne was a quick study. She might not have expected to have sex tonight, but she'd add a new key phrase to her repertoire....

*Naughty girls are always prepared.*

In the past, she'd found condoms an intrusive and somewhat awkward necessity, but apparently that was in her pre-Nick era. Now, as a naughty girl playing naughty games with a naughty boy, a condom took on a whole new sexy significance.

"Let me," she said, and his gaze glinted approval as he handed her the foil package. "Hold me, please." Weightless was fine and dandy, but if she leaned too far back and overbalanced, she'd land on her head and Nick would likely sustain damage to a critical body part in the process.

He obliged, wrapping his fingers tightly around her waist while she scooted down his lap just enough to allow his erection to slip up from between her thighs and spring free. She felt him shiver beneath her.

"You do things to me I didn't realize could still be done, Jules."

Slipping the condom from its wrapper, she studied it to

make sure she had the right side facing out. "Oh, like what?"

"Like testing my control."

Something in his voice made her glance up to find him watching her with a serious expression that seemed out of sync with the moment. They were having a responsible conversation while swinging in a love swing. She wore hoochie-mama undies and his erection popped through his fly. She *hoped* she tested his control.

"You ain't seen nothing yet," she said lightly, trying to coax a smile back on his face.

"After that striptease, I believe it."

She wished she could do something to really knock his socks off, like roll this condom onto that impressive erection with her mouth. Not only was it logistically impossible in their current positions, but she thought that skill required at least some practice before going live. At least if she didn't want to end up looking like an idiot.

She settled for rolling the condom on the old-fashioned way, while he contemplated her with an intensity that made the dark theater melt away, left only this small part of the stage where the two of them sat so intimately together.

The condom was no sooner fitted into place when Nick's hands slid from her waist, rounded her hips and then clamped under her backside to lift her.

"Oh." Julienne gasped and grabbed his arms for support. Once steady, she slipped her hands between them, stroked the head of his desire against her wet heat.

His gaze blazed a midnight fire that mirrored the intensity of the moment, their attraction. She saw only appreciation and hunger, felt the strength of his need pour through her body like a hot wave. Then he pushed up into her warmth, a groan on his lips as her greedy muscles welcomed him, stretching, unfurling, as he drove his hot male length deeper…deeper still.

His gaze never left hers. The shock of him rocked her, a giant shudder that ran from her head to her toes, chasing all thoughts away beneath a driving need to relieve the ache inside. And Nick must have shared her need, because suddenly he lifted her up, only to draw her back again in a long sweet stroke.

Julienne's chest constricted with the potency of the sensation, her skin burned and her thoughts scattered. Reality narrowed to the way her body connected to his, to her throbbing, wet senses that gathered and built and lifted her with his strokes, made her shiver when he growled aloud his own pleasure.

Suddenly his hands were slipping up her back, pulling her against him, breasts crushing his chest and driving his heat even deeper inside her. He caught her mouth and kissed her possessively, stealing her breath and her reason as he drove into her with one blinding stroke after another.

With the swing balancing her in midair and lending her a freedom of movement she'd never experienced before, Julienne locked her legs around his waist, created leverage to ride him, to meet his powerful thrusts, to create more friction exactly where she needed it most.

The swing rocked wildly, lending momentum to their motions, passion and urgency. The feelings were so intense she could do nothing more than meet each stroke as they built, finally splintering in an explosion that ripped a moan from her lips and dragged Nick right into the fire with her.

Every muscle in his body went rigid and he growled out his satisfaction against her lips, thrusting again and yet again with decreasing frequency as Julienne collapsed against him. Their hearts thundered against each other's, her bare breasts clinging to his sweat-dampened shirt.

She couldn't have spoken even if she'd had the will to try. She didn't. Something about this moment, this utterly beautiful moment where she lay fulfilled and clinging to this incredible man, begged not to be disturbed with anything so trivial as words or thoughts or reason.

Now was the time to inhale Nick's masculine scent, to feel his hands caress her as though he cherished her, to imprint this moment in her memory forever.

There would be time enough later to untangle themselves from this swing, to stand on trembling legs, to face awkward goodbyes and the sobering reality that naughty sex with this naughty boy had surely ruined her for any other kind of sex ever again.

# 5

*The morning after*

JULIENNE STRODE into the kitchen to find Uncle Thad at the table with the Sunday newspaper spread around him.

"Good morning, my dear. Late night last night?"

Her vocal chords couldn't possibly work until after coffee. She blinked eyes scratchy from lack of sleep and nodded.

"So how was the closing performance at the Risqué?"

Of course Uncle Thad had been up since the crack of dawn and wanted to hear all about her night, so she poured a mug, sipped gratefully and willed her body to respond to the caffeine.

"Hair curling," she ground out.

His faded blue gaze lifted to the mop residing on her head—*mop* being the operative term—as she brushed back curls weighted with styling products that had once transformed her hair into a sexy mane. Shimmer dust had stopped shimmering hours ago, sometime between dragging herself out of Nick's arms in the Risqué's parking lot and the time she'd stumbled into bed with a full face of makeup. Now she'd transformed back into plain old Julienne and her next order of business after caffeine was a hot shower.

"You've done something to your hair," Uncle Thad said.

"Ramón's been after me to cut it forever so I finally gave in. It looks nice when I don't have bed-head."

Uncle Thad smiled. "It looks nice even with bed-head."

She smiled back. He was such a dear man and she was so fortunate to have him in her life. Another hot gulp and she launched into details to satisfy his curiosity. "The performance was good last night...." She told him about the play, the party and meeting Nick Fairfax. "I met him and his senior project manager. You should hear their ideas for the theater. It's going to be fabulous when it's done. I think Nick's attention to detail might rival yours, and the Arts Council has given him carte blanche, regardless of how many tax credits he can qualify for."

"Nick, hmm. You sound quite impressed by the man."

Julienne stared into her mug, relieved she couldn't see her reflection in the inky depths. She didn't want to know if a blush went along with the warmth in her cheeks, or the tender aches all over her body that reminded her of just how impressed she'd been by Nick Fairfax last night.

"He's a very impressive man," she said simply. "I liked his senior project manager, too. No wonder ADF has earned such a wonderful reputation."

When Uncle Thad didn't reply, she glanced up to find him regarding her with a frown. "Come sit down, Julienne. I think we should discuss Dr. Fairfax."

Either sleep deprivation still clouded her brain or the memory of her delicious night in Nick's arms had crowded out the ability to think clearly. Either way Uncle Thad's tone of voice sparked a reaction close to panic. He couldn't possibly know what had happened between her and Nick last night. Or could he?

"Why?"

"Come sit." Uncle Thad motioned to the chair across from him. She did as he asked and he continued. "I'd like to share some thoughts that just occurred to me."

Julienne sipped her coffee and braced herself.

"Given that both you and Dr. Fairfax are in the field, it's not inconceivable that you'll run into each other while he's in town. You and I both know that given the extent of renovations, he'll be here awhile."

He paused as though collecting his thoughts. "You're a beautiful woman, Julienne, and you've recently come out of a long engagement. I'm sure you'll eventually date again—"

"Are you cautioning me against Nick?" she asked, so surprised the words popped out of her mouth despite her intention to wait for an explanation.

Uncle Thad nodded. "I know you're an intelligent woman, my dear, but a reminder to be careful around a man like Dr. Fairfax can never go amiss."

"A man like Dr. Fairfax?" He made it sound almost as though Nick was guilty of committing a crime. "Uncle Thad, are you telling me you don't approve of him?"

His mouth thinned into a frown, disappearing into his white mustache and beard. "To be honest, my dear, I don't."

"But I thought you admired him."

"I admire his work a great deal, but as man I think he may be lacking character. The more I've learned about him through the years, the more disappointed I've become."

Julienne set her mug down with a thunk. "I didn't realize you'd met him before."

If she had thought for one second that Uncle Thad knew Nick, she'd have never gone to the Risqué decked out to flirt.

"I don't know him personally, but I know his type. Very well, in fact. I've been following Dr. Fairfax's career ever since he founded ADF. I've heard things from my friends and associates in the field. If I had any questions about his character before, the media blitz when he accepted the presidential appointment only confirmed them. Dr. Fairfax is a man who charms women, moves on and doesn't look back. Trust me, Julienne. He's a heartbreaker. A man who can't commit has a problem.''

Julienne swallowed hard, biting back a retort about not being able to believe everything the media printed, but wondering instead why she felt compelled to defend Nick. She couldn't exactly argue the point now, could she?

Picking up her mug, she considered her uncle. She knew him to be an astute judge of character who would never steer her wrong. He'd liked Ethan but had concerns about her accepting a marriage proposal and hadn't been sorry when they'd ended their engagement.

Julienne couldn't deny there was a lot to be said about a man who'd seduce a woman within the first few hours of becoming acquainted. And a woman who'd let herself be seduced.

A blush warmed her cheeks again and she fought back a wave of chagrin. A healthy sexual appetite was a natural, healthy thing, she reminded herself.

*Naughty girls have the courage to explore their desires.*

She'd had the courage and she shouldn't feel bad. After all, finding a naughty boy had been the whole point of last night. She couldn't have anticipated her original plan of flirting with Nick and getting asked for a date would fly right out the window once they'd met. She hadn't expected the extraordinary attraction between them. Or that self-hypnosis would have her feeling so passionate she couldn't resist his provocative invitation.

But her one-night stand was over. Uncle Thad had nothing to worry about. Unfortunately, she couldn't explain why. Not in so many words, anyway.

"I appreciate your concern and I'll heed your warning."

He nodded. "You're a good girl, Julienne. I know you will.''

She blew him a kiss across the table and he caught it in midair, a game they'd begun so long ago, she couldn't even remember when, yet a game that still made her feel loved.

Julienne mentally sighed. If closing night had gone as she'd planned, she may have flirted her way into a date with Nick, which would mean inventing an excuse to cancel. She couldn't have him showing up on their doorstep now, knowing how Uncle Thad felt.

But her plan hadn't gone as designed and Julienne wasn't sorry at all. She and Nick had gone from start to finish in their relationship in one delicious night. She had memories to savor and her uncle had absolutely nothing to worry about.

*Three days later*

NICK CAUGHT SIGHT of the street sign that read Casa de Ramón and swung the rented sport-utility vehicle into the parking lot. The salon sat right in the middle of an upscale row of historic townhomes that had been converted into businesses. A tailor, a boutique, a children's specialty store.

Maneuvering into a parking spot, he tossed the gearshift into Park and gazed through the windshield at the Victorian row home—his one and only clue to the niece of a retired materials conservationist who'd completely knocked him for a loop.

How in hell had he confused Jules with a one-night stand? Nick could only reason that his brains had taken up temporary residence in his crotch and that making love with her had rendered him brain dead. But he was in full control of his faculties now and couldn't deny that only the biggest idiot on the planet would have let her leave without a way to reach her again. He knew she worked in education, but no last name equaled anonymity in Savannah's large school system. Why had he let her go without getting her number?

Okay, Nick could answer that question. Pride. Jules obviously wasn't interested, because when he'd asked her last name, she'd simply given him one of those amazing kisses and told him they shouldn't spoil a night of fantasy with reality.

Even so, he still didn't have to let her go. He didn't have to walk her to her car, kiss those wine-red lips or let her drive off in a glow of red taillights. He hadn't even had enough brain cells left to write down her license plate number.

Days had passed since closing night and all his brain cells still weren't up and running yet. And those that were…well, they couldn't focus on anything but her.

Fortunately, work hadn't been too taxing. He'd settled into his new place and directed the movers to clear out the theater. Props, sets and all salvageable items had been stored.

Nick didn't see his condition getting better anytime soon. Every taillight he saw still brought to mind Jules's red-devil dress and when she'd slipped that dress off to reveal a body straight from his fantasies. The way she'd danced for him, so bold and uninhibited…his mouth still went dry thinking about it.

Pride be damned. He wasn't going to worry about Jules's reaction, not when he didn't know if he could even find her or whether she'd see him if he did. But he'd damned sure try to convince her.

Thrusting open the car door, he walked the short distance to the salon and went inside. He took in the stylish Art Deco interior just enough to appreciate the clever use of geometric design and tile to incorporate the hair salon basics. Then he headed straight for the reception desk.

"May I see Ramón?"

"Do you have an appointment?" A beautiful young blonde lifted her bright-blue gaze to his.

"No."

She stared at him, wide-eyed and unblinking, as if he'd asked her to accomplish a task as unlikely as cleaning the grout lines of all this tile with a toothbrush.

"I met him Saturday night and he told me to come in," Nick added impatiently, whipping out the salon's business card and holding it up as proof.

She stared at the card and her expression transformed to one of such tragic horror that Nick glanced down at the card, wondering what was wrong. Nothing, as far as he could tell, and only when she raked her gaze over him and shook her head sadly did he realize she must think he'd come to Ramón for something other than a haircut.

Nick winced. He opened his mouth to defend his sexual preference, but remembered he wasn't interested in this fluffy little blonde. He was after much sultrier prey. Who cared what this woman thought of him if he got back to see Ramón?

"Ask him if he'll squeeze me in. I just need a trim."

As she rose and circled the desk, she cast another disappointed glance his way. At least she thought he was a loss. Nick supposed that counted for something.

Not two minutes had passed before an ear-shattering squeal peeled out louder than the blow dryers. Nick spun toward the sound in time to see Ramón practically flying through the busy salon, looking like a giant bat with his arms raised and some sort of black coat flapping behind him.

"Dr. Nick, Dr. Nick, you came." he said. "Of course I'll squeeze you in."

Every damned head in the shop turned to see whose arrival had inspired such enthusiasm and Nick forced a smile and thrust out his hand to stop Ramón dead in his tracks before he got too close.

"I appreciate it." He shook Ramón's hand, unable to miss the way the man's gaze traveled straight to his hair. Ramón frowned, prompting Nick to explain, "I just need a trim."

A bald lie as he always cut his hair before starting a job, so he didn't have to worry about finding a decent barber in a new town for a few weeks.

"So I see. I'm processing a perm and have a few minutes free. Come on back."

Nick almost changed his mind when he spotted the shampoo bowl and realized Ramón intended to perform this little ritual himself, but the man proved to be the epitome of professionalism, regaling him with questions about his plans for the theater.

Once in a styling chair and caped for action, Nick got straight to the point. "Where can I find Jules?"

Ramón met his gaze in the mirror, his widening smile reflecting both understanding and delight. "So you're interested in her, are you?"

"Yes."

"But you don't know how to reach her?"

"No."

Nick's answer seemed to give Ramón cause to consider. Reaching for the clippers, he lapsed into silence as he edged the line at the back of Nick's neck. Finally he asked, "All right, Dr. Nick, shoot straight with me. How is it you managed to part company without her phone number? Didn't you ask for it?"

"No."

Ramón grimaced and Nick laughed dryly. "I know, stupid."

"I would *never* use that word on a paying customer, but it does sort of work, doesn't it?"

"Unfortunately, yes." Nick scowled hard, which earned him an appreciative laugh.

"Did you at least ask for her last name?"

"As a matter of fact I did." There, he wasn't as big a fool as he felt at the moment.

"Then you're not looking hard enough." Ramón paused with the clipper in his hand as he met Nick's gaze again in the mirror. "I happen to know Jules is in the book."

"Which would work if I actually knew her last name."

"I thought you just said—"

"I asked for her last name, but she didn't give it to me."

When Ramón arched a meticulously shaped eyebrow and dropped the clippers on his station with a thunk, Nick knew his request had been denied. Ramón grabbed the blow dryer, clicked the power on and effectively ended their conversation.

Nick sat there, forced to reformulate his strategy. Hell, he couldn't blame the guy. He wouldn't want Ramón arbitrarily passing out Jules's information to just anybody. But Nick wasn't just anybody. She'd stripped for him on the Risqué Theatre's stage. He'd made love to her in a love swing and hadn't been able to think about anything else since.

"Listen, I understand your position," he said when Ramón shut off the dryer. "I realize you don't know me from Adam. Just for the record, I'm not a stalker or a serial killer. I want to send her flowers. How about I have them delivered here and you call her so she can pick them up. Deal?"

Ramón gave a laugh and extended his hand. "Deal."

JULIENNE'S DAY on Indian Knoll Island had been a long one. She'd instructed her interns on mapping and numbering floorboards, conducting moisture readings and other necessary processes in a one hundred and thirty-six-year-old church.

The church had been built a year after the Civil War's end, almost a year to the day when the first stone had been laid for the Risqué. The irony didn't escape her. In fact, nothing connected to the Risqué had escaped her notice the past few days.

No, her brain seemed mired in memories of *that* night and of the man who now conducted similar studies at the theater. Despite her uncle's warning, she'd had Nick on the brain in a big way.

Julienne sighed, envying Nick his project. Today had concluded her students' trip into the field, yet so much still needed to be done on the church, so many facets of preservation she wanted to share with her students.

Unfortunately, most preservation architects weren't eager for students to run around their work sites asking basic questions. Julienne had earned herself a reputation for instructing students who were both proficient and useful, which had resulted in a variety of invitations to some great projects. But the invitations were never for more than the time it took to complete individual tasks that only comprised a small percentage of the overall job.

She had great interns who needed seasoning in the field. They needed to experience a real renovation, the mystery of opening a building up without knowing what to expect, how many pieces of the antique puzzle might be missing and how they might put the puzzle back together with modern materials.

Neither the lab nor the classroom could prepare them for the interactions of restoration architects, structural engineers, materials conservationists, millworkers, bricklayers, masons, contractors and apprentices, all of whom played such crucial roles in preservation work. None of her students had had the benefit of being raised in the field with an uncle who specialized in materials conservation.

Oh, well. These past few days had provided a good experience, anyway—definitely a tiring one. Maybe tonight she'd actually sleep. But Julienne doubted it. Her nights had been filled with dreamy memories of Nick Fairfax and the love swing and other sundry fantasies of what else she'd like to do with him on the Risqué's stage, or in a bed, or on the shores of Indian Knoll Island, or wherever they happened to be. The rich strains of his humming had been her constant companion these days past, both awake and asleep.

Julienne rolled her eyes. She hadn't read anywhere in *The Naughty Handbook* that naughty girls were supposed to get all hung up on their one-night stands. She was hopeless.

Placing her briefcase and laptop beside the hall tree, she toed off her muddy workboots so she wouldn't track dried mud and other various organic matter through the house. Just as she was making her way down the hall toward the kitchen for a bottle of spring water, the phone rang. When it continued to ring she guessed Uncle Thad must be in his office, screening calls before allowing himself to be disturbed. The recording began, Uncle Thad's voice stating that neither he nor Julienne could pick up the phone at the present time, but to leave a message after the tone….

"I asked you to call me, Jules sweetheart, but you're holding out on me," Ramón's voice rang out over the recorder. "What happened between you two that night?"

She made a wild leap for the phone and snatched it up before Uncle Thad overheard anything incriminating. "What makes you think something happened?" she blasted into the receiver.

"Dr. Divine showed up in my chair today with nothing on his head to cut. I almost felt guilty charging him forty bucks to clip his sideburns."

"Ramón, you didn't."

"It's business, sweetheart. Of course I did. He handed me a fifty and told me to keep the change. The man's a class act. He gets my vote as the new guy in your life."

"You didn't tell him anything about me, did you?"

"Absolutely not. Quieter than your confessor, remember? I did agree to let him deliver *dozens* of the most ravishing roses I've ever seen. Coral roses, Jules, do you know what they mean? Desire, sweetheart," he continued without waiting for a reply. "And oodles and oodles of money, because those suckers are expensive and there must be three dozen here. But he'll get his money's worth trust me. I left them at the front desk and we've all been making trips up there to admire them. Oh, and there's a card. I didn't open it, of course, but I did hold it to the light. He wrote down his number. Are you going to call?"

That snapped Julienne from her daze. "Ramón."

"Don't get all prissy on me. Remember turning over a new leaf? You've got to take advantage of that new haircut."

She huffed, directing her exhalation at the wispy bangs in her eyes. One sober discovery about this new hairstyle was that a ponytail no longer swept all the hair back from her face. "Oh, I don't know." She tried to sound nonchalant, unaffected.

"What do you mean you don't know?" Ramón grumbled. "Didn't I just give him my seal of approval. What could you possibly not know about that divine man?"

Ramón was right; Nick was divine, *too* divine. She was way out of her league here. Even Uncle Thad knew it. "I'll swing by to pick them up on my way to the university tomorrow."

"No way, sweetheart. You need to go to bed with these on your night table to make you dream sexy dreams about that utterly delicious man. Tell you what, I'm getting ready to close the shop and you're on my way home. I'll just drop them by.''

How would she explain three dozen roses to Uncle Thad. ''That's not necessary—''

''It most definitely is if you're seriously contemplating not returning the man's call. He's positively gaga over you, sweetheart. Everyone in the salon noticed. I only wished Dr. Ethan had been here so I could have introduced them.''

''Ramón.'' Julienne's heart had begun to beat wildly. ''I appreciate what you're trying to do, but don't.''

''Then promise me you'll call him.''

''I will. I have to thank him for the roses.'' After she hid them in her bedroom.

''For more than thanking him for the roses.''

''I'll think about it.''

''What's there to think about?'' Ramón demanded. ''Just what exactly are you afraid of?''

''I'm not afraid of anything,'' she lied.

''That's good, because the worst I see happening if you let that exquisite man have his way with you is getting wined and dined, gifted with some expensive roses and maybe even some more expensive sparklies and ending up having all kinds of yummy sex. Live a little, Jules, before you're too old.''

''I'll think about it.''

''Yeah, well you've got exactly twenty minutes to think because I expect a yes when I get there or I'm telling Uncle Thad that you're too much of a weenie to live.''

Uncle Thad would be the last person to lend his efforts to the cause, but she didn't tell Ramón that. ''Cut me a break.''

''No breaks. Buck up, sweetheart. See you in twenty.''

The line clicked. Setting the receiver back in the cradle,

Julienne rested her brow against the wall and closed her eyes. She had to think. Coral roses? Desire? Nick wanted her to call him?

*Oh puh-leeze, girl.* That voice in her head cried out. *You know exactly what this means. Nick Fairfax wants to continue the one-night stand. Question is what are you going to do?*

Julienne inhaled deeply. In the span of one phone call, her exhaustion had gone the way of the red-eye and left her with an adrenaline rush that made her blood pound so loud she couldn't hear the sound of Nick's humming anymore.

Okay, think. Use the old brain. Nick wanted to continue the one-night stand. The self-hypnosis-induced ache inside gave a needy little clench at the idea of seeing him again. But how could she? Uncle Thad would be mortified if she got involved with him.

She was thirty, for goodness sake. The time for rebellion had been back in her teens, when she could claim youthful stupidity for her indiscretions and Uncle Thad had been young enough to withstand the stress without potentially serious side effects.

*So when do you get to explore your sensuality, girl?* Her inner voice reminded her. *You're not looking for a relationship. You just ended one and look where it left you —alone and feeling as though you didn't possess a passionate bone in your body. Nick proved you wrong. Sure you don't want to explore the opportunity at hand? Why not try again to make sure that night wasn't a fluke?*

Did she dare? What came after a one-night stand, anyway? Leaving the kitchen, Julienne beelined for her bedroom to retrieve *The Naughty Handbook* from under her pillow.

Sitting down on the edge of her bed, she thumbed through

the pages, looking for the chapter on relationships. Ah, there it was...a torrid fling came after a one-night stand.

*Naughty girls take advantage of the moment.*

She couldn't possibly. Uncle Thad didn't respect Nick. But her uncle was thinking marriage material. Julienne wanted passion. Exactly what Nick offered.

All right, what was the worst that happened if she had a torrid fling with Nick Fairfax? She would lose her heart to a naughty boy who wouldn't think twice about her when he moved on.

*But you'll have had your turn, at least.*

All right, all right. *Julienne* was obsessing here, not the woman who'd stripped on the Risqué's stage to the sound of a handsome man humming. *That* woman wouldn't be worrying about what her uncle thought. Or about what happened after a torrid fling ended. The woman who'd wished she could roll a condom onto Nick's penis with her mouth wouldn't be wondering whether she'd be able to get over him after he'd left.

No, *that* woman, the woman Nick knew as Jules, would toss her mane of hair, grab his crotch and eat him for supper.

Sure he'd move on to another woman, *eventually,* and sure he'd ultimately leave town *forever,* but Jules would make sure she'd gotten her fill of him before he did.

*Naughty girls take advantage of the moment.*

Should she miss the opportunity to develop her naughty girl skills in a torrid fling with the perfect naughty boy? No!

But what about Uncle Thad? She could never blatantly go against his wishes—no matter how much she wanted to make love to Nick again. Explaining to her uncle that she wanted to use Nick for sex was out of the question. No, she had to come up with a way of making a fling look like it wasn't a fling.

Tumbling back onto her bed, Julienne thumbed through

*The Naughty Handbook* for inspiration. Something that would convince Uncle Thad that being around Nick posed no threat.

Unfortunately, scripts for sexy telephone conversations and names of stores that sold sex toys provided no ideas whatsoever. With a sigh, she finally slipped the book under her pillow and sat up, tucking her knees beneath her chin in a fetal position of sorts that didn't stir her imagination, either.

But that was before she noticed the grass and muck-stained knees of her ratty blue jeans, and…tada, a compelling reason for becoming involved with Nick waltzed fully formed into her head. *If* she was daring enough to try it.

Julienne launched herself up, positively inspired, and headed for her briefcase chanting, "Naughty girls take chances."

# 6

*The following morning*

NICK ROLLED OUT from the crawlspace to stare up at Dale, who towered above him in the damp basement. "It's ugly."

"No surprises there. So what's the verdict?"

Nick dragged his industrial halogen lamp from the crawlspace and squinted against the light. "Since we need the electrical and plumbing systems up to modern standards and this one-hundred thirty-seven-year-old patchwork job is a wreck..." He shook his head. "We might use the same conduits and openings as the original heating system. The rest is a bust."

"Ouch." Dale scratched some notations on his pad, absently extending his hand to help Nick to his feet.

Ouch was right. The Risqué Theatre would require an upgrade of seismic proportions. The original structure had been added to and modernized through the years, which made the building a fusion of eras and technologies.

Even worse was the damage sustained by a fire in the concession area sometime during World War II. Elaborate plaster ceilings had collapsed, hardwood floors had buckled, decorative wallpaper had been stained and mahogany paneling had warped. The outward damage to the west portion of the lobby had been pieced together cosmetically, which left him with structural damage that had been deteriorating for sixty-plus years.

Needless to say, restoring this theatre without marring its historic character would be a challenge. But it just so happened that Nick needed a good challenge right now—to get a woman named Jules off his mind.

The sound of approaching footsteps ringing out on the stone floor drew his attention.

"What's up, Betty?" he asked his administrative assistant, a divorcée with grown children, who claimed to enjoy traveling with Nick's team because she could wear sweats to work and didn't wind up babysitting her grandkids too often.

"A professor from the University of Savannah is here."

Grabbing a cloth, Nick wiped his hands. "Did he say what he wants?"

"*She* only said she wants to see you."

"All right. As long as you're here, Betty, go through the morning's notes with Dale and take them back to transcribe."

"Do you want to give me your recorder, too?"

He shook his head. "I'll drop it off later."

He left, hoping this professor from the University of Savannah didn't want him to lecture. Until this project got underway, his schedule would be erratic to say the least.

When Nick exited the building to blinding sunlight, he blinked to ward off the effects of a morning spent playing the mole. But even despite his flawed eyesight, he immediately noticed the woman standing in front of the trailer.

She stood with her back to him, presumably reading ADF's mission statement that, along with his company's logo, comprised a large portion of the trailer. Something about her seemed familiar, but perhaps only his disadvantaged eyesight made her seem so, because when he took in the tailored bronze suit and neat hairstyle, he couldn't place her.

Then she stepped back, moving out from the shadows of the trailer's overhang. Sunlight sparked on her hair and Nick realized the wine-red mane that had shimmered with glitter dust on closing night now twisted up in an elegant sweep.

*Jules.*

She looked so different from the red devil in his memory, he was glad he'd seen her before she'd seen him, giving him a chance to school his surprise. But this was his Jules all right, perhaps another side of her, a side just as beautiful in the sunlight as she'd been in the darkness, just as tempting in a business suit as she'd been in red leather.

"Hello, beautiful."

Spinning around, she fixed her gray gaze on him, a gaze that had seemed smoky in the shadows but shone clear as quicksilver in the daylight. In fact, for as sultry and gorgeous as she'd been in a dimly lit theater, she was ravishing now. Wisps of that incredible hair fringed around her face, a face more natural and classic without the addition of dramatic nighttime makeup.

And her smile...a slow upturning of her oh-so sensual mouth landed a punch right to his gut.

"Hello, Nick." Sunlight had no effect on her voice, the same sultry sound that had haunted him for the past five days.

"A professor?" he asked.

"Dr. Julienne Blake, professor of historic preservation at the University of Savannah. Pleased to meet you."

When she extended her hand in formal greeting, Nick's senses snapped to attention. Instinctively he reached out and slipped his hand beneath hers, brought it to his lips to brush a kiss across her knuckles.

Ah, she hadn't been a figment of his imagination, after all. And he supposed he shouldn't be surprised she taught historic preservation, given her knowledge base.

"Julienne," he whispered, unwilling to let her go. "A beautiful name for a beautiful woman. Is Jules a nickname?"

She only nodded, her quicksilver gaze revealing their touch impacted her as much as it impacted him.

"I'm very glad you came today."

"The roses are beautiful. Thank you."

"My pleasure."

The longer he held her hand, the stronger the impact on him, and her, judging by the tiny sigh that slipped from her lips. What was it about the attraction between them that sparked like a match to dry wood?

Nick rallied his senses first, with the wry thought that he might otherwise still be holding her hand and staring at her by the time Betty returned if he didn't say or do something.

"Please come inside." He let her hand slip away. "I'd like to talk about seeing you again." Pulling open the trailer door, he allowed her to precede him up the steps.

Whether she wore red leather or bronze linen, her smooth curves affected Nick the same way. His pulse kicked up and sent his blood crashing south. An effect that multiplied exponentially once inside the close confines of his mobile office.

She inhaled sharply when he brushed past her, a fluttery...almost *shy* sound that reminded Nick of closing night. What he'd only suspected then became a certainty now. Jules wasn't nearly as used to flirting as she pretended to be, which begged the question—why had she allowed him to seduce her?

He intended to find out, because this breathless quality of hers drove him wild. Moving around his desk, he sat, as much to give her space as himself. "Please." He motioned to the chair in front of the desk. "I'd like to see you again, Jules. I want to know all about the woman who fascinated me with her architectural knowledge and danced for me on-stage.''

A faint hint of pink touched her cheeks at the reminder of the intimacies they'd shared and Nick couldn't help smiling. ''I can't stop thinking about you.''

''I've been having the same problem,'' she admitted softly.

''What are we going to do?''

''I've been giving the solution some thought.''

She sounded so serious, as if she'd analyzed and reasoned through their various options with careful deliberation, that his smile deepened. ''What have you come up with?''

She stood, clearly unable to sit still, cocked a hip on the edge of his desk, and stared at him. Nick leaned back, pleased with her intensity, as eager to hear what she had to say as he was to touch her beautiful body again.

''For the past three days I've had my class in the field,'' she said. ''We've been conducting moisture analysis and some other preliminary tests at a historic church on the coast. I've got great interns, Nick. They're smart, enthusiastic, willing to work hard—''

''Interns, Jules?'' he asked, not realizing he'd cut her off until the words were actually out of his mouth. He laughed wryly. ''Excuse me for interrupting you. But you said your interns. What exactly do you teach?''

''A curriculum for advanced practical and professional skills. I require my students to explore critical and contemporary issues in our field. I teach undergrad and grad classes and I'm supervising the internship of a select group of grad students.''

''Internship? Grad students?''

''You're surprised.'' It wasn't a question.

''You just seem awfully young to be teaching grad students. If I'd have been guessing, I'd have pegged you as one yourself.''

Her chest rose and fell beneath her pale blouse, firing his tastebuds with the memory of her delicious breasts. "Thank you. I'm often very close in age to my students, sometimes younger."

"So how does such a lovely young woman become a professor of grad students older than she is?"

She smiled. "Remember the uncle I told you about?"

He nodded.

"Well, he's technically my great uncle, and I took over his position on the faculty when he retired."

Nick issued a low whistle. "Nifty trick. I don't think I know too many historic preservation professors who are much younger than your great uncle sounds."

"I, uh, brought unique qualifications to the position."

Steepling his hands before him, he watched her hands flutter idly, as if she didn't know what to do with them, and settled back to hear her remarkable explanation. "Such as?"

"Fourteen years in the field."

Nick blinked. *He* barely had fourteen years in the field and he had to be older than Jules. "How did you manage that?"

"My uncle brought me up after my parents died. He's a materials conservationist, so I traveled with him."

Then it hit Nick. *Blake.* He knew that name, but she couldn't possibly be referring to… "Who's your uncle?"

"Thaddeus Blake," she said so casually Nick could only stare. "You may be familiar with some of his work. I know he's familiar with yours."

*May* be familiar with? He'd been studying Thaddeus Blake's work ever since college. An icon in the field, the man commanded a respect that prompted students, including Nick, to model their entire careers on. In fact, ADF's mission statement and the pledge Nick made before starting every job had been based on something Thaddeus Blake had once said in a lecture Nick had attended.

*When the fate of the past, of history, is in your hands, you're responsible to do your best to preserve it for the future.*

"I've heard of him," Nick said. "I knew he'd left the field to teach, and now that you mention it, I recall hearing he'd settled in Savannah. He dropped out of sight and I just never put two and two together when I contracted this project."

"He retired."

Nick met her gaze. "You've been renovating buildings all over the world with Thaddeus Blake...for exactly how long?"

"Since I was six."

And on closing night he'd wondered if she'd been genuinely interested in his architectural renovations. "Well. I'd say you did bring unique qualifications to your position."

She laughed, her smile making his blood pound harder....

And then a horrible thought struck him. He'd seduced Thaddeus Blake's niece. The man he'd admired for his entire career, a man whose work he'd respected to point of damned hero worship, and Nick had seduced his protégée, his *niece*.

"Jules, why didn't you tell me who you were?"

Folding her arms across her chest, she looked uncomfortable, but she held his gaze steadily when she said, "I wanted to enjoy the night with no strings."

"Did you know I'd be at the performance?"

"Yes."

A simple word that revealed so much and changed everything.

"You wanted to meet me?"

She nodded, gave him an almost sheepish grin. "I'm also an admirer of your work. But I never expected to..."

"Make love to me." That was the truth. He couldn't forget her dismay at realizing she didn't have a condom. Or her pleasure at finding out he did. "Are you sorry?"

"What do you think?"

Their gazes locked across the desk, connected them, making this transition from fantasy to reality and the attraction they felt for each other seem physical.

Fair enough. No one understood *no strings* better than Nick, and he certainly wouldn't condemn her for following the credo he lived by, even if for some reason knowing she'd walked off without looking back tweaked his pride.

Or had she?

"Why did you come today?"

"Because I decided one night with you wasn't enough."

Her admission filtered through him, an onslaught of awareness that she wanted him, a woman who shared his same interests, a woman who'd experienced a lifetime in the field with the greatest preservation architect of the century.

A woman who turned him on so much he couldn't look at her without the seam of his jeans cutting into his crotch.

Pushing the chair back, Nick stood and moved to the desk, close enough to take Jules in his arms. "One night's not enough. Not nearly enough."

With a sigh, she slipped her arms around his waist and whispered, "We could have a torrid fling."

*A torrid fling?*

Okay, he'd never heard the phrase before but it worked. When he gazed into those clear eyes, at those lips just begging for his kisses, Nick would have agreed to anything that allowed him to kiss her and become better acquainted in the daylight.

Her lips parted beneath his as though she'd been waiting forever. He felt as though he had. He burned so hot for this woman that when she ran her hands up his back, anchoring him close, he thrust his tongue in her mouth and kissed her with all the pent-up hunger from a very long five days.

Her tongue met his, a delicious swirl of warm-velvet skin, curious caresses and hot sweet breath that shot his pulse into the red zone. He wanted to lay her back on his desk and explore every inch of her, wanted to prove they could burn even hotter in the daylight than they had on closing night.

Making love wasn't an option. Not only could Betty, or anyone for that matter, walk in, but Nick intended to wine and dine Jules the right way. Empty stages had their appeal, but this woman needed to know how much she'd affected him.

He forced his mouth from hers, sat there brow to brow, his heart pounding. "What were you saying about your interns?"

"I want to bring them on site with your team."

That wasn't what he'd expected. "Really?"

"Don't say no just yet, Nick," she said earnestly. "Hear me out first."

He bit back a smile that she was so sure he'd deny her request. "All right, I'm listening."

"I've got a great group of interns. They've done an enormous amount of fieldwork. This city is a giant lab with all its historic districts, but they're only seeing bits and pieces. I want them to experience a project from start to finish."

"How many interns?"

"Eight."

"Why do I need eight interns roaming around a site where I'm renovating a theater that's crumbling around my ears—"

"Think grunt work." Slipping her hands from around his waist, she waved them to emphasize her point. "Think all the necessary stuff you hire locals to do. The kind of jobs I used to do for Uncle Thad. I could scrape paint and run analysis by the time I was nine."

For some reason, the thought of a young Jules, with her wine-red hair and big gray eyes, running around a work site taking paint samples made him smile.

"I'll be solely responsible for my students and their work," she said. "They won't get in anyone's way. I promise. And they wouldn't be on site all the time, either. They're required to spend a certain amount of time in the classroom and lab each week. Not to mention that I teach some undergrad classes, as well, which means I have to be at the university, too. Look, I brought a list of all the preservationists I've worked with, the Historic Foundation and the Development and Renewal Authority." She leaned out of the circle of his arms and grabbed her purse from the chair, and then she fished through her bag to withdraw a folded sheet of computer paper. "Have your secretary call them. Every one will tell you I run a tight team."

"Will they now?"

"Absolutely. Think about what this will mean to the students, Nick. How many graduates can say they've interned with the appointee on the President's Advisory Board?"

"Sounds rather impressive, doesn't it?"

She nodded. "It would mean so much to them. Not only for their resumes but just to watch you and your design team at work. This is a chance of a lifetime."

He'd never been anyone's chance of a lifetime before. "Will Uncle Thad come visit the site?"

"I can ask."

"That's good enough for me, Dr. Blake." He pressed a kiss to her brow to seal the deal. "Welcome to my team."

# 7

*A day later*

JULIENNE HADN'T BEEN this excited about working on a project since Uncle Thad had supervised an aerial photography shoot to create a photogrammetric map of Alcatraz Island. Grabbing her briefcase, she hopped out of the van while mentally chanting, *Naughty girls play it cool.*

"All right, guys, gather around and listen up," she addressed her students as the last one piled out of the van into the parking lot. "You know the ground rules. We've got a once-in-a-lifetime opportunity here, so let's make the most of it. I know you'll all show Dr. Fairfax and his design team you're a group of professionals who will be an asset to his team."

Julienne treated herself to a deep cleansing breath and led her students into the theater.

*Naughty girls play it cool.*

She was completely cool by the time they tracked Nick down—or at least his bottom half.

She might not have recognized the straight jean-clad legs and workboots protruding from the heating conduit had it not been for the way the worn jeans molded his very attractive backside. She could see the flashlight beam slicing through the darkness inside as he inspected the shaft. She motioned her students to silence and waited for him to resurface.

"I don't remember these conduits being such a mess from your report, Dale, but I think we can use this one," Nick called out. "Hand me the infrared glasses, would you?"

Julienne wasn't Dale, but as Nick's senior project manager wasn't around, she took it upon herself to do the honors. Handing her briefcase to Wendy, a bubbly woman whose sooty black pixie haircut framed a face perpetually fixed with a smile, she scanned a nearby table for the equipment.

As she reached into the conduit, she had the naughty urge to run her hand over those cute buns, but had to settle for touching Nick's fingers as she passed him the glasses, a touch that revealed she wasn't his senior project manager.

His head reared up as he twisted around to see her in the tight conduit and a loud thunk echoed, quickly followed by his growl. "Damn it."

Several of the students laughed, but a glare from Julienne quickly brought silence again. Struggling to keep her expression even, she watched Nick back out of the conduit in an erotic shimmying of solidly muscular legs and tight butt. He finally sat up to face her. His gaze caught hers and she couldn't mistake the pleasure she saw there.

"Hello, Dr. Fairfax," she said.

"Hello, Dr. Blake." His gaze lingered on her only an instant before swiveling to the tightly knit group of students, all staring down at him as if they'd been struck by lightning.

Nick made a move to stand, and Julienne extended her hand to help him, schooling her expression the instant their fingers met. Her every contact with this man felt charged and judging by the way his mouth compressed into a tight line, she wasn't the only one who felt it.

To segue through the moment, she introduced Nick to her students. "They're in their sixth year with the program now, and I interned while they were my uncle's students. I officially became their professor two years ago.''

They were great students, responding to Nick's questions with deference and enthusiastic promises to work hard.

Nick was pleased, she could tell by the way he relaxed. ''We'll need all the help we can get around here, trust me. We haven't scratched the surface of this job yet and this theater is already full of surprises.''

''I wasn't sure if you'd have anything special for us to start on today,'' she told Nick. ''So I worked up a game plan of possibilities so you can decide where we'll best fit in.''

Nick gave her an appreciative nod, and she motioned Wendy to hold up her briefcase, while she fished out her proposal.

''You're the first group of interns any of ADF's senior design teams has ever hosted,'' he explained, clearly at ease with the group. Though she wasn't sure why that surprised her, given his credentials as a lecturer. ''We're based out of California and have a local division that sponsors preservation programs with a university there. The rest of our teams work in the field.''

She handed Nick the printout and stood back while his black gaze raked over the page.

''You're right,'' he finally said, and she experienced a pleasurable little zing when he smiled in approval. ''Why don't you assess the seating and once it's done and moved out, you can map the floor.''

''All right, guys,'' Julienne said, commanding their attention. ''We'll begin assessing at the orchestra pit and work back from the stage. We'll set up home base...'' She pointed to a stretch of wall south of an emergency exit and looked to Nick for confirmation that they wouldn't be in anyone's way. He nodded. ''Right over there. Grab your gear and get the lights up. Wendy, please take my briefcase. I'll be right over.''

She turned around to face Nick, feeling edgy as he watched her students head across the auditorium, his profile dark against the shadowed backdrop of the balcony.

''Were you ever that enthusiastic?'' He didn't turn to look at her, but continued watching her students, most of whom were on their knees unpacking gear.

''I grew up doing this,'' she replied honestly. ''By the time I trained formally this was all old news. I think that's why I enjoy the students so much. Seeing the work through their eyes keeps me fresh. How about you?''

''Yeah, I think I was.''

Judging by his wistful smile, Julienne guessed he might be feeling some of that enthusiasm again.

Then his expression faded and he turned to her, back to the here and now. ''I'll be around all day, if you need anything. Direct questions to me, or Dale. He's around here somewhere, too.''

''All right.''

His gaze shifted to a point above her head, and Julienne turned, wondering what had made his eyes crinkle in amusement. Turning, she followed his gaze to the stage, which had been cleared of props, backdrops and curtains and the love swing. She sighed.

Nick chuckled. ''Have fun, beautiful.''

''I will.'' She fought back an overwhelming need to lift up on tiptoes and press a kiss to his tempting mouth.

She managed to quell the urge, focusing her energies instead on assigning her students work. They would dismantle the seating, one seat at a time, assess the condition of each, then note the damage on an evaluation sheet Julienne had created last night. While the students worked, she supervised and assisted their efforts, pointing out damage they may have overlooked or asking questions to get them formulating opinions about what parts of the seats would be salvageable.

"Dr. Blake, look at this," Wendy said, motioning to the seat her boyfriend Brit held up for their inspection. "These grooves are deep. Brit doesn't think they'll sand out."

Julienne knelt, following Wendy's immaculately manicured fingertips with her own, tracing the grooves in the oak.

"They're deep. What do you think about filling them?"

"Yeah, that'd work," Brit said. "Once they're filled, sanded and stained, no one will notice."

"I agree. But I have a question." Grabbing Wendy's hand, Julienne inspected her French manicure. The magic Katriona had worked on her own nails was seriously showing the effects of her work in the field. A week ago she wouldn't have thought twice about it, but now that she'd officially signed on for a torrid fling... "How do you keep your nails looking so good? You've been digging around in the same muck I have."

"Acrylic." Wendy laughed. "I visit Delia's manicurist."

"Every Saturday morning at nine," Brit said, rolling his eyes. "No matter how late we've been out the night before."

"That's real commitment." She might just give Katriona's suggestion for "real" nails a little more thought, when she had spare brain cells to devote to her manicure.

As it was, she spent her time on her knees working with her students or discussing the history of the Risqué Theatre.

"Who took the time to review the packets I sent home yesterday?" She was pleased to see that everyone nodded or raised a hand in the air. "Great. Then who can tell me how many of these seats we'll be assessing?"

"A total of 1,446—892 on the orchestra level, 136 on the mezzanine and 148 in the balcony."

"All right, Wendy. Take five points for your daily field report."

Wendy smiled smugly at Brit, who sat close by and added, "The city acquired the Risqué in 1974."

"And 2.6 million people have attended performances since the city's acquisition," Melissa piped in.

Julienne laughed. "Ooh. You all are so cool. But I've got one that'll get you. How long is the longest employment tenure with the theater?"

"A century?" Charlie, the comedian of the group, offered.

"Right. Try forty-five years. Esther Lou Quincy worked in the box office from 1924 until 1969."

And so the day went.

Removing and assessing theater seats was tough, dirty work. Her students worked in pairs, two sets of untrained eyes usually catching what one set alone might overlook, two pairs of unskilled hands managing a task that may have been unwieldy for one, and two enthusiastic brains meeting in a clash of inspired ideas, observations and interpretations.

This group of interns interacted well together. Wendy and Brit, who'd begun dating in their second year with the program, worked nearby, sitting close and murmuring in the hushed whispers of lovers. Charlie worked in the thick of things, cracking jokes about the various organic matter staining the seats after over a century of theatergoers watching sexy performances. Mild-mannered Melissa sat beside him, the only one of the group with any patience for his humor.

Julienne's loner was Steve, a student who preferred to work by himself but could usually be persuaded to pair off with quiet Ralph, her technowizard, when the need arose.

Fashion plate Delia managed to look glamorous even when scrambling on hands and knees over a dirty floor and her partner Jackson had been tutoring her in the program's stringent math requirements while rallying the courage to ask her for a date.

Julienne oversaw their progress to make certain the work met her standards and each item catalogued was an accurate assessment Nick would find viable and valuable. Nick or Dale periodically popped by to see how their work progressed, and she could see they were formulating their own opinions about how reliable and useful the students' data would be.

"We're logging our findings and making recommendations here." She handed Nick an evaluation sheet she'd just signed off on.

He read through the findings, his gaze scanning each notation quickly before falling on the additional comments she'd added at the bottom with her initials. "You're confirming each evaluation?"

She nodded.

"I like this data sheet." He flipped the page as if looking for a form number. "I can assess the damage-to-salvage ratio right up front. Is this some sort of educational form?"

She felt a decided sense of satisfaction when admitting, "It's one I worked up."

His gaze grew so warm with approval she couldn't help but smile. "Would you be willing to share it?"

She'd share a lot more than this form. "Yes."

"Walk me through it, so I can present it to my team."

Casting her gaze over her students, she decided on Wendy and Brit, who'd begun dismantling a new seat from the row.

"We want to watch you go through this one, guys," she said, noticing how they went on alert after glancing up to see Nick.

Nick must have noticed, too, because he knelt beside them, running a finger over the bracket that had fastened the seat to the floor. "You did a good job removing the bolt and bracket without damaging the flooring. They're rusted through."

"Some of them sheer off," Brit said. "But Dr. Blake showed us how to loosen the bracket from the floorboard. If they're rusted, the bracket comes up with the bolt still attached."

Nick's gaze shot up to hers. "You're just full of nifty tricks, aren't you?"

He glanced at the stage, a private reference to the nifty tricks she'd performed there. Fighting back a smile, she said, "I've assisted in theater renovations and expansions before."

"But never one quite like this, I'll bet," Nick said.

"Granted, this one's unique." The tremor rippling through her mirrored the excitement she saw flash deep in his eyes.

Wendy and Brit examined the seat, armrest, backrest and the working of the reclining mechanism. They discussed their findings before making notations on the evaluation sheet and finally announcing, "This one's salvageable."

"What about the broken reclining mechanism?" Julienne asked.

"A nonissue." Brit glanced at Nick. "Right?"

"Right. The mechanisms will have to be replaced on whatever seating we keep. What about the armrest?"

"We'll replace it with one from an unsalvageable seat. Dr. Blake told us that even though we don't know the details of your budget, we can safely assume you'll want to recycle as many parts as you can. We're running a salvageable parts list."

"Dr. Blake is absolutely right." Reaching for the pen

Julienne held, he initialed the evaluation sheet with a bold penstroke. "This is the exact call I would have made."

Standing, he gave them an approving smile and walked off, leaving Wendy beaming with pride for her classmates to see, Brit trying to look cool and unfazed, though he was clearly just as pleased, while Julienne savored her own pleasure quietly, a delicious feeling that made her feel yummy all over.

NICK SAT in the last row of the mezzanine, where he could relax for the first time since arriving at the site at five this morning. Reaching for the hero sandwich Betty had provided for lunch, he took a bite and watched Jules work unobserved.

Hair had slipped from her ponytail, leaving wisps around her face. A soft look, different from the professional one she'd sported yesterday or the wild one she'd worn on closing night.

She'd shaken up his routine, and the diversion was welcome. He hadn't realized his work had become so mundane, but for a while he'd felt that his social life had. Though he'd never admitted it to Dale, he'd enjoyed the break when he'd temporarily retired from the dating scene to divert the media's interest. For the past few years, he'd found himself curiously unfulfilled, the women he'd dated not quite worth the effort of the chase.

The fault was his, Nick knew. He worked hard and played hard and made no apologies, but he expected too much. A woman couldn't be everything to a man, especially when she didn't have long to get acquainted.

Maybe if he'd lived more conventionally, with a job he came home from every day, he wouldn't have found fitting a woman into his life so difficult. Then again, living a more conventional life didn't guarantee two people would share their interests, either. He'd seen proof enough of that while growing up.

His parents had reared him in a very conventional upper-middle-class lifestyle and look what marriage had done for them...taken two people who must have loved each other at some point and turned them into indifferent acquaintances.

They still plugged away at marriage. His dad, a federal judge, spent sunup to sundown in his chambers, emerging only to head off to some golf tournament weekend with his power buddies or his latest mistress, while his mom filled her days with endless rounds of volunteer functions, charities and friends.

Nick honestly didn't remember the last time he'd seen his parents sit down together for a meal, or head out together to see the opera or a play. If they hadn't both resided at the same address, they might have been strangers.

Long ago he'd decided that repeating his parents' lifestyle was not what he wanted from life. Nick had steered clear so far. When he was with a woman, he devoted himself to her completely and expected her full attention in return, which explained the short lifespan of his relationships. Even though he ran a large company, he still liked to go in the field with his team and a woman couldn't be expected to hang around until he came home again.

Taking another bite of sandwich, he watched Jules retreat from her students to dig out a bottle of spring water from her gear. Was her interest in his work what fascinated him?

Perhaps. But in truth she'd captivated him from the minute he'd laid eyes on her. She'd had his blood pumping double time before she'd ever opened her mouth to express an interest in architecture. An *honest* interest.

She was intelligent and beautiful and so hot she made simply tipping her head back to drink from her water bottle a crotch-inspiring display. And given the progress Jules and her interns had made with the seating this morning, he'd been wise to invite them onto his team. Not only because he could use the extra hands with the theater, but for the first time ever, Nick looked forward to involving a woman in his work and seeing where that sort of closeness might lead.

# 8

*NAUGHTY GIRLS TALK THE TALK.*

Julienne let today's key phrase fill her mind as she lay on her bed and exhaled through her mouth, forcing all the air from her lungs. Then she inhaled through her nose, slowly, slowly, allowing her abdomen to expand with the effort of taking a good deep breath. Then she repeated the process.

Since the last of Nick's team had arrived in town late this afternoon, his night had been occupied with a staff meeting, but he'd told her to expect a telephone call before she went to bed.

She was content with a phone call as she didn't want to raise Uncle Thad's suspicions about her personal relationship with Nick. Though he'd taken the news of their working relationship well enough, claiming to see the benefits of the educational opportunity for her interns, he'd restated his concerns about Nick's character. Julienne knew his concerns—were she looking for a husband. She wasn't, of course, but she couldn't tell Uncle Thad that without explaining that Nick the naughty boy served her desire for a fling perfectly.

She'd tried to reassure him, instead, without resorting to outright lies and had wound up in her bedroom for an intense round of self-hypnosis to contain her guilt. For the moment, she seemed able to reconcile her need to explore her sensual self with keeping the truth from Uncle Thad.

She'd soon quelled the good girl within and managed to divert her energy into preparing for Nick's call. *The Naughty Handbook* stated that breathing exercises would help her achieve a sexy voice reminiscent of Marilyn Monroe or Lauren Bacall, so she'd combined a self-hypnosis session with the breathing exercises.

*Naughty girls talk the talk.*

The key was relaxation. *The Naughty Handbook* claimed that the more excited she became, the shallower her breathing, which resulted in a high-pitched voice that didn't sound sexy. Especially over a telephone, where her voice would be her only tool to seduction.

She wanted to seduce Nick tonight, remembered when he'd talked sexy to her on closing night, not X-rated, four-letter-word sexy, but bold, suggestive sexy. She hadn't been turned on so much by what he'd said—although he'd definitely made some very erotic suggestions—but more by *how* he'd said it, with that run-his-voice-down-her-spine huskiness that had made her go all weak in the knees.

*Can you imagine my hands on you, Jules? I want to slide them down your creamy neck and along your shoulders.*

*Mmm.* She had no problem imagining his hands on her now, or remembering how that hot velvet voice of his had made the blood slug through her veins like molten lava. She planned to have a similar effect on him tonight. She planned to talk sexy and get his imagination running wild. She wanted him all hot and bothered and yearning for when they could be alone again. And she stood a good chance of accomplishing that goal, since she didn't have to worry about him seeing her blush.

*Naughty girls talk the talk.*

When the phone rang shortly before eleven, Julienne was armed with *The Naughty Handbook's* sexy suggestions and ready to breathe very deeply.

"Hello, beautiful."

His voice sent a thrill through her and she bounced up onto her bed, cradling the phone close to her ear. "Hello, Nick. Did everyone get in okay?"

"No problems. The meeting ran late though."

She'd guessed as much. "You're just getting home?"

"Just put my briefcase down and haven't even taken off my shoes yet. This isn't too late to call?"

"No." She took a deep breath, liked that he'd been eager to talk to her. Liked that he didn't mind admitting it.

Fluffing her pillows, she settled against them to pay close attention to what else he might admit. In the meantime, she'd make an admission of her own. "I waited up for you."

Nick didn't miss a beat. "I'd hoped you would. I want my voice to be the last thing you hear before drifting to sleep."

"I'll be sure to have sweet dreams."

She heard a zip and a rustling in the background and guessed he stripped off his pants. Her mind became fully occupied conjuring up that image, or at least her imagination did, since to date he'd seen much more of her than she had of him.

"Am I keeping you from anything?" he asked.

"Sweet dreams about you." Deep breath. "I'm sitting on my bed, propped up with lots of pillows, wearing my jammies. They're long and silky. They feel really good against my skin."

She didn't mention the open book propped beside her, listing at a glance suggestions for *talking the talk* such as describe what you're wearing, compliment a body part or tell your lover what you'd like to do to him and vice versa.

"Hmm, silk jammies." His voice dropped, one husky

note that reassured her she'd conveyed the image loud and clear. "One piece, two piece or negligee?"

She had to give the man credit. He jumped in feetfirst. If she'd ever turned a conversation like this on Ethan, he'd never have played along. Once over the shock, he'd have scheduled her for a battery of psychological tests to evaluate her sanity, no matter how much he'd claimed to want more passion in their lives.

"Two piece." She reminded herself that the past was indeed the past and she had a torrid fling to enjoy right now. "Long clingy pants and a spaghetti strap top."

"What color?"

"Flesh colored. Darker than ivory, but not as deep as cream. Resembles the color of my skin."

"You have lovely skin."

"Thank you."

"Hang on a sec. Don't go away. I've got to put the phone down to get this shirt over my head."

Like she'd actually leave when he was on the other end of the line getting undressed. Now he was teasing her, Julienne knew, and the realization vitalized her. She wanted to strip off his clothes, a piece at a time, acquainting herself with his naked body by sight...by smell...by touch.

There was a racket on the other end, and then Nick's voice, "I'm back."

"I'm glad." She was, *very.*

"I missed seeing you tonight."

Such an intimate admission surprised her, made her tingle with awareness. Another deep breath. Her chest rose and fell beneath her pajama top and she focused on the way her nipples slid against the filmy fabric, rose to attention as she rallied her courage to *talk the talk.*

"I missed you, too. I've been thinking about you all night, Nick, imagining your hands on me. About how much

I wanted to feel them slide down my neck and along my shoulders.''

Those were his words from *that* night and using them seemed the perfect way to break the ice.

''I want that, too, Jules. Having you so close today made me want to touch you every time I walked by.''

A thrill zipped through her, sent her snuggling against her pillows to relax and enjoy the sensation. ''Hearing you admit that does amazing things to me. I wanted you to touch me, too.''

''Where?''

Oh, this man had the naughty thing down cold, and Julienne actually shivered as her mind wrapped around her sexy reply.

*Tell your lover what you'd like him to do to you and vice versa.*

''Right now I'm wishing you could free my breasts from this skimpy top and touch them. I can imagine your mouth on my nipples.'' She gave him his own words back again, letting their familiarity transport her into this new world where naughty girls embraced their sensuality and didn't give in to the ordinary. Deep breath. ''Just thinking about you touching me drives me crazy.''

He gave a wry laugh. ''Hearing you talk about it is doing quite a number on me, too, beautiful.''

''I want to do a number on you, Nick. If you were here, I'd peel off your clothes piece by piece and use my mouth to become better acquainted. I didn't see nearly enough of you on closing night. I *felt* you, but I want the freedom to *explore* you.''

*You go, girl.*

She closed her eyes, the tingling in her breasts spiraling downward. ''I wish I was with you now, so I could kiss my way from your mouth, down your neck...over that hard chest I could only feel through your shirt the other night. Would you like me to do that, Nick?''

His breathing echoed through the receiver, before he answered thickly, ''Yes.''

''Good, because I want to taste you and touch you. I want to run my hands over your skin. I want to know if you have hair on your chest, and if you do, is it blond or black like your eyebrows? We never undressed you on closing night. I'm not sure which will feel sexier, rubbing my nipples against smooth muscles or lots of silky hair. I can't wait to find out.''

His labored breathing echoed over the line, fueling her boldness with the sound, recreating the image of his face, heavy-lidded with wanting, sculptured lips parted...

''Touch yourself, Jules.'' Nick proved he could meet her challenge and planned to give as good as he got. ''Since I'm not there, I want you to slip your hand into your pants and tell me what you feel. Give me the vicarious pleasure of touching you.''

Julienne lost her fragile hold on her growing confidence. Poof. Gone beneath a zip of excitement and daring that actually sent goose bumps down her arms.

She wondered what he made of her continued silence, hoped his anticipation mounted and he hadn't realized he'd thrown her off balance with his request. She supposed she should have seen it coming. After all, she was playing naughty with a man who'd honed the concept to a science.

''Okay.'' She brushed aside her pajama top with suddenly trembling fingers. ''I'm heading under the waistband, skimming my fingers down my tummy. My skin feels warm, flushed.''

''With excitement?''

''Mmm, hmm. I'm pretending these are your fingers touching me like you did the other night. Your hands are a bit rough and they created this friction on my skin, made me squirm.''

"You're making me squirm right now." The sound of rustling in the background reinforced his admission.

"Good." Deep breath. Her sultry laugh sounded as though she'd caught her balance again. "I like the thought of you squirming. It means you want me."

"You have no idea."

"Oh, I think I do, I know how much I want you. I've got this ache between my legs that's making my thighs tremble...." She grazed a light touch over the hard knot of nerve endings right at the forefront of her sex. "Oooh my, I better not touch *there*, or this conversation will be over too quickly."

Nick's laughter echoed in her ear. "Move on then, because I'm not getting off this phone yet."

Julienne smiled, couldn't stop a chuckle at the longing in his voice, didn't even try. Not when her fingertips were lightly parting the folds of her moist flesh, a gentle but daring touch that made her feel decadent, made her sex clench with longing. "I'm very soft, Nick, and very...*wet*."

His breath hitched over the line and Julienne's smile deepened. "Why don't you join me? Why don't you wrap your hand around that big boy—he is hard, isn't he?"

She thought the gravelly sound that barked over the line might have been a laugh, or at least an attempt at one.

"Why don't you wrap your hand around yourself and give a little tug, pretend I'm touching you. And while you're doing that, I'm going to dip my finger in here, just a bit, as though I'm making myself ready for you."

The ensuing crash blasted through the receiver and startled Julienne so much she actually jumped, all thoughts of sex and sexy sensations flying out of her head as the mattress squeaked and *The Naughty Handbook* fell to the floor with a thump. Her eyes flew open, shooting straight to the locked door, and she worried Uncle Thad was there, even though she knew he'd never enter without knocking, couldn't get in even if he'd tried.

But then Nick's curse dragged her attention back to the phone, and when she heard a loud rattle and another bang, she guessed what must have happened.

"Damn it," he growled, as if from a distance and then she heard more rustling before his voice became clear again. "You still there, beautiful? I dropped you."

Julienne chuckled, willing her pulse to slow. "I'm here."

"I got busy hanging on to other…things."

"Mmm. I wish I were hanging on to other things, too. I guess I'll just have to dream about you." She sighed a bit dramatically. "I can't go any farther without putting down this phone to free up my hands, and I'd much rather you satisfy me."

"You're making me crazy."

"I want you to want me so much that tomorrow seems like forever away."

"Mission accomplished."

Jules laughed, a deep sexy laugh that exploited her new-found breathing skills and made Nick groan on the other end. This was sexual power and she liked it. Very much indeed.

"I thought maybe we could go away this weekend, Nick," she suggested, implementing the next phase of her plan.

Her best friend Kimberly worked for a major airline. She often had layovers in Atlanta and Julienne frequently drove there for impromptu slumber parties. Uncle Thad wouldn't think twice about her spending the night away. "Can you get away Saturday?"

"I'll make the arrangements." He laughed thickly.

"Don't satisfy yourself until then, Jules. Let that be my pleasure."

"You'll wait, too?"

His groan suggested she'd asked him to do something criminal like swinging a wrecking ball at the Risqué. "I'll wait, too," he finally agreed. "But I want you to know waiting might kill me."

Julienne laughed, a husky, Lauren Bacall sound that proved the breathing exercises were working. "I have a lot of things planned for you, Nick, but trust me, dying isn't one of them."

*The next morning*

NICK HUMMED as he exited the University of Savannah's drive-thru welcome center, hanging the visitor's pass from his rearview mirror and glancing at the campus map. He made a right at the administration building and hoped he could find a parking space near the science building and Jules's office.

He got lucky and found a space in a nearby lot. Climbing out of his sport-utility vehicle, he smiled at a group of students whose gazes darted to the foil wrapped package he held tucked under one arm.

Perhaps he should have waited until Jules arrived at the site this afternoon, but they'd have had a hard time finding a place to be alone. With an uncharacteristic eagerness he attributed to his deprived libido, Nick didn't see the point of waiting. Especially when he couldn't concentrate on anything but giving her his gift.

She'd flat-out blown him away on the phone last night. He'd *never* gotten that turned on by talking to any woman before, had never known anything that resembled this kind of anticipation to see her again. What was it about Jules?

Nick didn't know. He didn't care. But he'd damn sure make the most of every moment with her.

He found the fourth floor of the science building easily enough, but then wandered through corridors, past busy labs and occupied classrooms, without a clue where her office was. The numbered doors led him on a circular goose chase, starting and stopping each time he turned a corner. Fortunately, the next turn brought him directly to the sound of voices.

"I'm not saying you're not qualified for your position, but your connection to me didn't hurt. Or to your uncle, either," Nick heard a male voice say. "In any event, I wanted to tell you I'm pleased you've scored such a coup for the university."

"And without your help, too. Thank you, Ethan."

Nick stopped, recognizing Jules's voice, his senses on red-alert at her clipped tone. Sure enough an office door stood ajar and a plaque on the wall read Julienne Blake, Ph.D. Nick didn't hesitate, but knocked once and pushed inside.

Jules stood behind a small desk, where a computer monitor sat amid neatly ordered stacks of papers. She wore her professor persona, as he'd come to think of it, her hair braided back from her face and a tailored suit that while professional, couldn't hide the tempting curves below. She stood tense and wary, until her gaze fell on him. She smiled.

The dark-haired man standing in front of the desk turned around and Nick found himself the recipient of a blue gaze that narrowed sharply when it landed on his package.

"Hello, Dr. Blake," Nick said in his most cordial tone. "I hope I'm not interrupting."

"Of course not. I'm delighted to see you. Let me introduce you to a colleague of mine, Dr. Whiteside. He's a professor with the college of behavioral sciences. Ethan, this is Dr. Fairfax.''

Ethan Whiteside's deepening frown told Nick he didn't like any man showing up in Jules's office with a gift any more than he liked her pleasure at the intrusion.

Then it hit him. This must be the ex-fiancé. A man in serious need of his own psychological services to have let a woman like Jules get away.

They shook hands in greeting.

"I heard about your affiliation with the preservation department on Rebel Radio," Ethan said. "I came by to congratulate Julienne."

"Rebel Radio?" Nick directed his question to Jules.

"Our campus station. Wendy and Brit are producers. They're broadcasting how great it is to work for you."

"I'm glad I didn't scare them off."

"My interns like a good challenge."

"Like their professor, hmm?" He slanted his gaze back to Ethan. "Well, Dr. Whiteside, my design team and I scored quite a coup getting Dr. Blake and her interns to help us out on this project." He tossed the man's own words back at him to clarify he'd overheard their conversation and considered Jules's affiliation an asset.

Judging by Ethan's scowl, he got the point.

"Do you usually bring gifts to your guest professors?" Ethan asked.

"I've never had a guest professor on my team before. Dr. Blake is my first."

"That sounds like quite an accomplishment given your advisory position on the national council." Ethan's stare didn't waver. "If you don't mind my asking, exactly how did this come about? Do you know Julienne through her uncle?"

Nick shook his head. He did mind Ethan asking, didn't

like what the guy seemed to imply and had no intention of sharing the details about how they'd gotten together.

But Nick noticed Jules's frown, a puzzled expression that suggested she hadn't recognized that Ethan was jealous.

"Dr. Fairfax doesn't know Uncle Thad, but I've promised to introduce them."

"If you're through." Nick dismissed the guy. "I need a minute of Dr. Blake's time before she heads off to class."

"It was nice of you to drop by," Jules said to Ethan.

With nothing to do but leave, Ethan left, but he clearly resented his lack of options. Nick barely waited until he cleared the door to shut it behind him.

"The ex-fiancé?"

"How'd you know?"

"A lucky guess." Nick couldn't figure how she'd missed her ex-fiancé's disapproval but he didn't know enough about the reasons behind the demise of her engagement to comment. And quite simply, he didn't want her thinking about any man but him.

Striding across the office, he handed her his gift. "This is for you, beautiful. A thank you for last night."

"Really?" She lowered her gaze to the package and Nick couldn't miss the pink blush that brightened her cheeks.

"Open it."

He half sat on the edge of her desk, watched as she slipped a finger through a seam and carefully removed the paper, then the box top. The pink staining her cheeks deepened.

"Oh, Nick." She chuckled, lifting out a telephone headset. "You bought one for yourself, I hope."

"I did."

She finally lifted her gaze to his and he knew how much she had enjoyed making him lose control to the point he'd dropped the damned phone. That one gaze told him how much she wanted to make him drop it again.

And right on cue his pulse pounded.

"There's another in there."

She gingerly lifted out a pair of shiny blue balls hanging by a loop. She must have felt the weights within, because she shook them, arched a wary brow.

"I'm guessing this isn't a Christmas ornament."

Nick laughed. "Payback for last night. Kegel balls."

She may have never seen a set before, but she apparently understood the word Kegel well enough. "You keep a supply of sex toys handy, do you?"

"I made a trip out after we got off the phone."

"You're kidding?"

"You didn't think I'd be able to sleep after the way you left me hanging, did you?"

"Oh."

Leaning across the desk, he tapped a finger against the bottom ball, making it vibrate suggestively. "I want you to use this until we leave. It'll level the playing field."

"You don't think I want you enough already?"

He lifted his hand to that lovely lower lip, traced his thumb across it. Jules's blush belied her calm voice but Nick enjoyed her show of bravado.

"Not at all. I like the thought of knowing you're thinking about me with every step you take."

"Do you think about me with every step you take?"

"I do indeed, beautiful, and it's a constant battle to keep everyone I run into from knowing, too."

Jules's gaze slipped to his crotch and a slow smile curved her lips. His crotch swelled when she pressed that delicious mouth against his in a quick kiss.

"You're on. But I've got to get to class."

"Mind if I tag along?"

She glanced meaningfully at his crotch again. "I don't want my students to know you're thinking about me."

Nick rubbed the heel of his palm against his erection as if pressure would relieve the trouble. "Give me a minute."

She glanced at her watch and winked saucily. "If I hurry, I may have time for a quick trip to the ladies room." Grabbing the Kegel balls, she dropped them into her jacket pocket and circled her desk in a fluid burst of motion that hindered his best efforts to subdue his erection. "Room 438. See ya."

"See ya, beautiful," he said, as she disappeared.

Willing his blood to slow, he paced his breathing until he could comfortably leave the room to tackle locating Jules's classroom. Running into Wendy and Brit ended his search.

"Dr. Fairfax," Wendy said. "What are you doing here? Aren't we still coming to the Risqué this afternoon?"

"I'm expecting you." Nick extended his hand to Brit in greeting. "I dropped by to work out some details with Dr. Blake."

"She's a great teacher," Brit said. "If you want to attend her lecture, she'll make decay processes interesting."

"I'm there." He followed the two into a classroom. "I could use a little enthusiasm about decay, given what I'm tackling on the theater's facade."

Jules stood behind a podium, reviewing notes, the addition of a pair of tortoiseshell glasses catching Nick's attention.

"Hi guys," she said, her clear gaze shifting above the rim of the glasses in what Nick thought was a very sexy look. "Enjoyed your broadcast today. You'll have student enrollment sky-high if you keep up all this excitement." She inclined her head in greeting. "Dr. Fairfax, I'm glad you're joining us. Today's lecture should be right up your alley.

We're discussing outdoor atmospheric pollutants and some new conservation treatments.''

''I'm riveted.''

Wendy giggled and Jules said, ''Why don't you and Brit introduce Dr. Fairfax to the students and find him a seat.''

The couple headed toward the rows of elevated seating and Jules smiled as he passed, a smile that suggested she'd made her trip to the ladies room and now enjoyed the effects of his gift.

He smiled in reply, feeling an intimate connection in that instant, a connection that made the entire classroom with all its shuffling students and lively banter fade into white noise. But the moment was over when Wendy and Brit explained that the class was made up of students from Jules's grad and undergrad classes, and introduced him around.

They took their seats and Jules soon addressed the group. Watching her move in front of the whiteboard, discussing the difference in the effects of weather on granite set in lime mortar versus cement while imagining the Kegel balls vibrating with her fluid steps, left Nick with a grin and wondering what the deal was with Ethan Whiteside.

On closing night, he'd gotten the impression from Jules that the decision to end her engagement had been mutual, but what Nick couldn't figure was what could possibly make a man give up a woman like Jules. He mulled a few possible answers, but each led him back to the fact that Ethan Whiteside was an idiot—until Nick realized the implication of where his thoughts traveled.

Was Nick setting himself up to be an idiot, too? He didn't do long-term. He'd never even considered it. So why was he all of a sudden giving thought to how he'd feel when the time came for him and Jules to part company?

He wasn't even going there. He lived for the moment and

would enjoy Jules while they were together and not cloud the issue by heading down this path.

Fixing his gaze on her, Nick forced himself to imagine those shiny blue balls swaying gently with her fluid strides. The awareness that shot through him was simple, uncomplicated. He wanted her. She wanted him. What they shared was that easy.

What had Jules called it? *A torrid fling.* Torrid flings didn't involve worries about special women getting away. The phrase "torrid fling" didn't imply a choice.

The classroom door opened, distracting Nick from his thoughts. A man walked in without awaiting an invitation, a stout man barely taller than Jules with a shock of white hair that stuck out at odd angles. He walked with an energetic step, despite his obvious age. Nick recognized him instantly.

*Thaddeus Blake.* He kissed Jules's cheek and waved to the students, who all seemed delighted at his arrival.

"Yo, Uncle Thad," one called out.

"Hey Dr. Blake, where've you been lately?" another asked.

Wendy's hand shot into the air, an unnecessary formality given she was already half out of her seat. "Are you going to tell us a story? We're doing outdoor atmospheric pollution on stone. Have you got one for that?"

Dr. Blake cupped his chin as if deep in thought. "Let me see. Outdoor atmospheric pollution on stone, hmm?" He slanted a twinkling gaze at Jules, who smiled fondly.

"Uncle Thad has a story for everything." She handed her great uncle the dry erase marker she'd been using. "So without further ado, I'll turn over the floor." Before she retreated to the podium, she whispered something to her uncle, and his gaze shot straight to Nick.

Nick nodded in greeting and before long Dr. Blake had

them all laughing over the absurdities of dealing with bureaucratic red tape while renovating a courthouse.

The star of his story was an eight-year-old Julienne, who'd overheard several employees from the archival department blaming each other because they couldn't track down the images of an outer wall's original construction.

She'd barged into the meeting and addressed a table full of bureaucrats and preservation architects as if they were crazy. Reminding everyone the building was historically significant, she dragged a textbook from her bookbag and showed them a picture of what the wall had once looked like.

"Out of the mouths of babes," Dr. Blake said with a chuckle. "And the moral of this story is that sometimes the solution is as simple as the nose on your face, if you don't let all sorts of other nonsense distract you."

Nick laughed with the rest of the class but Dr. Blake's words echoed in his head. Glancing at the woman standing at the podium, a wry smile on her face as she gazed fondly at her uncle, Nick thought that moral might apply to more than preservation work.

Maybe being with Jules could be as simple, if he just didn't let the other nonsense distract him.

# 9

*Later that day*

AFTER SPENDING the afternoon working at the Risqué, Julienne knew Nick hadn't leveled the playing field with his Kegel balls as much as he'd managed to make her crazy. The constant friction of the rocking weights had kept her on edge and marked their every interaction with an intimacy that only amplified the needy ache between her legs.

When he'd asked her for a local place to take his team out after work and invited her crew to join them, she'd decided he must enjoy watching her squirm. And if she had to spend her night squirming, she'd at least squirm someplace she enjoyed—the Olde River House. The neighborhood bar offered a place where working people could get together to shoot pool, shoot the bull and even cut loose on the small dance floor by the jukebox.

Nick had also invited Uncle Thad, whom he'd offered to tour the Risqué when she'd introduced them after her class earlier, which sent Julienne's tension spiraling off in a less pleasant direction. Uncle Thad had accepted the invitation, apparently eager to keep his eyes on Nick.

Her interns were thrilled at the prospect of socializing with Nick's group, though, their first experience at being considered "part of the team." As a result, Julienne found herself squirming in the driver's seat of the preservation department's van while squiring the group through Friday night traffic.

She could have headed back to the university to let her interns pick up their own cars, but she'd designated herself the driver. Although all her students were well above the drinking age, they were in high spirits and she wanted them to have a good time. They'd worked hard this week and they deserved one.

*Someone* should have a good time and she wouldn't be enjoying herself in her present state. Not when every step she took reminded her of how much she wanted Nick and how she was deceiving her uncle to get him.

"I didn't realize we'd test the seams of the place with ADF's group," she said to Uncle Thad, when they entered the tavern and saw the size of the crowd.

"I'm sure the owners are grateful for your recommendation, dear. ADF will be in town awhile, and this is an appropriate place for preservation architects to relax and enjoy themselves."

No denying that, but she couldn't help notice that Uncle Thad looked less than thrilled. His gaze scanned the crowd, zeroing with unsettling accuracy right on Nick, who stood at the bar talking with Dale and a woman who appeared to be on staff with the tavern, a manager perhaps. Judging by her uncle's frown, he clearly thought this off-site get-together was sufficient cause to worry. As much as she'd have liked to, Julienne couldn't attribute his worry to anything else. She'd never known him to be so vigilant and his displeasure certainly had nothing to do with the crowd inside the tavern.

A privately owned inn, the Olde River House had originally been built as a warehouse almost two hundred years before. The turn of the last century had seen a devastating fire raze the original structure, and the existing building had been rebuilt into a riverside inn with over 700,000 flame-resistant bricks.

Her uncle had always enjoyed visiting the place and Nick, too, looked pleased by the accommodations as he worked his way through the crowd toward them. He smiled in greeting and Julienne reacted instantly, feeling warm inside, a sort of unfamiliar glow that radiated outward and made her school her expression, when she sensed her uncle's gaze on her.

"Your suggestion to come here was perfect, Julienne." Nick dropped the familiar form of her name, apparently for her uncle's benefit, and she wondered if he'd sensed the need to tread lightly around Uncle Thad. "Dale's already talked the owners into touring the place and I got them to rearrange the floor plan so we have a section of tables in the back. I'm glad you made it, sir."

When her uncle responded with a reserved smile, Julienne issued an inward sigh of relief. Nick led them to their tables and she found herself flanking him with Uncle Thad seated on his other side. She'd already met most of his design team and many came and went between the bar, pool tables and jukebox, until Nick rallied the troops to order dinner.

Her interns appeared to fare well. Charlie had found a kindred spirit in Nick's engineer, a mid-fiftyish man with a wicked sense of humor. The two entertained their table with amusing observations about what put the risqué into the Risqué Theatre, which had the group bursting out in noisy appreciation.

Wendy and Brit, joined at the hip as usual, sat with Delia, Jackson and Melissa at another table, where Dale and several senior members of the design team generously answered their questions and expressed interest in their plans for the future.

All in all, they were a merry group throughout dinner and

by the time Nick stood, requested silence and raised his beer
in salute to his colleagues and guests, everyone was fed,
watered and smiling back at him.

"All right, team, we're onto our next project, but since
you all know the drill, I'll skip the pep talk, because this
time out, we've got company and an opportunity to show
off what we do." He flashed a dashing grin, caressed her
with his gaze for a moment, before glancing at her interns.
"Trust me, we like to show off, because we're *that* good."

His team hooted and cheered, mugs and glasses raised
and clinking together in a tinkling of rims. Nick waited for
them to quiet again before he continued.

"We also have the responsibility of setting a good example for these preservationists who'll take our places in
the field one day. Every one of my employees knows that
ADF operates on a very simple premise—to preserve and
protect." He flashed a decidedly sheepish grin. "That's not
an original slogan, I redesigned it to suit my purpose. But
the premise is important."

Julienne glanced askance at her uncle to gauge his reaction, hoping his opinion of Nick might be raised a few
notches.

"My employees also know ADF's mission statement was
founded on the words of a much admired and respected man
in our industry. He's a man who has inspired and challenged
many next-generation preservation architects to live up to
his exacting standards by the example of his work and his
commitment to preserving and protecting our nation's history. So I want to share his words and hope you'll take them
to heart when it's your turn to take up the torch." Nick
raised his beer to Uncle Thad. "He said, 'When the fate of
the past, of history, is in your hands, you're responsible to
do your best to preserve it for the future.'"

"I said that?" her uncle asked, surprise clearly written on his ruddy face.

Nick nodded. "You did, sir. In your Design Challenges in Historic Development lecture at Berkeley back in 1985."

"You founded the mission statement of your company based on something I said?"

"Yes, sir, I did."

The moment was so powerful, so enormous. A moment where one man honored another, the very silence rich with the implication of how people often inadvertently shaped others' lives, exerted influence that might never be acknowledged. But without the slightest hesitation, Nick had seized his opportunity to acknowledge the man who'd influenced him. He began to applaud.

Tears stung Julienne's eyes as chairs scraped across the wood beam floor and one by one Nick's team got to their feet. Even her interns stood to honor the professor they were so very fond of and she rose, blinking furiously, and joined them.

Though Uncle Thad may not think much of Nick outside of work, he did respect Nick's work. A great deal. She hoped he'd also respect the enormous compliment Nick paid him.

Uncle Thad smiled his absent smile and said matter-of-factly, "Then I'm one fine lecturer and you're one bright student."

Julienne blinked back tears, touched by Nick's actions and her uncle's gallant response, and hoping a bittersweet hope that Nick never discovered the man he admired held such a hard opinion about his personal choices.

But Nick laughed, obviously pleased with her uncle's response, and the cheering began all over again, so loud, Julienne wondered if the Olde River House's owners would throw them out for disturbing the other guests.

When the applause faded and everyone took their seats again, she cast her gaze between her uncle and Nick, found them talking together in low tones. She exhaled a sigh of relief that they'd segued through the moment and hoped they might even learn a little more about each other.

*Think torrid fling, girl.* Her inner voice reminded. *You just have to get through the night. You're not looking for anything more than a fling with Nick.*

Julienne told herself to heed the advice. She shouldn't even be thinking about the rapport between these men. Nick would leave town after the renovations and Uncle Thad would no longer have any reason to object to him. Problem solved.

But as she pondered the man who'd been so generous with his praise for her uncle tonight, what she felt had nothing to do with flings or sexy gifts but everything to do with a warm swelling sensation centered right in her chest.

"Ready to rack 'em, Nick?" Roy, ADF's senior engineer called from a nearby table.

"Do you play pool?" Nick asked, turning to her as calm and unfazed if he hadn't just given her uncle a gift beyond price.

She shook her head.

"Uh-oh, honey," Betty said loud enough for the whole table to hear. "You're in trouble now. Mr. Hot Cue thinks it's his duty to share his talent with the underprivileged."

Nick shot his administrative assistant a wry glance. "As if your game didn't need work. Get me a table, Roy, I'm giving lessons. Come on, Julienne, I'll teach you how to play." He stood, leaving her no chance to decline his invitation before he glanced down at her uncle and asked, "Sir, would you like to join us?"

"No thank you. I'm ready for coffee."

While Nick flagged a waitress, Uncle Thad eyed them

stoically. Julienne reassured him with a forced smile before Nick led her off to the table Roy had claimed for them.

"Is your uncle okay?" Nick asked.

"Fine, I'm sure. He just wants to relax and enjoy visiting." *He just wants to sit at the table where he can watch us to make sure you're behaving.* "You were very kind to him."

Nick just shrugged and that crazy swelling feeling in her chest didn't seem to care that Uncle Thad was watching.

"Are you wearing them?" he asked, a gleam in his eyes.

"The crazy balls?"

When he laughed at her name for his gift, she couldn't help but smile. "I am."

"Good." He set his mug on the rail of the pool table. "So tell me how you managed to avoid playing pool growing up on architectural sites with a bunch of men?"

Julienne waited as Nick moved to the wall to choose a cue. "Uncle Thad had very decided ideas about what constitutes appropriate behavior for a lady and he was absolutely determined I grow up to be one."

Nick lifted a cue from the rack, a fluid exertion of muscle that stretched the blue cotton shirt taut across his broad back and reminded Julienne of how firm his skin had felt beneath her fingers. That ache between her legs gave a nagging little tug.

He circled back around the table, grinning broadly. "Mission accomplished," he whispered against her ear as he passed, before leaning over the table to rack the balls.

*If he only knew the half of it.*

She experienced another little tingle at direct odds with the ever-present guilt that ate at her. Scanning the tavern to make sure Uncle Thad wasn't watching too closely, she found his eyes riveted on her, though he appeared to be engaged in conversation with Melissa, Steve and Ralph. She smiled, hopefully to reassure him, disliking that he was pre-occupied watching out for her when he should have been enjoying the visit with his former students.

She'd worried about him becoming isolated after his retirement and wanted him to make the most of their outing tonight. No matter what their reasons for being here, getting out of the house was good for him, even if she had to walk a fine line between being the good girl her uncle knew and the naughty girl of Nick's acquaintance.

But dodging Nick's steamy glances beneath her uncle's watchful gaze was proving a problem as Nick seemed completely oblivious to her uncle's scrutiny. And when he slipped his arms around her to teach her how to aim the cue, she suffered a moment of absolute panic.

*Naughty girls don't lose their cool.*

She mentally chanted the key phrase, trying to act casual as though the heat from Nick's body wasn't radiating through her and intensifying the ache between her legs. As if her every inhalation wasn't filled with the scent of his skin, a totally masculine scent, faintly musky from an afternoon spent on a work site, a scent that permeated her senses and made it even more difficult to act unaffected.

"How are you holding up?" he whispered against her ear.

For a moment she wasn't sure what he referred to. Had he noticed that Uncle Thad had been giving them the once-over ever since they'd left the table? When he brushed his crotch against her backside, just one slight, barely noticeable—she hoped—motion, she realized he was asking about her sexy gift.

"Oh, I'm doing just dandy," she replied in a tone low enough to melt into the tavern's background noise and the blaring music from the jukebox. "If you don't count this throbbing between my legs.'' *Or my uncle eyeing us like this scenario is his worst nightmare come to life.*

With his fingers lightly around her wrist, Nick guided her arm back in a slow motion that mimicked the other players on the tables around them. And as he did, he blew into her ear, just a gust of warm breath that sent ribbons of sensation spiraling through her. ''That's good, because I want you to pretend it's me touching you, that I'm slipping my finger inside you, to make you ready for me.''

Julienne recognized the words as her own from their telephone conversation last night, and though she didn't have a telephone to drop, she knew the cue stick would have hit the table had Nick let her hold it. He didn't. With a throaty chuckle he straightened and was gone, leaving her still bent over the table, her sex engaged in one long pull of desire.

Mr. Hot Cue, hmm. She certainly wouldn't argue that.

Especially when he bombarded her with sexy glances and some very hot beneath-the-breath promises that had Julienne so wet she feared she might lose her grip on the crazy balls. Just the image of the shiny blue balls slipping down her pant leg and onto the floor in full view of Uncle Thad and this crowd gave her heart palpitations.

But, Julienne decided, his sneaky whispers were a double-edged game, since the effect on him was much more noticeable than on her. After all, if the crazy balls did slip out, she could kick them under a table and pretend they belonged to someone else. Nick, on the other hand, couldn't pretend that bulge testing the seam of his jeans belonged to anyone but him.

And thankfully he seemed very aware of the fact as he skirted the table to hide at the far end when Wendy and Brit showed up.

''Dr. Blake,'' Wendy said, breathless from dancing.

"They have him here. He's on the jukebox. I couldn't believe it."

"Francis Albert?" Julienne decided to cut Nick a break by blocking Wendy and Brit's path around the table.

"Come on. Dr. Fairfax would you dance with Dr. Blake? She never lets her hair down and it's her favorite song. Brit already put the money in and you two look so good together you just have to dance," she said on the edge of a long breath.

Nick arched a dark brow skeptically. "Francis Albert?"

Julienne arched her brow right back. "Frank Sinatra."

"Oh."

"Oh, is right." Brit grimaced. "Whenever we're in the university van, she forces us to listen to this oldies station and then cranks up the volume until we're begging her to slow down so we can jump out the windows."

"Deejays and radio producers have to be accommodating, Brit. You and Wendy go dance as practice, or you just might lose your listeners at Rebel Radio," she said with a light laugh. The last thing Uncle Thad needed to see was her dancing with Nick.

"If the listeners are into the Rat Pack, I don't want them."

"There it is. There it is." Wendy waved wildly toward the dance floor when the music segued from a pop tune to a sultry swing beat. "Go on. Dr. Fairfax, make her dance."

Brit nodded to Nick. "Better get her out there, before someone pulls the plug and comes after us."

"Very funny," Julienne said, but she never heard Brit's reply, because Nick guided her toward the dance floor, leaving her no chance to resist.

"So you like the oldies, do you?" He swung her into his arms and led her in a slow dance more reminiscent of their night on the Risqué's stage than the swing tempo filling the tavern. "I suppose you can dance all those oldie dances, too."

"Mmm, hmm." She slanted a gaze toward Uncle Thad, still sitting at the table regaling a crowd with some story or another. What were her chances of getting off this dance floor without him noticing she'd ever been on it? "The Lindy, the Jitterbug... I can even Tango."

"You'll have to teach me then, because my dance moves are limited to bumping and grinding and that won't work tonight." Nick followed her gaze. "I guess you heard lots of oldies while you were growing up."

No, a bump and grind wouldn't work tonight and thankfully he'd noticed. "I did. Uncle Thad's a big music lover."

"A traditional music education is important for a lady."

Julienne wouldn't exactly have called Frank Sinatra's swing music traditional, but she liked that Nick thought she was a lady. Following his movements easily, she fought to resist melting into his arms. His thoughts must have been traveling a similar path because he said, "So we look good together, hmm?"

"I was hoping no one would notice."

Nick lifted his head and eyed her with a steely gaze. "You mean that in a strictly professional sense, I'm sure, because I'll be crushed if you're ashamed to be seen with me in public."

His chiseled jaw was set in a tight line, his smile had faded. He sounded so...possessive.

What could she possibly say? Only the truth would enlist Nick's cooperation in keeping their fling low-key in front of everyone she knew. "I don't usually flaunt my torrid flings under my uncle's nose. And I don't like questions about professional ethics, either."

"Professional ethics? You're an adult."

He must have accepted her concerns about her uncle, because he didn't question her further. "True, but I'm still young compared to many of my colleagues. Questions sometimes arise about my job qualifications."

"There's a story here. Is this the conversation I walked in on with your ex this morning?"

She hesitated. A torrid fling meant maintaining a level of superficiality that didn't delve into pasts and personal troubles, and they'd already crossed a big line by aligning themselves professionally. But since he'd accommodated her interns so kindly, Julienne supposed the least she could do was answer honestly.

"Ethan credits himself and my uncle for my successes."

"Do he and your uncle deserve the credit?"

"Well, like Ethan reminded me this morning, my connections to both of them haven't hurt in getting the university administration to take a chance on me. But not only am I qualified for my position, I'm good at it. I work well with the students…"

"Very well."

"I brought a lot of experience to this position and a unique perspective. The fact that I'm young is a good thing."

"A very good thing." His mouth softened its stern line.

She met his gaze. "I sound defensive, don't I?"

"No. You didn't this morning, either. Or at least during the part of the conversation I overheard. Why didn't you defend yourself to Ethan?"

That might have been a tough question to answer had the crazy balls not been knocking around inside her, reminding her of exactly why Ethan had been relegated to her past. "The time for defense is past. I'm not worried about what Ethan thinks anymore."

Something flared in Nick's expression, some emotion she couldn't name. "How long did you say you were together?"

"A little over five years."

"Many relationships before that?"

"I dated."

*Liar, liar pants on fire.* That voice inside her head said. *You call what you did dating? Nice men who met Uncle Thad at the house when they picked you up and kissed you on the cheek when they dropped you back off again?*

Julienne willed that voice to shut up. Admitting her limited dating experience to the man she was honing her naughty girl skills on simply wasn't part of the plan.

They lapsed into silence again and she focused on the moment, on the feel of Nick's arms around her, the heat of his body radiating against hers, his intimate gift making her want him with every move they made.

Frank Sinatra's song ended and segued into a popular ballad, but Nick made no move to let her go.

"We should go back—"

"No."

She couldn't exactly break away without drawing notice, so she tried to act casual... "Where are we going tomorrow?"

"It's a surprise."

"Anything special I need to know about dressing, so I'll know what to pack?"

"Don't bother packing. You won't need clothes."

His low voice issued a sensual promise that sent a shiver through her, made it difficult to remember they were on a dance floor in full view of Uncle Thad, her interns and Nick's team. So difficult, in fact, that she jumped, startled, when Dale showed up to tap Nick on the shoulder.

"Mind if I take a turn with the gorgeous Dr. Blake, buddy?"

Nick's darkening expression suggested he minded very much.

*Ooh, girl, he looks like he might bite. He doesn't want to take his hands off you.*

Propriety dictated that Nick allow Dale to cut in and he did, but not without making his displeasure known. "Shouldn't you be touring the place with that blond manager?"

"Her name's Nancy. And we're continuing the tour after her shift's over."

Nick scowled and Dale took her hand and guided her away in a sort of sweeping box step.

"Thanks for dancing with me," he said.

"Thanks for asking me." And she was very glad. At least now Uncle Thad wouldn't think her dancing tonight implied any favoritism.

"Couldn't resist. You're my idea of the perfect woman, and since the boss man plans to monopolize your time, I should keep him on his toes."

"What about Nancy?"

"My heart belongs to you, gorgeous."

She forced a chuckle. She had another ladies' man on her hands, much like the handsome man who'd returned to the table, scowling. That ladies' man clearly didn't like sharing his lady and judging by her uncle's expression, he'd noticed, too.

Uncle Thad didn't look as much disapproving as he did...*stricken*. Julienne caught his gaze and shook her head, silently telling him not to worry, while the sane voice in her brain chided, *good girls don't disappoint their uncles*.

But even the thought of disappointing Uncle Thad didn't slow her racing pulse. She was caught up in Nick's unexpected possessiveness, very caught up, in fact.

She forced herself to remember her uncle's warning.

*Trust me, Julienne. He's a heartbreaker. A man who can't commit has a problem.*

Looked like Nick wasn't the only one with a problem. She had a few herself, not the least among them was trying to reassure Uncle Thad he didn't have to worry about her. And if that wasn't enough, she'd have to step up her self-hypnosis sessions to add another key phrase to her repertoire.

*Naughty girls don't fall for their lovers.*

# 10

*Saturday afternoon*

NICK HAD CHOSEN Tybee Island as the out-of-town destination to get away with Jules because he'd wanted her all to himself. He liked the thought of making love to the sound of the surf, of walking along the beach together and sharing the ocean sunrise as the canvas behind the island's historical buildings.

With its lighthouse, present structure circa 1773, and beach cottages, circa 1910, Tybee Island struck Nick as the perfect place to indulge their interests without the shadow of students, uncles or work to distract them.

He wanted a break from distractions. He'd waited a week to get her alone again, to make love to her and solve the mystery of why she affected him the way she did.

He was seriously affected.

With a sidelong glance, Nick watched her walk along by his side, long hair lifting up on the wind. They'd decided to walk along the beach and she looked relaxed, content with the crashing surf, the wind and the throaty cries of the gulls filling the silence between them.

A University of Savannah sweatshirt kept the twilight chill at bay, but she'd removed her sneakers and socks and rolled up her cuffs to walk through the sand. She fit in as naturally on this beach as she had when mingling with strangers on closing night. Jules went with the flow and made the most of each moment. Nick found her easy to be around, her quiet independence refreshing.

"Coming here was a wonderful idea." She tightened her grip on his hand.

He squeezed back, liking the intimate simplicity of holding hands. "I want you all to myself, beautiful. I'm tired of sharing. All I've done this week is try to act like I don't want to be touching you when I do."

She only smiled, a flash of white in the deepening dusk.

The boardwalk beckoned them in the distance, a pavilion filled with sound and bright light that glowed in the black night, reflected against the cold surf nibbling at their feet.

"You hungry?" he asked, directing Jules to a bench and motioning her to sit while he plucked her sneakers from her hand and knelt before her.

"Not as hungry for food as I am for you. I don't feel like doing the restaurant thing after last night. Do you mind?"

"That you're hungry for me instead of dinner? Ah, no. In fact, that fits neatly in with my fantasies about you." Propping her slim foot on his lap, he brushed the sand from her toes.

"Fantasies, hmm? Can I make your dreams come true, Nick?" She shot him a sultry smile.

"You already are." Lifting her foot, he pressed his open mouth to her ankle, smiled when he felt her shiver in reply. "I want to replace my gift inside your lovely body. Just the thought has been driving me crazy."

Her eyes gleamed, looked smoky and sexy in the glow cast by a streetlamp on the boardwalk. He twirled his tongue around her anklebone, tasted the salty sea spray on her skin. "I want to explore every inch of you tonight, discover what makes you shiver and sigh...."

"Talking this way works." Her eyes had grown heavy-lidded, their smoky depths gleaming with desire. "I'm surprised you even suggested a walk along the beach."

"Are you?" He worked the sock onto her foot, her red polished toenails vanishing beneath the soft white cotton. "I want to romance you. Especially since we've been working backward."

"Working backward? How's that?"

He slipped her other sock on, sat back on his haunches and gazed up into her face, liking the way the streetlamp cut her features into fragments of glowing light and shadow.

"Topping last week is going to take some doing so we can make the most of our *torrid fling*."

Her brows drew together. "You're making fun of me."

Bracing his hands on her thighs, he ran them up the expanse of cool denim, felt her muscles. "I find you charming and very, very sexy." Sliding his hands upward, he braced to stand. "I'd never make fun of you. I want to have fun *with* you."

"I don't know if I'd go right to fun with these little drive-me-crazy balls."

He placed her sneakers beside her on the bench and retrieved his own. "I would. I've had lots of fun knowing you're constantly reminded of how much you want me. Builds the anticipation. If you haven't found wanting me just as fun, you'll hurt my feelings."

"My, my, Dr. Fairfax. What a big ego you have."

"The better to pleasure you with, my dear." He sat so close their thighs touched. "I perform much better when I think you want me more than anything else in the world."

"I do."

Her admission whispered above the whipping wind, but those two softly spoken words arrowed their way inside him, warmed him more than a shot of vermouth on a cold night. "I want you, too."

The moment became charged with rich implications and unspoken admissions. The wind faded beneath the hum in his ears, the chill suddenly unnoticed beneath the heat warming him from the inside out. Her gaze locked with his, her soft lips parting slightly.

Any appetite for food disappeared. "Since you're not hungry, let's skip the boardwalk and head back to the cottage."

Jules gifted him with a smile and before he'd realized what she was about she'd yanked her socks back off, shot up from the bench and took off, calling, "I'll race you."

Claiming a head start, she ran down the beach, long hair whipping out behind her, sexy laughter filling the night and fueling his efforts to catch her.

He quickly overtook her and by the time they reached their cottage, they were breathless and sweaty and primed to play.

"Come on, beautiful." Nick led her toward their porch, where a sturdy hammock provided a great view of the surf.

"I want to hear all about your fantasies, and I happen to have one of my own I was hoping to indulge."

Jules had a fantasy? Just the thought rocketed his pulse rate, no small feat given he'd just sprinted a good mile.

"Your wish is my command. Can I indulge you out here, or would you rather head inside?"

Jules peered out at the moonlit surf. Upon their arrival she'd decreed their cottage charming, and obviously designed for sex with the tropical jungle of palms, oleander and hibiscus that separated their slice of beach from their neighbors. With the moon gleaming silver over the black water, Nick agreed.

"Out here," she delighted him by saying.

"My thoughts exactly." Pulling open the door, Nick

waved her inside. "Get what you need. I don't want interruptions."

With her hair tumbling over her shoulders, she gave a saucy shake of her head and disappeared inside. Nick followed, grabbing condoms, and not one, but two blankets, just in case the temperature continued dropping.

But when he stepped back outside and met the quicksilver gleam in Jules's gaze, Nick didn't think he'd have to worry about getting cold anytime soon.

"Ever since that night, I've wanted to peel off your clothes." Her husky admission sent his blood draining to his crotch. "Will you let me do the honors?"

"Will I let my fantasy woman undress me? Hmm, let me think." Tossing the blankets on the hammock, he turned back around in time to notice Jules's smile of pure feminine satisfaction.

That expression, a sultry confidence that hinted at how much she liked being his fantasy woman, excited him on a level he'd not known before looking into her silvery eyes and discovering he had the power to arouse her with his desire.

Being with Jules was so different than his usual diet of light and sexy affairs. The undercurrent between them made each glance, each word, each kiss, carry such weight that he'd become preoccupied with devising ways to win her smiles.

Nick had no experience with feelings that sucked him along like the Atlantic's undertow, so he extended his hand to reveal the foil packets he held, and said honestly, "I'm honored you want to strip me, *and* I'm prepared for where it will lead."

Grinning, she dug into her back pocket and held out two more foil-wrapped squares. "Me, too."

"You're very good for my ego, beautiful."

She gave a jaunty toss of her head, which sent that mane of hers tumbling over her shoulders and down her back in a fall of shadowy waves. "Well, you did say you'd perform better."

In one sinuous move that brought images of her sexy striptease crashing in on his senses, she closed the distance.

An abundance of layered clothing blocked skin from touching skin, so Nick settled for the only bare part of her he could reach. Her feet. Balancing awkwardly, he dragged his toes over hers, outlined the sweep of her foot and the slim curve of her ankle, enjoying the contrast of the chill air and her warm skin.

She snuggled against him, reached around to grab his hand and pry the condoms from his fingers. He relinquished them, preoccupied with playing footsie and inhaling the scent of her hair mingled with the briny smell of the sea.

He laughed when she tossed the condoms onto the hammock and they skittered in all directions. "So you don't need those yet."

"Not yet. I plan to undress you, Dr. Fairfax."

"Undressed sounds good." But when he reached for the bottom of her sweatshirt, she danced away.

"I said I plan to undress *you*."

Meeting her gaze, he recognized the challenge deep in her moonlit eyes. "Work your magic, beautiful."

Instead of dragging the sweatshirt over his head, Jules just headed straight for the button on his jeans. Her gaze held his, daring, almost defiant as she unfastened the button, worked the zipper down. "I'm so curious. I've spent a week imagining what you keep hidden under all these clothes. You looked so handsome in your tux…." She parted the fabric and tugged his shirt out. "And your butt looks scrumptious in jeans."

As she reached for the waistband, her fingers skimmed

his bare skin, and he sucked in a sharp breath that made his stomach retreat from her touch. Instinctively he moved to help, but she brushed aside his hands again. "Let me."

He clasped his hands behind him, determined to indulge her fantasy, give her control over the moment. She worked his jeans and underwear down his legs, kneeling before him, head bowed to her task, wind whipping her hair around like a fury, dragging it across his bared thighs and tossing it into her face and mouth.

The contrast of her warm hands and cold air blasted him, a strange sensation that intensified dramatically when she helped him pull his clothes away, left him standing with the wind whistling in his ears and across his bare skin.

Jules tossed his jeans away, then rocked back on her haunches to survey him with an appreciative smile. His erection jumped, performing, and her smile grew wider.

Nick forced himself to stand there, legs braced apart and exposed to the raw air. His hands itched to drag her against him, to strip away her clothes and to seek shelter from the cold with their warm bodies pressed tightly together, his erection cradled between her sleek thighs.

Drawing his fingers into tight fists, he resisted the urge, until Jules bent forward and pressed her mouth to his thigh. An electric touch that made his hips buck, his skin ache with the contrasting heat of her mouth and chill night air.

Her gaze shot up to his face, searching, and he had no ability to hide what he felt, not when the sensations coursing through him were so intense he could only focus on standing, keeping his hands from dragging into her hair.

That daring glint in her gaze suggested she found the moment as exciting as he did. A moment where anyone could walk along the public beach, catch him standing bareassed above her, his erection begging her to take advantage of her position.

Without a word, she did.

Stroking her fingers along his thighs, featherlight touches that made sensation coil in their wake, she traveled down his thighs, over his knees, along his calves. She massaged her hands over his feet, dipped her fingers between his toes.

He swayed slightly, the moment filled with such a richness of sensation, such simple touches that shouldn't have impacted him like this, but had his body quivering with the hope that she wouldn't stop, that one simple touch would lead to another....

She circled him and he held his breath. Jules was full of surprises, hot surprises, innocent surprises. He didn't know what to expect. Certainly not the sweet open-mouthed kisses she pressed along the backs of his knees.

She trailed those wet kisses up his thighs, and the wind stung each one, made him ache. She followed the same path with her hands and her caresses became less sweet, and more purposeful. Kneading his buttocks with long firm strokes, she brushed her tongue so lightly along the cleft that he shivered.

When she nipped his buttock, his hips bucked hard of their own accord, need arrowing straight through him in a blaze that made him struggle hard to keep from sinking to his knees and pulling her beneath him. And when she slipped her hands around his hips and cupped those magic fingers beneath his scrotum, Nick didn't think he'd be able to last.

The weight of his skin in her hot palm made his erection jump. She laughed, a soft sound that shouldn't have carried over the wind but melted against his senses. Then she swiveled around him, her faced tipped to his, her gaze glowing with pleasure. When a slow smile curved her lips, Nick knew, he knew with every nerve ending in his body what she intended to do.

Her tongue lashed out with such purpose he couldn't react, couldn't think beyond the slow wet stroke swirling up the underside of his hot flesh.

His blood pumped. His legs shook and his knees finally gave way. Sinking back against the door, only vaguely aware of the icy glass against his ass, he braced his legs apart to offer himself willingly to her ministrations.

''Ah, beautiful.''

If this was her fantasy, Nick decided he'd died and gone to heaven, because he'd never felt like this before, had never known any woman who could strip him of all control.

He had none when she sank her fingers into his hips, urged him close and sucked the head of his erection into her sweet mouth with one long hot pull.

# 11

JULIENNE'S INDECISION about whether to bring Nick to fulfillment or bring him to his knees resulted in a sort of unintentional tease that made her slow her efforts each time she sensed him about to climax.

She should have known he'd get tired of her indecision. Growling a sound of the purest frustration, he startled her so much that she didn't even think about resisting when he pulled away and hauled her to her feet.

His black eyes glittered. His jaw clenched so tight Julienne wouldn't have been surprised if he'd cracked a few molars. The intensity of his need staggered her, and as reason returned, delighted her.

*Naughty girls feel good about feeling naughty.*

Watching Nick rip the sweatshirt over his head with jerky motions made her feel very, very naughty. She stood back and enjoyed the show, delighted to discover that he did indeed have hair, a light furring of silky black that nestled on all the muscles of his powerful chest.

Her gaze locked on the picture of the man before her, an image so magnificently sculpted she'd have been content to just admire him as the night passed, until the tide went out and sunrise stained the horizon in wispy shades of pastels.

But Nick left her little time to admire. Whirling around, he grabbed the blankets and spread them over the hammock, muscles rippling, body parts dangling, completely comfortable with his nakedness in that uniquely male way.

She'd obviously had him feeling very aroused, but Julienne didn't feel too bad—not when she'd been walking around with his crazy balls. That thought inspired her to new naughtiness. Sure she'd teased him by not bringing him to fulfillment and sure he was clearly *very* horny, but did that give him the right to get all huffy and start dictating what happened between them?

*Naughty girls take advantage of the moment.*

The phrase no sooner blossomed in her mind when Julienne leaped into motion. In one energetic jump, she cleared the porch and took to the beach, her bare toes clawing the sand for wild purchase as she ran toward the water.

She heard Nick growl, "What the hell…" but didn't stop. Pulling her sweatshirt over her head, she tossed it back his way before sending her shirt and bra flying after it.

With the wind whipping her hair into her face and numbing her skin, she laughed in sheer abandon of the moment, the freedom to be impulsive and follow wherever her desire led. On *that* night desire had led her into Nick's arms, and while this breakneck striptease didn't remotely resemble her earlier dance, Nick didn't seem to mind the differences. Bellowing her name, he charged after her.

Julienne wasn't about to stop and fiddle with removing her jeans. Not when Nick tore after her, sand kicking up around him, a scowling, and very naked, madman.

Plunging into the moonlit water, she yelped at the shock of the cold but kept going, deeper and deeper, the waves breaking against her legs, making her weave drunkenly.

"This water's like ice," Nick roared from behind her, and she spun toward the sound, experienced a surge of excitement to see him so obviously disgruntled and so gorgeously naked.

"California boy," she taunted. "It's only September."

She could see his scowl, even from this distance, and

recognized trouble. Julienne dove in to get away. The ocean enveloped her in a blackness that locked the breath in her lungs, slowed her motions with the cold. She circled around, knowing she couldn't stay under for long.

Resurfacing behind him, she launched her arms around his neck, tried to drag him down into the water. The impact of her icy breasts against his broad back made her gasp. "You need to cool off, Dr. Fairfax."

Nick was bigger, stronger and obviously not as put off by the cold as she'd supposed. With an unexpected shifting of his weight, he sent them both sprawling into the water. They sank like stones, and she barely sucked in a breath before the frigid water closed over her head again.

With one nimble twist, he broke free and shot away. The sodden weight of her jeans made her movements slow and clumsy and by the time Julienne came up sputtering, he'd already gained his feet and hauled her against him.

"Crazy woman. You're going to give us pneumonia and we'll have a helluva time kissing with oxygen tubes up our noses."

Julienne might have replied with some rejoinder about how he'd followed her on this moonlit dip of his own free will, but his hands were suddenly everywhere, grazing her shoulders, her breasts, thumbing the icy tips, skimming her ribs.

As his erection was no longer erect, her ploy had succeeded in cooling him off. But not for long. Caught in the wet tangle of her hair, they stood waist deep in the ocean while he stoked a fire inside her, the waves breaking against their bodies, his caresses tantalizing and languid by comparison to the wind and the waves thrashing around them.

When he said, "Enough with the Polar Bear Club," and scooped her into his arms, she didn't argue. Primarily because she was too busy kissing the corded muscles of his neck and she didn't intend to stop. Not when his skin tasted all slick and salty and only the meager warmth radiating from all his glorious muscles kept her from hypothermia.

Let him weave through the sand like a drunk. Let him carry her like a bride to their honeymoon suite. Nick did. He didn't put her down until they were back on the porch.

"Do you want to go inside and shower?" He draped a blanket over her shoulders, before pulling another around himself.

"That depends," Julienne said boldly, suffering from a serious case of sex-on-the-brain with so many condoms scattered over the hammock. "Can you warm me up if we don't?"

His smile flashed in his tanned face and his black eyes gleamed. "My pleasure, beautiful."

But by the time she'd struggled out of her wet jeans, a feat that left her exposed to the wind and even colder than before, she re-evaluated Nick's idea. A shower would feel really good right about now.

And that's exactly what Julienne told him as she raced inside. Once in the bathroom, she flipped on the tap full blast in the shower, dropped the blanket and got in, sighing as the water saturated her hair and flooded her body with liquid heat.

"Join me, if you want," she called out, hoping Nick could hear her over the pounding pulse of the jets.

"I plan to."

His reply came from inside the shower, and Julienne jumped, eyes flying open to discover his head popping in through the shower curtain. His gaze traveled over her slowly, purposefully, making her skin tingle and that persistent ache between her legs, which had subsided compliments of the cold ocean, renew throbbing in force.

She shot him her most alluring smile. "Come on in then, the hot water feels great."

He did, his athletic body a striking show of muscles and tanned skin against the backdrop of white tile. "Let me under."

She backed up until he could share the spray, both surprised and touched when he rinsed, then reached for the soap, not to cleanse himself, but her.

He lathered his way down her neck, his caresses firm, yet gentle and so infinitely arousing that Julienne shivered.

"You're crazy. Do you know that? The sharks could have eaten you out there."

"What sharks?"

"The sharks that swim around at night waiting for beautiful women skinny-dippers. Didn't you ever see *Jaws?*"

"I saw it." She feigned indifference. But there was nothing indifferent about her body's response to his ministrations, the tender way he stroked his strong hands over her curves. "I didn't get eaten."

He shook his head and then bent over to lather her thighs. "You're still crazy."

"I wouldn't complain too loudly, if I were you. If I wasn't crazy, we'd never be together right now."

"How's that?"

"I'd have to be a little crazy to let a stranger seduce me that night."

His hand trailed between her thighs, his smile widening when his fingers brushed the loop of the crazy balls, his soapy fingers curling around it, teasing her with a light tug. The weights knocked around, making her sex clench needily.

"But I wasn't a perfect stranger, beautiful. And I'm not complaining at all. Just making sure you know."

She knew all right, knew she was going to scream if she

didn't find some relief from this sexual torture soon. Okay, fair enough, she may have already been satisfied had she not insisted on a moonlit swim, but enough was enough already.

With her hands on his shoulders, she urged Nick to stand, intent upon pressing her body full length against him, coaxing his mouth into a sexy kiss and getting this show moving, but now Nick didn't want to be rushed.

With a smile, he deposited the bar of soap back in the holder and reached for a bottle of shampoo. "Turn around."

Julienne acquiesced, allowing herself to be distracted only because this particular task had to be completed if she expected to get a comb through her hair.

With even pressure of his fingertips against her scalp, he lathered her hair in silence, directing her back under the spray to rinse, before reaching for the conditioner and working it through the long strands with expert strokes of his fingers.

"You know so much about women, Nick." The observation just popped out, and she wished she could take it back, didn't want him to think that the past or future factored into their relationship.

Nick just chuckled. "I don't know nearly enough about you, Jules, and you're all I care about." With his fingers anchored in her hair, he tipped her head back until she could look in his eyes and his black gaze seemed very resolute. "Trust me, I intend to spend the night answering all my questions."

The steely promise in his voice sent a sizzle through her, made Julienne wonder whether he took the time to find out about all his women. Wasn't it possible she might be different?

She waited for that voice in her head to agree or disagree, but the sound of Uncle Thad's voice drowned out all others.

*Trust me, Julienne. He's a heartbreaker. A man who can't commit has a problem.*

And if Nick did fall for her, he'd have an even bigger problem, Julienne thought wryly, because she relied on hypnotherapy techniques to awaken what little passion she had.

But she wasn't about to spoil her mood with thoughts about her shortcomings or their relationship's inevitable conclusion. Torrid flings meant enjoying *the moment.*

Shoving all thoughts of self-hypnosis from her mind, she pressed her backside against Nick, gratified to feel life signs stirring in that once-impressive erection. No matter how she accomplished becoming passionate, she aroused this man. That was all that counted.

When he finished working the conditioner through her hair, Julienne grabbed the soap and decided she would concentrate only on what his skin felt like beneath her soapy hands, on how her palms glided silkily along each rise and fall of sculpted muscle. She'd imprint this moment in her memory, the way his black gaze captured hers, revealed with one dusky glance how much he enjoyed her hands traveling over him.

With that resolution came renewed purpose to imprint an equally lasting memory in his mind. No matter where Nick Fairfax went in his life, Julienne intended to be a woman who could put a smile on his face whenever and wherever he thought about her.

Sweeping her hands boldly along his penis, she remembered how he'd tasted of hot satin in her mouth, how his erection had thickened and jumped beneath her tongue.

Nick's breathing grew ragged, his chest rising and falling in uneven bursts. Circling him, she admired the spray of hot water sluicing down his broad back, over a nicely shaped butt only slightly paler than the rest of him.

She trailed a finger along the cleft, smiled when he shivered. Emboldened, she shimmied her fingers inside that sexy gap, forcing him to spread his legs apart to let her in. Then she lathered his backside with an intimacy that made *her* shiver.

"That's it. I'm done in here." Nick reached for the shampoo and dispensed a glob into his palm. Stepping out of the spray, he savagely lathered his hair and said, "Rinse off."

Julienne did, then stepped out of the shower and grabbed a towel. She'd no sooner dried off, when he pulled the shower curtain aside. In a burst of tanned muscle, he stepped out of the shower and gave one of those full body shivers that reminded her of a big Labrador shaking off the water after a swim. He reached for a towel and wrapped it around his waist. Without a word, he marched her out of the bathroom, heedless of the water trail he left behind him.

"It's my turn, beautiful." Bypassing the bedroom, he guided her into the living area to sit on the leather sofa. "Sit here and don't move. I'll start a fire and get us wine."

"Is this another fantasy?"

"Everything about you is my fantasy."

And then he disappeared, leaving Julienne feeling all warm and fuzzy as she tucked her feet beneath her and tried not to drip onto the sofa. When he reappeared, wearing a dark blue robe, he knelt in front of the fireplace, stacked two logs and glanced inside an antique brass coal pot, presumably for some other fire-starting accoutrements.

"I don't think you realize just how much you've been calling the shots since that night," he said.

"What do you mean?"

"You, me, us, beautiful."

She could tell she commanded about half his attention as he wadded up a sheet of newspaper and lit a match, but she waited.

"You've been steering me like a crane operator. You

dance and I drool. You talk all sexy on the phone and leave me with a hard-on I could use as a load-bearing beam.''

She bit back a grin at *that* image and shrugged in pretend innocence. ''You dropped the phone.''

He shot her a dark glance beneath an arched brow. ''Then you strip off my jeans and drive me nuts with that incredible mouth of yours and then haul ass into the ocean.'' He gave an indignant grunt. ''It's my turn now. I want you sitting there, just like you are, awaiting my pleasure.''

Julienne mulled his words as he fed the lighted newspaper into the grate, igniting scattered twigs of kindling. ''Just out of curiosity, Nick, if I've left you hanging so unfairly, what do you call these crazy balls jiggling around inside me?''

Rising to his feet in a fluid burst of shifting muscle, Nick covered the distance between them in two long strides. Julienne could hear her heart pound in the silence as he raked that black gaze from her face to her toes and over every barely covered inch in between.

''Who said anything about being unfair?'' Reaching out, he curled his work-rough fingertips around her chin, forced her to meet his gaze. ''Trust me, I'm not complaining. I just want equal time. I want to explore your sweet body and make you gasp. Can you handle it?''

She replied with a smile. He smiled back. Then he let his fingers slide away and disappeared into the kitchen. Julienne tightened the towel that had slipped over her breasts, settled back into the corner of the plush sofa, and waited. The sound of his sexy promises rang in her ears accompanied by the clink of glasses and other sundry noises emitting from the kitchen.

*Equal time?* That voice inside her asked. *He's hooked, girl. Show him you can handle anything he has to offer and then some.*

Hooked? Torrid flings weren't about getting hooked, Julienne reminded herself, and by the time Nick returned with two glasses of wine, she'd resolved to get her fling back on the torrid track before the sun rose.

"Try this." Nick handed her a glass. "It's merlot."

She took a sip. "Tasty. Is it time for your fantasies yet?"

Sitting down, he directed her to sit between his legs, and she sank back into his embrace, relaxed against his hard body. Sipping his wine, Nick just held her, saying nothing, doing nothing, but somehow infusing the silence with expectation.

Then he trailed one hand over her tangled hair, over the towel that clung damply to her skin. With each passing minute, Julienne felt her awareness grow until the ache between her thighs pounded harder and her skin grew flushed from the warmth of the fire. Then again, perhaps the way she felt had nothing to do with the fire, but everything to do with Nick's gentle touch.

She didn't expect the spray of tepid liquid that splashed on her breasts, jerking her rudely from her dreamy state. Glancing up, she found Nick holding his glass poised over her shoulder while he drizzled wine over her nipple. Her heart pounded sharply.

"I want wine and I want you," he said in reply to her unasked question, his deep voice promising not only sex, but sex as she'd never known. "I couldn't decide which first."

Placing the glass on the end table, he slipped off the couch and resettled himself in front of her, the robe parting over his tanned thighs. His gaze trailed to where her towel gaped at her breasts, and he peeled it from her body, exposing her.

"You're so beautiful," he said, a simple but potent observation.

Julienne recognized the pleasure softening the line of his

jaw, felt her breasts tingle in response, felt as beautiful as he claimed she was.

"Here, let me in." He guided her thighs apart with a casual touch, the sheer nonchalance of the gesture making her so aware of all the naked skin between them...the weight of her breasts as they grew taut beneath his heavy-lidded gaze...every inch of her bare body within easy reach of his skilled hands; his mouth...

When he lowered his head, she noticed how his hair dried in wheat-colored strands around his hairline, but that was the last thing Julienne noticed before his mouth fastened onto her breast.

Drawing on the tip, he sampled the wine with his rough velvet tongue. Her sex clenched greedily around the crazy balls at the sight of him poised over her, his face so dark against her pale skin, his action so possessive. He lapped the wine from the valley between her breasts and paused to press open-mouthed kisses there that made her ache with a need she'd never known before Nick.

Tonight was to be a seduction of the senses to imprint in her memory to savor long after their torrid fling was over. She'd remember the feel of his mouth on her skin, his hands...

Slipping his fingers beneath one breast, he cupped her in his palm as though weighing her soft fullness. His smile gleamed white as her nipple peaked toward his mouth, but he ignored its silent plea, peering up at her instead.

"That's one fantasy down." He darted his tongue out and flicked that greedy pink peak. "You like this."

Nick knew, oh, he definitely knew how deeply he affected her, because he couldn't miss the head-to-toe shiver that rippled through her when he tugged at her nipple with his teeth.

"Relax and enjoy, beautiful, because I'm still thirsty."

The wineglass reappeared and then the warm satin ooze of wine as it dribbled over her skin, pooled in her navel. He chased the trickles down her ribs and over her stomach, each silken stroke of his tongue making her muscles vibrate.

She'd never known anything like this ache, her whole body hot, her breast arching hungrily into his hand as he squeezed her nipple between his thumb and forefinger.

Julienne closed her eyes with a sigh. This was sex as she'd dreamed about it, the reality better than the fantasy could be. She'd never been gifted with such lavish attention, every inch of her skin cherished as though Nick felt privileged to touch her.

When his tongue dipped into her navel, scooping up the tiny puddle of wine onto his tongue and sucking it down with a noisy slurp, she practically jumped off the sofa.

"Hmm. You're ticklish, too." His breath gusted over her skin, a hot whisper.

Another low moan slipped from her lips but she kept her eyes squeezed tightly shut, couldn't bear to see him smile as he learned all her most intimate secrets.

When he drizzled that wine between her legs, Julienne couldn't think at all. He followed the trail of wine over her oh-so-sensitive skin and his wicked tongue flashed over her in one long stroke. A pitiful yelp escaped her and she arched wildly, but Nick held her in place. He wasn't about to let her escape, no matter how intense the pleasure.

No, he planned to worship her. With his tongue. With his hands. And she could only lie there with her hands sinking into the leather cushion to keep her from reaching for him, when he separated her woman's flesh and dipped his tongue into her heat.

His thumb slipped down to join the game, unerringly zeroing in on that tiny knot of nerves and massaging her with such skilled precision that a shock wave lifted her up off the sofa again.

She heard his muffled laugh, felt his warm breath caress her flesh, and then Julienne was lost in the steady pressure of his thumb, the wicked curls of his tongue.

She rode against him, unable to stop herself. His chin offered leverage against her sex while the crazy balls rocked gently inside her, filled her with a friction that lifted her higher, higher, until she poised on the edge of an orgasm so intense her body gathered, ready and waiting.... Nick caught the loop of the crazy balls with his teeth and tugged.

One round ball stretched her aching passage and slid out with a moist pop. He tugged again and the second followed.

Julienne crumbled beneath an onslaught of sensation so powerful she gasped aloud, a sound that was half sob and half moan, and she shrank from his touch as another barrage, and yet another, crashed through her.

"Oh, Nick," she ground out, the words sounding as though they'd been wrenched from her with a crowbar.

Just as she hung there, pleasure rolling in on her, proving beyond any doubt that her instinct had been right—there was no comparison between tepid sex and its naughty counterpart.

*Naughty girls feel good about feeling naughty.*

Julienne did. So good, she couldn't open her eyes until the echoes of that incredible orgasm finally faded away. Then she opened her eyes to the sight of Nick, his robe parted around an impressive erection and the crazy balls dangling from the tip of his finger and his expression, so infinitely satisfied that he'd brought her such pleasure, undid her completely.

She wanted to smile boldly—after all, naughty girls loved to come—but all she could do was lift her arms to him, needing to be held, to feel solid muscle and warm skin to reassure herself he was real and not some figment of her passion-starved imagination.

Sinking into her arms, he held her, crushed her breasts to his chest, pressed his erection against her stomach, twined their bare legs together. Julienne's breathing raced, but his breathing remained steady, an anchor in this blitz of emotion. She told herself that hypnosis had unleashed her feelings, but the tiny still-functioning part of her brain warned she was in big trouble.

Nick seemed to sense she was shaken, because he just held her, his hand sliding up to brush away wisps of hair from her cheek. He gazed down tenderly at her.

"I'm going to make love to you now, Jules. No sex swings, no more crazy balls, nothing fancy. I just want you underneath me. I want to sink inside you and hear you sigh."

Oh, man, Julienne was so gone. How could she not be when he admitted how much he wanted her with such quiet pride?

"Oh no, we left the condoms outside." A diversionary tactic to distract her from the way her heart melted. She needed a moment to collect herself, to rein her emotions under control, and she didn't stand a chance wrapped in Nick's arms.

Backing out of her embrace, he reached behind him to grab something from the end table. "Not all of them." He flashed a foil-wrapped square triumphantly.

*So much for being prepared,* that voice in her head whispered with a wry laugh, a laugh completely at odds with the quiet desperation she felt inside.

Stripping off his robe, Nick tossed it aside, faced her breathtakingly naked. "I'll do the honors." Tearing the packet open, he withdrew the condom, discarded the packet the way of his robe, and rolled the sheath on with such a practiced move that Julienne could only blink.

How could she tangle with a man who'd forgotten more about naughty than she'd ever know and not get hurt?

"Kiss me, Jules."

Her womb gave the odd clench, and after the fullness of sporting the crazy balls, she felt emptier than she ever imagined possible, empty and ready to feel this man inside her.

Her mouth caught his hard, and he obliged her with a need that both aroused and frightened her. Their tongues tangled, dueling wildly, while he wedged her thighs apart with his hips, rubbed the head of his magnificent erection against her wet sex, until she moaned and arched against him.

He used his hand to guide himself inside her and Julienne's sex unfolded around him in grateful degrees as he sank deep, a hot sleek stroke that made her sob out a broken gasp, made Nick whisper, "Ah, Jules," against her lips.

Once inside he just held her as though savoring the beauty of the moment, the feel of their bodies joined intimately, his heat warming her from the inside out.

Then he withdrew slowly, stealing the breath from her lungs, before he pressed back again, another smooth stroke that applied pressure exactly where she needed it.

Julienne had thought he'd wrung out every last drop of feeling with that incredible orgasm but she was wrong. She couldn't resist his sweet assault, each slow stroke of his body contrasting so exquisitely with his demanding kisses.

His broad shoulders blocked out the world, cocooned her in a place consisting of only him, his damp skin, his deep thrusts that lifted her right along with him. Each thrust made her yearn for the next, made her fear he might slow down and she'd lose her grip on this precious sensation. But her pleasure mounted, hopelessly tangling her physical response with her emotions.

When Nick's thighs began to tremble and his throaty growl burst upon her lips, Julienne clung to him as she splintered again, dragged into another climax that left her body vibrating and her mind asking a desperate question....

How could she not fall in love with this man?

# 12

*One month later*

No MATTER how hard she tried, no matter how many key phrases she chanted, Julienne couldn't help falling in love with Nick. How could she resist being swept into a fantasy with the man of her dreams?

*She* couldn't, but her naughty alter ego didn't have the same trouble. In fact, the increased sessions with self-hypnosis only helped Jules enjoy her time with Nick without a thought for life post-torrid fling.

For Jules life couldn't get any better. Spending weekends with Nick, exploring towns around Savannah while exploring each other had become the focal point of her week. Tension mounted steadily from Monday through Friday at the work site and at night via steamy telephone conversations and an occasional late dinner.

Julienne, on the other hand, tried to balance work and weekends away without arousing Uncle Thad's suspicions, all the while adding new key phrases to her repertoire, which ran along the lines of...

*Naughty girls don't confuse lust with love.*

Life became a series of chanting these phrases and telling herself she wasn't in over her head, that each new day and each kiss wasn't making Nick more important to her. Jules had her emotions under control, so why couldn't Julienne manage the same?

*Naughty girls live for the moment.*

Try though she might to believe that, Julienne was barely treading water. Worse yet, she suspected she wasn't the only one going under. Nick didn't just make love to her, he seduced her senses. He romanced her. And he didn't seem about to let up any time soon.

Julienne walked a fine line between spending time with Nick and keeping her uncle's suspicions at bay. She wasn't entirely successful in either endeavor. Nick wanted more of her time. Her uncle wanted to know why Kimberly was spending more time on the ground in Atlanta than in the air and seemed to be waiting for her to fess up and tell him the truth.

Julienne didn't. She *couldn't.* How could she confess to her beloved uncle that she'd done exactly what he'd cautioned her against—she'd fallen in love with a naughty boy? So she continued avoiding the issue, telling herself that if she'd just put forth more effort, she could figure out what to do to make everyone happy and everything all right again.

But in her saner moments, the moments in between passionate bouts in bed, she knew she should end her relationship with Nick before they got in any deeper. If Nick was beginning to care for her, she couldn't let him fall for a woman who was a lie. Without self-hypnosis, she was just plain old Julienne. Unfortunately with self-hypnosis, she had no willpower to resist him. *Jules* just wouldn't stand for it.

She'd made a mess, as Uncle Thad always said, and she felt guilty, guilty, guilty. For lying to her uncle. For misleading Nick. When it came right down to it, she'd even used her job to cover up her fling. Although her students benefited from their affiliation with ADF, she couldn't exactly feel guilt-free about her intentions. There'd been nothing noble about wanting to be closer to Nick.

Julienne didn't know what to do. She'd thought about

discussing the problem with Kimberly but knew exactly what her best friend would say—come clean and let the chips fall where they may. But every time she opened her mouth tell Uncle Thad about her fling, she found her throat closing up with panic that he'd be so disappointed he wouldn't even be able to look at her.

And every time she opened her mouth to tell Nick about the self-hypnosis, she wound up kissing him. Every time she tried to tell him they shouldn't see each other anymore, she wound up kissing him some more.

So Jules ran the show, leaving Julienne to hope she'd find the strength to end their relationship. Or that naughty boy Nick would tire of the game and move on. Or that Uncle Thad would stop grilling her about her weekends away. Or that she would somehow turn into the passionate woman she pretended to be.

*Naughty girls can learn to live the part.*

Couldn't they?

NICK WHISTLED as he swung the door to the construction trailer wide, almost nailing Dale, who was on his way inside.

"Jeez, buddy." Dale took a quick step back to avoid a broken nose. "Watch where you're going, would you?"

"Don't count on it," Betty called from her desk behind him. "And don't rag on Nick, either, Dale. He's been pleasant lately and we all like the change. Let the man whistle."

Dale snorted.

"Sorry," Nick muttered, mulling Betty's observation while stepping off the last riser to let Dale head inside the trailer.

But Dale motioned him to close the door. "I don't need to go in. I was looking for you."

"What's up?"

"I should be asking you. You were just whistling and now you've got a frown on your face. All I did was blink."

Nick shrugged, moved away from the trailer to gaze toward the river, where a ship cruised lazily past. "I think Betty knows about me and Julienne."

"Good guess," Dale said, irking Nick with his flip reply. Something of Nick's annoyance must have shown, because Dale continued. "Well, don't even bother denying that your mood isn't affected by whether or not you're getting laid regularly."

Nick scowled, unable to deny the accusation and wondering when he'd become so shallow and predictable. He didn't have an answer, but as usual, Dale didn't need one.

"Besides Betty knows everything around here," he said. "She figured out what you and Julienne were up to a long time ago."

"What about the others?"

Dale shrugged. "With the way you and the gorgeous professor shoot those steamy looks at each other all day? Not to mention those trips out of town every weekend. What do you think?"

"They know."

"Of course they know. They're happy." Dale shot him a dry look. "We just want to know how the breakup will affect your working relationship. Or are you planning to send Julienne and her interns packing?"

Nick's brain locked on one word and didn't move beyond. "Breakup?"

"Yeah, breakup," Dale repeated as though that answered his question. "The day you move on from the gorgeous Julienne to greener pastures. Out of curiosity, when will that be?"

Truth was, Nick hadn't thought about moving on. Not once. He couldn't help but wonder if Dale brought the subject up because he wanted to make a play for Jules himself. The thought sucker-punched him in the solar plexus. "What, did Mallory leave you already? Or were you dating Madison this week?"

"Mallory is old news. Morgan's this week. No Madison." He shrugged. "I'm having a run on the letter *M*. Do you want Mallory's number, buddy. She'll help you get over Julienne. Trust me."

Nick scowled.

Dale smiled. "You're a bitch to be around when you're not getting any, so as long as you're walking around smiling, no one cares who you sleep with."

"Do yourself a favor and don't let Julienne's name and another rude reference to sex come out of your mouth again."

To Nick's profound annoyance, Dale just laughed. "What, you're telling me she's somehow different from all your other bedroom buddies? If that's the case, then I suggest you stop treating her like one. If you only keep her in the bedroom, people are going to think she belongs there."

Nick found the charge unbelievably offensive. Dale's offhand comments made his knuckles ache to connect with bone to stop from hearing another one. But no matter how much Nick disliked the casual references to sex he couldn't fault Dale.

"She's different, so shut up about her."

Dale's gaze narrowed, but he didn't heed Nick's suggestion. "Listen, buddy. I'll be the first to tell you Julienne is out of the ordinary. Hell, not only is she a looker, but she knows what an escutcheon is. There's a combination you don't find every day. But if you're seriously giving in to the love bug, then you're going about this all wrong. Didn't your mama teach you the difference between the kinds of girls you sleep with and the kinds you marry?"

Actually, his mother hadn't ever acknowledged there'd been any other kind of girl but the marrying kind. His father had been the one to distinguish the differences, and explain how the two could mesh while keeping a marriage intact.

"Damned shame Julienne isn't a woman you might actually stand a chance with. She knows all about life in the field and might just have the patience to put up with your obsession with ADF. She's crazy about you, too. That's obvious. Damned shame you're not worthy of her."

"What makes you say that?"

"You're a slut, buddy. She's a nice girl. You've got to treat nice girls with respect and you don't have a clue."

Nick scowled, staring out over the river and the bright blue sky beyond, wondering when he'd become so self-serving. He'd never even given a thought to how his dating history would affect Jules. And now that he thought about it, he couldn't remember ever giving a thought to how any of his dates would be affected. Except for the time the press had hounded him. Then the baggage he brought to a relationship had been too noticeable to ignore.

Nick didn't like what that said about him. He also didn't like that his team believed his mood depended on his sex life. Where they wrong?

*No.*

When he thought about this past month with Jules, Nick had to admit not only his mood, but his work had benefited. Jules and her students had renewed his enthusiasm in a way he hadn't realized had been lacking.

But dating her hadn't *renewed* anything, because Nick had flat-out never experienced anything like the effect she had on him. He routinely found himself making dozens of excuses a day to walk through the auditorium. He liked the way she interacted with her students. She instructed them with a calm logic that encouraged input and made them use their heads. She always respected their answers, viable or not.

*Respect.* Was he treating Jules with less than she deserved? Was that why she would only see him outside of Savannah? She hadn't actually come right out and admitted she wanted to keep their relationship secret, but Nick read the signs well enough.

She wouldn't spend the night at his townhouse, hadn't once invited him to the home she shared with her uncle. Whenever they went out of town, she met him at a parking garage downtown and left her car parked there. She treated him exactly the way Dale had accused him of treating her. A bedroom buddy.

He didn't like the term one bit. He especially didn't like Jules treating him like one.

Turning to face his friend, he caught sight of the long white van emblazoned with the University of Savannah logo parked in the middle of the lot. Why wasn't he content to be Jules's bedroom buddy? Why was he consumed with waking up in the morning with her beside him? Why weren't Sunday mornings enough?

"I've been trying to get our relationship out of the bedroom. Either I'm not doing it right or she's just not interested."

"Well, here's a twist. A woman who won't give into your every whim. Maybe Julienne isn't so perfect after all."

"Oh, she's perfect all right," Nick said without thinking, earning a surprised stare from Dale.

Then Dale issued a low whistle and sat down heavily on the low wall separating the parking lot from the street. "What makes you think she's not interested?"

"Obviously she doesn't want to flaunt our relationship in front of her students. A personal connection between us could raise questions about her work ethics and job competency. I understand that, especially after meeting her idiot of an ex. She also told me she doesn't want to flaunt our fling in her uncle's face. I understand that, too. Hell, I don't want the guy to think all I want to do is sleep with his niece.'' Nick ran his fingers through his hair, frustrated that every time he reasoned through Jules's reluctance to get more involved he wound up back where he started—confused.

"You're missing the obvious."

"What?"

"I don't know how to say this diplomatically, buddy."

"Calling me a slut was diplomatic?"

Dale shrugged, a gesture of entreaty that made Nick brace himself for what was coming. "You're not exactly what I'd call the ideal guy to bring home to meet the folks. I mean, come on, Nick, you're not marriage material. What the hell's Julienne supposed to do? Her uncle's in the business so unless he's been hiding under a rock for the past decade or so, he knows your reputation with women—especially after your fifteen minutes of fame last year."

Dale leveled a steely glance, reminding Nick of some protective older brother laying down the rules for dating a beloved younger sister. "You're out of your league. Uncle Thad is a nice man who raised a nice girl. Julienne's not stupid. Bringing you home to her uncle would be synonymous with admitting she only wants to have sex. You've got her between a rock and a hard place. You see that, don't you?"

As clearly as he could see the crumbling eaves of the theater's roof. Nick had never made any apologies for the way he lived his life and now his arrogance bit him in the ass. "So what do I do, just continue being her secret fling?"

"What else can you do? Short of a marriage proposal, a ring and a date, Julienne isn't going to believe you're interested in anything but sex. With your past history, no one in their right mind would. Are you looking for a trip down the aisle?''

Nick blinked.

"Didn't think so. You said Julienne's different, though, so my advice is don't push it. If it comes down to you or Uncle Thad…I'm sorry, buddy, but you'll lose. No matter how satisfied you keep Julienne in bed, you've got to come up for air sometime. Uncle Thad's got a lot more going for him."

Nick ran his fingers through his hair again, annoyed at the truth in Dale's words. If he pushed Jules, he'd surely end up losing, so what did that leave?

"I'll just have to prove I want more than a bedroom relationship."

"You're going to prove you want to extend your normal bedroom relationship by a month or two? I'm sure that'll impress Uncle Thad."

Nick scowled.

Dale laughed. "You don't know the first damned thing about what takes place in a relationship outside the bedroom."

"I'm not stupid. I'll figure it out."

"Not now you won't." Dale hopped off the wall. "Your sex life has held me up enough for one day. Right now you're coming with me to look at the latest problem spot."

"Can't it wait?" He needed to visit the coffee shop for caffeine to clear his head. He needed to seriously think about what he wanted from Jules.

"No."

"Lead the way." Nick had no idea what Dale wanted him to look at but he hoped that wherever they were heading, they'd have to go through the auditorium to get there.

No such luck. Dale led him around to the front of the

building to talk about the cracked casing around the glass in the box office window, but they hadn't been talking long when Nick recognized a portly bearded silhouette heading toward them from the parking lot.

"Dr. Blake, great to see you." Nick extended his hand. Was it his imagination or did those piercing blue eyes seem a lot more piercing than usual? Or was guilt just making him feel that way?

Either way, Nick didn't like coming face-to-face with the sobering fact that the man whose work had profoundly impacted his life may not have a good opinion of him.

"Not a bad time for you, is it?" Dr. Blake asked.

"You're welcome any time."

"What brings you by today, sir?" Dale extended his hand.

"Just happened to be in the neighborhood and thought I'd pop in to see how you boys were doing. And my niece."

Dale shot Nick a look that suggested Dr. Blake's visit had more to do with ensuring his niece was still in one piece than how the renovations were coming along.

"I'll take you to see her." Nick ignored the gnawing sense that Dale was right. "We were just about finished here anyway."

Dale shot him a glance that said he didn't think they were even close but Nick ignored him, too.

"This way, sir."

Dale followed and Dr. Blake remarked on their progress at dismantling the lobby, lifting broken tiles and how much of the unsalvageable wallpaper they'd managed to peel away. The lobby of the Risqué no longer resembled its former grandeur, more like a grand old lady without her wig and makeup.

But Nick knew Dr. Blake could see right beyond this temporary state to the beauty that would emerge once they'd replaced the mildewing sections of wallpaper with modern reproductions, once they'd repaired the chipped and broken tiles.

Jules had said her uncle had followed his career but somehow that didn't take the edge off of realizing that no matter how highly Dr. Blake thought of his work, the man might not think much of Nick as a person.

When they reached the auditorium, Dr. Blake's expression lit up. Nick followed his gaze to where Jules was huddled with her students in discussion around...something, though Nick couldn't tell what from this distance.

"Uncle Thad," Jules called out, when she glanced around. Brushing her hands on her jeans, she hurried toward them, gifting them with a bright smile. "Hi, Nick, Dale."

She kissed her uncle on the cheek. "I'm so glad you're here. You're just in time for Rebel Radio's latest surprise. Wendy and Brit have been taunting us all day with some mystery broadcast that's airing at three. They claim it's going to launch Rebel Radio into the big league."

"Really, dear?" He glanced down at his watch. "Then I just made it, didn't I?"

"Just in time. My uncle's a nostalgic radio aficionado," Jules explained.

"With today's technology all those great old radio series have been restored," Dr. Blake said. "Julienne is a fan, too."

"Sure am. I'm a Sam Spade gal."

Dr. Blake smiled fondly. "Little Orphan Annie and Captain Midnight, too."

Dale laughed. "My father used to tell me Captain Midnight stories at bedtime."

Nick hadn't done the bedtime story thing with his own father, who'd been active in his high-power law career, which had ultimately led to his seat on the bench. But he was glad Jules had. He liked the old-time charm that living with her other-generation uncle had lent her. Frank Sinatra music, ballroom dancing, and yes, even old radio shows. He just couldn't figure out how her bold bedroom manner fit into the equation.

"It's on," Wendy yelled. "Come on, Dr. Blake and Dr. Blake, it's on."

They gathered around a boom box set to an AM radio station, judging by the tinny sound and untimely crackle of static. Then Nick heard Brit, in his role as radio commentator, announce the arrival at the radio station of a script telling the story of the anonymous *Hush-Hush Honeys,* a couple connected to a university who were conducting a clandestine, and very steamy, love affair.

Similarities between the campus in the script and the University of Savannah had convinced Rebel Radio to air the segment. Nick heard Brit start an on-air reading and motioned Jules back from the crowd, just enough to talk without being overheard, yet not far enough to draw notice. "Prerecorded?"

At her nod, he asked, "I tried to call you last night. It was late, around eleven. The recorder picked up but didn't record."

"I fell asleep," she admitted with a grin. "I don't know what's up with the recorder, though. I'll have to remember to check on it. A student told me she had the same problem when she tried to call yesterday."

"Doesn't matter as long as you were dreaming about me."

"I was."

The admission slipped from her lips in a sexy burst of breath that filtered through his senses like a warm breeze, stirring his body with responses that had no time or place on this work site. Or around her uncle.

Who, he discovered, was staring at the two of them with a disturbingly unreadable expression.

"Sort of reminds me of *Moon Over Africa*," Dr. Blake senior said, and Nick recognized the maneuver for exactly what it was—a way to draw Julienne away from Nick and back to him.

With one graceful step, she moved back to her uncle, never even giving him a second glance. "Do you think? No Congo drums."

"No, no Congo drums, or horror," her uncle agreed. "Unless I'm much mistaken, this seems to be a straight romance."

While radio broadcasts may fascinate this group, Nick preferred to focus on his own troubled romance than on the adventures of two people referred to only by the endearments My Love and Darling. He had some serious thinking to do, starting with how much he disliked the way he felt right now.

Thaddeus Blake had made his point, which only reinforced what Dale had said to him earlier. If Jules were forced to choose between him and her uncle, Nick would lose, and for some reason he'd better analyze, the thought of losing her bothered him a lot.

He intended to slip away quietly, intent upon taking some time to sift through this latest development, but hesitated when a reference to St. Simon's Island brought to mind his past weekend with Jules on the historic island.

*"Forced to meet in secret, My Love and Darling chose St. Simon's Island for their weekly tête-à-tête, a place where they could openly stroll hand in hand along the white sand beach, kiss while spiraling up to the top of the lighthouse and hide inside a bungalow to explore their passion…."*

Well, at least My Love and Darling had sense enough to enjoy their time together, Nick thought wryly, the mystery duo raising a notch in his estimation. He and Jules had done all those things on their visit.

Then he heard Wendy's voice chime in over the airwaves, *"Oh, darling, I wish we could hold hands at home. I want to show our love, tell everyone what's inside my heart."*

*"But, my love,"* Brit's voice shot back. *"We don't have that choice, not without hurting the people we care about...."*

Catching Dale's gaze, Nick cocked his head toward a nearby exit to signify his intention, then made his escape, leaving the group to enjoy what they considered a riveting performance.

Nick headed down the long hall back toward the entrance. Though the erotic artwork normally exhibited in the hall had been shipped to ADF's headquarters, where his restoration artists were hard at work, the molding along the hall caught his eye, a plasterwork Kama Sutra of greedy hands and thrusting genitals.

He wished he could see Jules tonight. Even sharing dinner would go a long way toward satisfying this ache inside him that proved he wanted to be more to her than just her bedroom buddy.

JULIENNE PICKED UP the telephone on the second ring around ten that night.

"Hello, beautiful," his rich voice filled the receiver, made her smile as she settled back against her pillows for what had now become a familiar nightly ritual.

"Hi, Nick. How'd your night go?"

"Accomplished a lot. Would have been more fun with you."

She sighed and Nick laughed, a sexy sound that sent awareness through her, made her notice the way her nipples beaded against the silk of her pajama top.

"Only three days until we can get away, beautiful. In fact, I think I'll cut out early this Saturday. We've pulled late nights every day this week. My team could use the break."

"Oh," Julienne said. "I hoped to get an appointment with Ramón on Saturday. It's the only day I can and I'll never make another week. That won't interfere with our plans, will it?"

"I have no plans unless they include you. I'm overdue for a cut myself. How about I give a call and try to get both of us an appointment before we head out of town?"

Julienne should say no. His-and-her hair appointments seemed too intimate, too much of a *couple* thing. While she and Ethan had patronized the same stylist, they'd never actually shared an appointment, which implied that she and Nick had definitely moved past *torrid fling* into the realm of *steamy affair.*

Nick must have interpreted her silence as assent, because he said, "I'll take care of it. And pack warm. I got us tickets to a nighttime football game."

"Okay," Julienne said, though she should have been canceling their plans, explaining that she couldn't see him off the work site. But how could she when that voice in her head kept chanting, *Naughty girls live for the moment?*

At this moment she simply wanted to enjoy the effect of Nick's voice on her senses, because he was having a definite effect. She'd put tepid sex long behind her and was actually *living,* really enjoying life for the first time in a very long time. How could this be so wrong?

She couldn't answer that question, needed to stop obsessing until she figured out how to fix this mess, but now…now was the time to enjoy being lovers.

"What did you think of Rebel Radio today?" A diversion.

His grunt told her he hadn't been nearly as intrigued as

she'd been, which came as no surprise given the way he'd left in the middle of the broadcast.

"It was almost spooky. I mean how many *Hush-Hush Honeys* were on St. Simon's Island this past weekend? Do you think we ran into them on the beach or during the plantation tour?"

"They're fictional, beautiful."

"They *may* be fictional. Wendy and Brit don't know for sure. The author alluded they might be real. But I don't think it really matters. People will think a couple sneaking stolen moments is romantic."

"Being with you is romantic. Going to a college football game this weekend is romantic. My Love and Darling didn't do much for me."

"My Love and Darling?" Julienne repeated, aghast. "Oh, now I get it."

"What?"

"This is my first official glimpse of Nick the cynic."

"I'm not a cynic."

"Oh, no?" She smiled at his indignation. "Then would you mind telling me what's so romantic about a football game?"

"The bleachers."

"The bleachers?" Clearly she'd missed the obvious.

"Yeah. I want to kiss you underneath them. I want to slip my hands under your sweatshirt and feel skin."

His hot promise made her tingle in reply, made the cool silk against her nipples create a needy friction. "Is this some sort of high school fantasy?"

"I'm making up for all the years I didn't know you, beautiful, and trust me, if I'd have known you in high school, I'd have made out with you under the bleachers."

Julienne rested her head back into the pillows, grateful

for the headset. Slipping her fingers beneath the waistband of her pajamas, she zeroed in on that tiny knot of nerves, shivered when she found it.

"So tell me about what we'll do under those bleachers."

# *13*

---

*Saturday morning*

JULIENNE HAD MARVELED at Nick's good timing in calling Casa de Ramón not five minutes after a haircolor touch-up had cancelled a coveted Saturday appointment. He'd managed to schedule ten and ten-thirty haircuts.

They arrived together at the salon shortly before their first appointment only to be directed into the reception area and told Ramón was running behind.

"He won't be long," Julienne assured him, sitting down on one of the sleek Art Deco benches that had been artfully grouped around the open reception area. "I've never had to wait more than fifteen minutes in the entire time I've been coming here."

"No problem, beautiful." Nick sat down beside her, so close his thigh pressed against hers.

His gaze raked over her reflection in a nearby mirror and his appreciative smile filled her with a sense of feminine pride. The last time she'd walked into this salon, she'd practically blended in with the decor.

"We're in no hurry," he added. "Our time's our own today."

No sooner had he said that than a familiar voice cried out, "Dr. Blake, Dr. Fairfax."

Julienne recognized that voice, even though it had absolutely no business being here. Sure enough, one glance into the nail area revealed a pixy-haired brunette with a bright smile on her face.

*Wendy.*

"Well, good morning," Julienne said, casually putting some distance between her and Nick. The last thing she needed was Wendy mentioning to Uncle Thad that she'd run into them away from the Risqué. "I didn't know Katriona did your nails, and we were just talking about this not long ago, too."

"Delia turned me onto her," Wendy said.

"I do everyone who's anyone around here, sister." Katriona shot her one of those you-should-have-known looks, then dropped her gaze back to Wendy's hand, which she held sandwiched in one of her large ones.

"I guess that makes me somebody." Wendy laughed. "So what are you two doing here this morning?"

"I don't have a barber yet, so Dr. Blake generously offered to share hers," Nick said, sounding so offhand Julienne breathed a sigh of relief.

"Where's Brit?" she asked, hoping to keep the conversation moving. "I don't often see you two apart."

"He's wiped from this week. I left him home sleeping."

"Am I working you too hard?" Nick asked.

Wendy shook her head, sending shiny hair ruffling around her face. "Oh, no. We've been working till the wee hours every night on the new radio series. You wouldn't believe the response we've gotten. The lines to the studio haven't stopped ringing with students wanting to know when the next installment airs.

"Brit wants to build momentum, so we've been rearranging the line-up to make room for the *Hush-Hush Honeys.* The author promised two new scripts next week, but he sent along some teasers to run until then. We just finished recording them last night. Well, this morning actually. We didn't get done until three.'' She yawned.

"The *Hush-Hush Honeys?*" Katriona commented. "Sounds like some sort of homey Southern dish, deep-fried in lard and guaranteed to put at least three new dimples in my butt.''

Nick winced and Julienne had to hide her laughter beneath a sudden cough. Wendy quickly corrected her.

"Oh, no, Kat. *Hush-Hush Honeys* is a really cool radio serial. It's about a couple of fictional lovers. At least we think they're fictional, we're not really sure. The author won't tell us. Brit's playing up the mystery angle, anyway.''

She launched into an animated explanation of the lovers' exploits that had Katriona pausing in her work to listen raptly. Nick just shook his head.

"Dr. Blake and Dr. Fairfax heard the first installment the other day,'' Wendy added, apparently unaware that Nick had cut out halfway through the broadcast.

"Sure did,'' Nick agreed. "Riveting.''

Julienne poked him in the thigh, below the edge of the bench so neither Wendy nor Katriona could see.

"Brit's hoping we'll win the college broadcaster's award if our ratings stay up. The deadline for the contest is next week, and he didn't think Rebel Radio would qualify this year.''

Julienne noticed how Wendy's smile faded. "I'll keep my fingers crossed.''

"Please do. Just becoming a finalist in the contest would look good on his record.''

Julienne sensed there was something more than just an ego boost behind Wendy's words but didn't have a chance to ask when Ramón whipped around the corner and practically skidded to a stop in the middle of the reception area.

"Jules, Dr. Nick, come back, come back. I'm so sorry to

make you wait. My first appointment decided to have an identity crisis when I'd only booked time for a trim. I've been off schedule ever since,'' he said on one long rush of breath.

Waving goodbye to Wendy and Katriona, they followed Ramón through the salon.

"Jules, grab that stool and take a load off," he said, once back at their station. "Let me get Dr. Nick out of the way, because I've got to think when I cut your hair."

Nick arched a dark brow skeptically, as if questioning where Ramón's attention would be while cutting his, but Julienne just smiled and took the opportunity to admire Nick's backside as he stalked off to the shampoo area.

Nick needn't have worried. In less than twenty minutes, Ramón had him back to his neatly trimmed self. Then he settled Julienne in his chair, where she explained, "I didn't realize I'd have to come back so often for trims."

"A minor inconvenience when you look so good. Book your next appointment before you leave today. It's easier."

Taking Ramón's advice, she scheduled her next appointment on her way out of the salon little more than an hour later. Nick followed suit, scheduling his next month's appointment back-to-back with hers.

"You want us to come together like we did today?" she asked as they left the front desk and headed out of the salon.

"And we'll come tonight like we did last weekend." His black gaze glittered and he shot her a grin nothing short of roguish. Linking his arm through hers, he guided her toward the parking lot.

Julienne didn't know what to make of his plans. If he intended to be around long enough to make their next hair appointment, then their relationship had definitely crossed over into steamy affair turf.

*Don't panic, girl,* that voice in her head said. *Just go with the flow and don't spoil your weekend. Things will work out.*

Julienne didn't have a chance to consider the advice before reaching Nick's sports-utility vehicle, where their weekend gear had already been packed for the drive to Athens.

Opening her door, Nick whistled a jaunty tune while he waited for her to settle in. Then he circled to the driver's side and climbed in singing, "We're off to see the bleachers..."

*Wednesday night*

NICK'S TELEPHONE rang shortly after midnight and he reached for it, expecting Dale or Betty to be on the other end, as he'd barely left the site a half hour before.

Jules was on the line.

"What's up, beautiful? Miss me? I got your message but I thought it was too late to call." At least when she should have been catching up on the sleep she'd missed in Athens. He still suffered the effects big-time, and he knew Jules had made two trips to a nearby coffee shop for espresso before noon today.

"Nick, we've got a problem."

The urgency in her voice bolted him to the spot. "What's the matter?"

"We're the *Hush-Hush Honeys.*"

A moment passed before Nick connected them to Rebel Radio's new broadcast. "That couple is supposed to be us?"

"It is us."

"They mentioned our names?"

"No, no, it's all still this big mystery thing—are they fictional characters or not—but that fictional couple spent this past weekend in Athens. They were making out under the bleachers, Nick.'' Her voice rose hysterically. ''Indulging some sort of high school fantasy.''

With a nasty chill zipping up his spine, Nick moved to the kitchen bar and leaned against it. ''Making out under the bleachers isn't all that uncommon of a fantasy,'' he said, more for her benefit than his.

''They've got everything else down cold. The university, how we're working together, then heading out of town on the weekends.''

''Did they mention specifics about our work?''

''No, but just insert the Risqué and you've got us. No question.'' She made a tiny noise that sounded suspiciously like a sob and Nick cradled the phone between his shoulder and ear, ran his fingers through his hair, trying to appease the urge to wrap his arms around her and comfort her.

''Do you have a computer with Internet access?'' She sounded resolute, though Nick could hear her voice tremble.

''Yes.''

''A dedicated phone line?''

''Cable.''

''Log onto the university Web site. What's your e-mail address? I'll send you the URL right now. You can download the program right off Rebel Radio's page and listen for yourself.''

''I don't doubt you, Jules.'' He gave her his e-mail address anyway, understanding her need for action as he struggled with his own feelings of anger.

He hadn't had time to assimilate the ramifications of their affair being broadcast under the guise of a fictional relationship, or even to speculate on how anyone could have discovered personal details about them. Why would someone even bother? But he wanted to be with her, to calm her fears and deal with this together.

Pushing away from the bar, he headed toward his office,

anger fueling his strides, irrationally not at the anonymous writer of the *Hush-Hush Honeys* scripts, but because he was standing in this townhouse when Jules was halfway across town.

"All right. I'm booting my computer now."

"Okay, I've loaded my e-mail program," her voice came back, a little less shaky now.

Within minutes Nick had picked up her post and clicked on the URL to Rebel Radio's home page. He navigated to the downloadable broadcasts, clicked on the latest episode of the *Hush-Hush Honeys* and sat back to listen.

Jules remained silent on the other end of the line, while he listened to Brit and Wendy play the parts of My Love and Darling. Nick wasn't halfway through the ten-minute broadcast before he knew with a feeling of gut-wrenching certainty that Jules had every right to be upset.

She was My Love and he was Darling.

Maneuvering the mouse, he clicked off the computer's media player. "Damn. That sounds like a guided tour of our weekend. We should check our clothes for surveillance equipment."

"Why would someone bug us, Nick? Or follow us? But how else could they know all this stuff? I haven't said a word to anyone."

He half expected her to ask if he had, but was both appreciative and relieved when she didn't call his integrity into question. "I haven't said anything, either," he offered, an additional reassurance. "Unfortunately everyone knows I've been heading out of town on the weekends. Dale's the only one who knows I've been going with you, but I haven't shared details."

"Why would someone do this?"

"We're both consenting adults. I don't see what can be

accomplished by making our relationship public. What's the point?''

"To broadcast that we like kinky sex."

If her voice hadn't sounded so shaky and scared, Nick might have smiled at the reminder that Jules, for all her delightful sexual bravado, wasn't nearly as experienced as she made out to be. Instead, he sank back in his chair, frustrated.

"There's no law against enjoying kinky sex, beautiful, as long as we're both over age."

She exhaled in exasperation, a huff that echoed over the phone line. "We might not be guilty of a crime, but do you know how bad this will look if people think we've been having an affair in front of my interns? If the university board hears?"

"If your uncle hears."

The silence on the other end confirmed Nick's suspicions.

He took the direct approach, steeling himself against the pang he felt at Jules's continued silence. "Listen, we haven't talked about this before, but I want you to know I'm aware how seeing me puts you in an awkward position with your uncle."

"Oh, Nick." She did sob this time and the teary sound filtered through him, almost numbing in intensity.

Nick stared at the telephone, openmouthed, wanting to say something to smooth away the raw edge to her voice. He didn't know what to say to make her feel better. Didn't have a damned clue. He was usually long gone before any woman would even think about crying around him, which begged the question: what could he possibly offer Jules now when she needed him?

This was a question he couldn't answer, not when her soft sobs were breaking over the telephone line, each one digging another trench in his composure, making him feel more inadequate.

"Look, I don't want to talk about this now," he finally said, spurred to action. Avoiding the problem seemed to be the only sane approach to take. At least until he had time to figure things out. "I just want you to know I understand. With my past history, it's probably best that your uncle doesn't know the details about us."

"It's not just your past, Nick."

Great. More problems. And those were definitely tears he heard in her voice. Nick could have kicked himself for bringing this up now. Dale was right. He was way out of his league. He tried for levity. "You're not going to tell me Uncle Thad would be happy to know we're having a torrid fling, are you?"

"No, no, of course he wouldn't. But it's not just you. It's me. I'm...I'm not—"

"You're beautiful is what you are," he said, a desperate attempt to steer out of these turbulent emotional waters. "And we're not going to talk about this now. Let's save it until the weekend, when we can lie in bed and discuss this face-to-face." That would give him a few days to figure out what to say. "Right now we have a crisis to contend with. Agreed?"

"Only if you'll promise me you won't assume all the responsibility yourself. I don't deny that your history is a problem, but I'm the one to blame here."

"Jules."

"No really, Nick. Promise me."

Those tears told him that she was barely hanging on. "All right, I promise. But forget about it for now. We've got to figure out who's sending those scripts and stop them before another episode airs."

"Do you really think we can?"

"Yes." He sounded a lot more certain than he felt, though.

But he'd given Jules something to latch onto and she grabbed it with both hands. "We've got to. I'll die if Uncle Thad finds out I'm one of the *Hush-Hush Honeys*. He's from a whole different era and I've never given him any reason to be ashamed of me. Nice women don't do things like this and he raised me to be nice."

He heard the panic rising in her voice again. The only thing he could think to do to reassure her was to hold her, and he couldn't do that across a telephone line. Nor could he stroll into Thaddeus Blake's home and wrap his arms around the man's niece. Not with the current status of their relationship. And he wasn't about to suggest Jules get into her car.

"Where's your uncle?"

"Upstairs asleep."

"All right, listen to me. Meet me on your front porch in twenty minutes. We'll take a walk and figure out what to do."

"I've been wracking my brain and I can't think of a thing. We can't ask Brit and Wendy to stop airing the episodes without them guessing we're the stars of the show. Oh no," she cried. "Wendy saw us together at Ramón's. What if she figures out we're seeing each other? She's bound to suspect we're the *Hush-Hush Honeys*."

"Don't worry. I've got a few ideas."

Which gave Nick approximately twenty minutes to clear his head and come up with something before he got to her house.

JULIENNE FLIPPED UP her collar as she sat on her front porch waiting for Nick. But even her wool coat didn't offset the effects of a chill that arrowed straight to the bone.

The night was black and crisp and clear. The stars glittered sharply, draped silver shadows over her quiet street. Each home in her neighborhood sat back on a well-maintained lot, the glow from porch lights and streetlamps illuminating slanted eaves, tiled roofs and wraparound verandas.

She and Uncle Thad had chosen this neighborhood because the turn-of-the-century homes were in need of constant maintenance, or in some cases even restoration, and over the past decade she'd watched subtle changes occur as the twin effects of age and maintenance campaigned to leave their marks on the majestic facades and weathered shingles.

A calm street, Julienne knew it would come to life in another week, when costumed children would swarm from front door to front door, calling out, "Trick-or-treat!"

She almost smiled at the thought. She and Uncle Thad always made it a point of being home on Halloween. She picked up bags of candy from the grocery store at least a week beforehand, lots of chocolate bars and red licorice—Uncle Thad's favorites.

She'd open two bags into a big bowl on the kitchen counter and watch the candy slowly vanish, a trick of her uncle's sweet tooth. Halloween night she'd produce the rest and Uncle Thad would smile slyly and marvel at the never-ending bowl that reproduced candy as he reached for yet another mini-chocolate bar.

This Halloween would be different. Uncle Thad never had much of an appetite when he got upset or anxious, and she suspected he wouldn't even want sweets when he discovered the niece he'd reared to be a good girl had ignored his warnings. Not only had she fallen in love with a naughty boy, but she was about to be busted for it in a very public way.

All because she'd wanted to lose her good-girl inhibitions.

Her plan had been perfect—*if* a one-night stand had remained a one-night stand. Her plan had major flaws when applied to torrid flings and steamy affairs and she'd blithely overlooked them, just to stay involved with Nick.

Uncle Thad had warned that Nick wasn't the man for her. She'd ignored him, too. Now they would all face the consequences of her choices, all the worse because Nick believed himself responsible. His lifestyle may have been a problem for her uncle, but she'd signed on knowing full well who Nick was and what he wanted from her. She'd believed herself capable of handling their fling. She'd thought she could keep their affair secret and everyone would have what they wanted. Uncle Thad his peace of mind. Julienne the freedom to explore her passion. Nick his sex with a naughty girl.

But Nick had thrown her a curve. He hadn't wanted just sex. He'd wanted more. How much more she didn't know— she didn't think even he knew—but she'd been naive to discount that life didn't always play by the rules. Predicting people's emotions could be very risky business. Now she was responsible for hurting the men she loved most.

Lights flashed at the corner. The familiar sport-utility vehicle swung onto her street and Julienne's heart mushroomed in her chest, a huge ache that stole her breath and made relieved tears prickle at the back of her lids. She blinked hard. She couldn't even do a one-night stand right, she thought morosely.

*Naughty girls don't confuse lust with love.*

Right.

*Give the pity party a rest, girl. Your knight in shining armor is here and the two of you will figure something out.*

Julienne hoped.

Nick pulled in front of the house and she met him at the sidewalk, feeling those stupid tears prickling at the back of her lids again when he walked straight up to her without saying a word and wrapped her in his arms.

Her cheek settled against the smooth leather of his bomber jacket, anchored in place by the kiss he pressed to the top of her head. He stroked her hair idly with one hand, while he locked her close with the other.

The heat and his familiar male scent oozed through her senses like a balm. He seemed to know that she needed to be held, needed to borrow his strength right now because her own faltered badly. And she just clung to him, the night enveloping them in shadow, shielding them—she hoped—from prying eyes.

She savored each nuance of the moment, each warm breath that burst softly against his jacket, the heat of his mouth still pressed to her head. She tried to convey through touch that she'd meant what she'd said earlier. Nick's relationship history alone wasn't responsible for her keeping their relationship secret.

But Nick was right—now wasn't the time to tackle that particular issue. Not when it meant explaining how a man he admired and respected didn't extend those feelings about the way he lived his life. Not when she'd have to admit to practicing hypnotherapy techniques to unleash her passion.

"You okay?" he asked.

No. But her lying heart promised she'd be okay as long as he held her. "I am now."

He tightened his grip around her and she stood there, arms clasped around his waist, the cold night making their breath come in misty bursts, imprinting each sensation in her mind, knowing deep down that their steamy affair would soon be relegated into the category of *naughty encounters-to-*

*remember.* She hadn't found the strength to end their perfect fantasy, but ugly reality would.

His fingers brushed her cheek, so warm against her skin. "Come on, let's walk. You're freezing."

They headed down her street hand-in-hand, bodies pressed close, just as they'd walked along the beaches and through the historic districts of the towns they'd visited. But this walk was markedly different. Carefree abandon and mounting sexual tension had been replaced by a foreboding sense of doom. They'd shut out the world long enough.

"What are we going to do, Nick?"

He gazed down at her, his expression set in grim lines. "We're going to find out who's writing these scripts and stop them. I'll talk to my attorneys and find out what kind of legal ground we're standing on, but hopefully we won't have to go that route. I hope confronting the author will be enough."

"How are we going to find out who the author is? Brit and Wendy are playing this secrecy thing to the hilt and I can't very well force them to tell me or go to the university president without raising everyone's suspicions. I've been racking my brain to come up with a game plan, but all I know is that I don't want to go to the police. Then we'd have to press charges. I don't have a clue for what...harassment maybe, or slander? It doesn't matter, either way, our fling will be splashed all over the news."

Nick nodded. "We don't want that. If anything, we'll hire a private investigator. But that'll take time we don't have. We need to investigate, starting first thing in the morning."

"Do you know how to conduct an investigation? I'm clueless."

"I heard somewhere you were Sam Spade."

She heard the humor in his voice, knew he was attempting to make her feel better. He cared and though she had no right to take pleasure or comfort in that, for the first time since listening to the latest installment of the *Hush-Hush Honeys,* Julienne felt a flash of something that resembled a flicker of hope. "Sam Spade would compile a suspect list."

He gave her hand a reassuring squeeze. "That's where we'll start then. So who knows about our relationship? Dale definitely. We've spoken about it. I believe Betty and some of my team assume we're dating. I've never discussed it with any of them."

"Ramón and Katriona. And Wendy may believe we are, which means Brit will, too. I don't know if they'd share speculation like that with my other interns."

"What about your ex?"

"You think Ethan might be responsible?"

Nick twined his fingers through hers, a gesture of reassurance at odds with his somber expression. "He goes on the list. Rebel Radio is a campus broadcast and he's connected with the university. We'll assume he suspects something personal between us, since I showed up in your office with a gift."

"A gift isn't necessarily personal."

"I'd bet money Ethan thought it was."

Julienne only nodded, unwilling to debate his reasoning, though she thought animosity suggested feelings that ran much deeper than anything Ethan had ever displayed for her. That had been part of their problem.

"Any friends you've told about us?" Nick asked.

"Just my best friend and she doesn't live here."

"What about your uncle? What exactly does he know about us?"

Julienne met his gaze, knew her reply would mean something. She wished with all her heart she could give some answer that didn't sound as though she'd kept him all to herself, her own guilty little secret. But she owed him the truth no matter how much it stung him and shamed her. "Nothing more than we're working together."

He didn't look surprised. "What have you been telling him when you leave town?"

"My best friend Kimberly works for the airlines. She has frequent layovers in Atlanta and I drive in to do the slumber party thing. I've just been telling Uncle Thad that I'm heading out of town and leaving him to assume I'm visiting Kimberly."

"We've been gone every weekend, Jules."

"I know, and I think Uncle Thad suspects something. But I can't tell him, Nick. He'll be disappointed in me and I don't want that. I've never given him any reason to regret taking me in and I don't want to start now. He's all the family I have and I don't want to hurt him...." She was babbling and she knew it. Judging by the furrow between Nick's brows, he knew it, too.

"Please try to understand. It's just...best right now. Given the dynamics of our relationship, Uncle Thad's much happier not knowing for sure, trust me. All he'll do is worry."

"If we get busted as the *Hush-Hush Honeys,* I imagine he'll do more than worry."

Julienne closed her eyes, fought back another wave of tears. "He's eighty years old. He's cared for me almost my whole life. He doesn't need this."

Nick tightened his grip on her fingers, lifted her hand and tucked it inside his jacket pocket with his. "We'll work this out. I promise."

Nick might not be able to commit, but he did care and knowing that he cared about a woman who'd been misrepresenting herself made her lose the battle. Tears squeezed past her lashes.

Nick pulled her close. "Don't cry, beautiful. Trust me."

That was the problem. She had trusted Nick. Despite what her uncle had said. Despite what her own common sense had told her, she'd jumped into a fling feetfirst and trusted Nick to play by the naughty rules.

Pulling away, she swiped at her eyes, unable to bear the tenderness in his voice. "I'm okay. So what do we have to do?"

He considered her thoughtfully and she knew he didn't believe she was okay any more than he believed the Risqué would be ready to reopen tomorrow night. But he didn't call her on it.

"Okay, then. The place to start is with Wendy and Brit. We've got to find out how those scripts have been arriving at the radio station. That will get them talking about the author and perhaps yield a clue or two. They have to know who the author is or else university administration would have pulled the plug on the show. Too much liability."

"I'll talk to them in the morning. If they haven't already guessed about us, they'll know something is up if we show up together and start grilling them about the scripts. I'll let you know what I find out as soon as I get to the Risqué. I expect to have us there by eight."

"Sounds like a plan." He pulled her to a stop beneath a streetlamp and dragged her against him. "Kiss me, Jules."

Julienne hadn't found the strength to say no to this man when she'd felt strong and she felt far from strong now. Sinking into his warm embrace, she lifted her mouth to his, wanting to feel the hot demand of his kiss, selfishly needing a taste of their familiar passion to reassure her.

"We can fix this," he whispered against her lips. "Everything will be all right."

As much as Julienne wanted to believe him, she suspected dealing with her uncle's disappointment would be easier than the reality of losing Nick.

# 14

*Friday morning*

NICK WAITED in the trailer when Jules drove the University of Savannah van into the theater parking lot. Through the blinds in his office window, he watched her slip from the front seat as her students piled out of the side. The instant he saw the downward tilt to her luscious lips, he guessed all had not gone well when she'd talked to Wendy and Brit.

He met them as they lugged their gear past the trailer. "Dr. Blake, have you got a minute."

She gave a quick nod, "All right, guys, you know the program," she said to her students. "Head inside and set up. I'll be along in a minute."

With waves and polite greetings, her interns took off in the direction of the theater's back entrance and he motioned Jules inside the trailer.

"Come on in," he said. "I sent Betty to the coffee shop for a couple of quadruple espressos. Thought you might need one. If not, don't worry, I'll drink them both."

She gave him a strained smile. He couldn't help but notice the dark smudges beneath her eyes and directed her to a chair.

"Have a seat, beautiful, and tell me how your talk went." He half sat on the desk in front of her. "I don't have anything to tell. It's still early on the West Coast, so I can't get through to my attorneys for at least another few hours."

She exhaled a tiny sigh, let him sandwich her hand between his. "They wouldn't tell me much, Nick. I got the impression they enjoyed my asking, though. Brit seemed to think if he could hook me, the rest of the campus must have been positively drooling to know who the *Hush-Hush Honeys* are. They haven't met the author in person and have been conducting business by fax. You were right. University administration has been very careful to make sure all the *I*s are dotted and *T*s crossed."

"They'd have to be. The liability here is enormous. But a fax machine is good news, beautiful. If we're not having much luck, a private investigator can easily trace the incoming and outgoing numbers." He smiled. "Have the scripts been arriving by fax, too?"

She shook her head. "Wendy said the first one showed up on the desk in the radio studio with the campus mail one day."

"That's a start. The author must be on the campus then."

"That's what I thought, too, but it turns out the second script and the teasers showed up on the desk at different times, so Wendy wasn't sure they'd come through campus mail. Honestly, Nick anyone could have walked in off the street and left them. Rebel Radio's studio is nothing more than a room in the tech building. A busy place."

Nick wound his fingers through hers, enjoyed the fit of their hands twined together. "Still a clue. Whoever left those envelopes either belongs on the campus or had to get a visitor's pass, like I do when I visit you. Maybe we'll luck out and the security guard will remember someone asking for directions to the radio studio."

Her gaze brightened. "You're right, I hadn't thought of that."

"Do Brit and Wendy know when to expect the next installment?"

"Probably Monday."

"Did the author suggest the *Hush-Hush Honeys* weren't fictional?" Nick asked.

"He said to present them as if they were, which of course convinced Wendy and Brit the couple must be real. Especially since the author refers to himself as 'an interested party.'"

The damned melodrama of the situation rubbed Nick the wrong way. "Interested party. Sounds like someone's having a good time at our expense."

Jules scowled. "Add Wendy and Brit to that list. They're elated by this whole situation. Apparently Brit's been having some financial problems that makes keeping his job with the radio important right now."

Now it was Nick's turn to scowl. "More problems?"

"More problems. Brit has been running Rebel Radio ever since he started school, but interning with me hasn't left him much time to work on keeping the ratings up. From what Wendy said, he's in danger of being replaced as producer, and a pay cut right now would make it difficult to keep a roof above his head while he finishes his internship. This whole *Hush-Hush Honeys* thing is making him look good. If he can win that broadcasting award Wendy mentioned, he'll be able to keep his job, no questions asked. Trust me, he's planning to ride this horse for as long as he can."

"I don't get it." Nick searched for answers in Jules's clear gray gaze. "What is the fascination with this serial? Who cares what two people called My Love and Darling do? And what the hell kind of name is *Hush-Hush Honeys,* anyway? It's sounds like something out of a time warp, archaic and ridiculous."

Jules exhaled a sigh. "People like to feel good, I suppose. Especially with so much bad news happening in the world.

It's nice to have something exciting to look forward to. You've got to remember that many of the students are still young and idealistic enough to love the idea of being in love.''

Well, that explained why he didn't understand. He'd never been young and idealistic enough to love the idea of being in love. But when Nick looked into Jules's face, noticed the way her expression had softened, he wondered if he'd ever really given love a fair chance.

Another question to add to the list of things he had to figure out.

''Whatever the reason, Nick,'' Jules said. ''Wendy wasn't exaggerating when she said the phones have been ringing off the hook. They didn't stop the entire time I was in there. The campus is buzzing about what's going to happen next with the *Hush-Hush Honeys*. It's quite a phenomenon.''

''We're a phenomenon.'' He lifted her hand and pressed a kiss to her smooth skin, wanting to reassure her.

She lifted her silvery gaze to his and he liked the smile in her eyes, the trust he saw there. She believed in him, in them, knew they could sort this mess out together. When she looked at him that way, Nick believed they could.

''What are your chances of getting away this afternoon?''

''Not good. I've got two classes scheduled as soon as I leave here. Why?''

''We need to visit Casa de Ramón. Ramón and Katriona both know about us and Wendy's a client there. She's connected to the university and that's a connection we can't overlook. Can you ask Uncle Thad to cover for you this morning so you can leave the site for a little while? Ramón won't be nearly as forthcoming with me as he will be with you.'' Nick hadn't forgotten the stylist could be damned hard-nosed when he chose.

She nodded, making wisps of hair from her neat ponytail thread along her sweatshirt. "I can give him a call."

While Jules called her uncle, Nick went to stand in front of a window, watched Betty climb out of ADF's pickup truck. She leaned back inside to retrieve the coffees and by the time she reached the trailer, Nick held the door opened.

"Thanks." She handed him a tall cup as she walked past. "I assume one of these is for you, Dr. Blake." She passed another cup to Jules before setting the cardboard carrier on her desk.

"Thanks, Betty." Jules sipped thoughtfully, before meeting Nick's gaze. "He said thirty minutes."

"Good, that'll be just enough time to let this caffeine get our brains functioning again. Betty, I need you to hold down the fort. I'll be heading out for an hour." He didn't mention that he and Jules would be going together.

"You got it, boss."

Less than an hour later, Nick had left the site, met Jules in the parking lot and headed to Casa de Ramón for the second time in less than a week.

Katriona claimed Wendy hadn't said a word about running into him and Jules together. She had apparently, gone on ad nauseam about how fascinating she found prying wood chips off the Risqué's floor and Katriona assured them she didn't find repairing the damage to Wendy's manicure remotely fascinating.

Nick thought they'd reached a dead end—until the manicurist sat back in her chair, tossed her hair over her shoulder and spun the conversation off in an entirely new direction.

"Guess who brought in his new girlfriend when he came for his manicure last night?"

The way Katriona's eyes fixed on Jules with a wicked gleam Nick suspected he knew the answer.

"Ethan?" Jules asked.

"You got it, sister. And he sat right on that bench." She pointed a long red fingernail to the very bench where he and Jules sat. "He made it loud and clear he's never been happier and wouldn't mind one bit if we shared that tidbit with the whole world. I knew he was referring to you."

Jules looked surprised, but before she could reply, Ramón's voice resounded above the drone of blow dryers and he descended on the nail area, a black buzzard in his salon coat.

"I hear you back here, you gossiping old biddy. Don't you dare say another word," he demanded. "Gossip is bad for business. You'll trash our reputation and our clients won't tell us their secrets ever again."

"Trust me, girlfriend, that man wanted me to gossip and he tipped me enough to make sure I would."

"Since when do we listen to what our clients want?" Ramón stared over the rim of his glasses. "You wouldn't want us spilling the beans on you two, would you? Quieter than a confessor, remember, Jules?"

"I remember," she said, but her blush suggested Ramón didn't refer to Ethan or his new girlfriend.

*Hmm.* What other secrets did Jules hide behind her blush? Ramón shot them another quelling gaze before he told Katriona, "Zip your lips" and marched back out of the nail area.

Katriona smiled, clearly unfazed by the interruption. "If you happen to run into Dr. You-know-who, just mention you saw me so he'll know I spilled the beans. I promise he'll be *thrilled* to fill you in on the details himself."

"You're a doll." Jules gave Katriona a peck on the cheek.

Nick waited until they were back in his car before asking, "Do you have any idea who Ethan might be seeing?"

"Not a clue. But why would he want Katriona to tell me?"

"There's one way to find out."

"Ask him?"

"Can you make up some excuse to visit? I want his spin on the *Hush-Hush Honeys*. It's too convenient that we walk into Casa de Ramón to grill Ramón and Katriona about Wendy and wind up hearing about Ethan instead."

Nick caught a glimpse of the tiny crease between her silky red brows before he shifted his gaze to the rear window and backed out of the parking space.

"If Ethan wants a response from me, I'd rather not give him the one he expects. I don't see the point in playing games. I'll tell him Katriona mentioned he was seeing someone and wish him well. If he wants to tell me about her, I've no doubt he will."

Nick didn't doubt it, either, but he could understand Ethan's annoyance about letting Jules slip away. From where Nick sat, the man had no one but himself to blame for that act of stupidity.

But Ethan's stupidity shouldn't be haunting Jules, which begged the question: would the man go so far as to write the *Hush-Hush Honeys* scripts to cause trouble for her?

"Do we have time to head over to the university now?" Nick wanted an answer to that question fast, because if Ethan proved to be their "interested party," he'd find himself dealing directly with Nick.

Jules glanced at her watch. "He'll be lecturing all morning. This afternoon would be better. I can talk to him between my classes later."

"I'll be there when you do."

"Is that a good idea, Nick? If Ethan does think there's something personal between us, he won't say anything incriminating if you're there—"

"I'll eavesdrop." Before she had a chance to object, he chucked her on the chin and said, "Hey, it worked the last time you talked to him and I wasn't even trying to overhear your conversation. Ask him what he thinks of the *Hush-Hush Honeys*."

"He may put two and two together and suspect us."

"Unless he's the scriptwriter, for all he knows he could be Darling and his new girlfriend My Love."

Nick could tell by her frown that she really didn't suspect Ethan of being involved. But Nick put him on the top of their suspect list. He just wouldn't worry Jules with his theory until after hearing her ex's spin on radio programs and new girlfriends.

"All right," she said reluctantly. "Be at my office at two forty-five."

He dropped a kiss on her pursed lips. "It's a date, beautiful."

*Later that afternoon*

JULIENNE PULLED the door to Ethan's office closed just enough to hide Nick who stood in the hallway, under strict orders to casually keep walking if anyone chanced by.

"Thanks for making time for me," she said to Ethan over the too-loud pounding of her heart.

She managed to walk naturally across the room, but found herself entirely too nervous to sit. Propping a hip against his desk instead, she gazed down at him. Ethan's penetrating blue eyes cut right through her and the smile playing at the corners of his mouth suggested he was very pleased she'd come.

"So what's on your mind, Julienne?"

His voice filled the small office, where shelves stood on three of four walls, stacked with psychology journals and texts, the latest in hypnotherapeutic models and conjecture. Though she'd listened to his voice for five years, and it was a perfectly good voice, somehow the sound wasn't as easy on her ears as Nick's, whose voice gave her a thrill each time she heard it, whether in person or over a telephone.

"I went to the salon this morning and Katriona mentioned you'd been in last night," she stated the words exactly as she'd rehearsed them in her mind, but before she had a chance to complete the thought, Ethan smiled.

"She told you about Honoria."

"Honoria?"

Ethan nodded.

"Honoria Bainbridge from the English department?"

"Yes."

"Oh. So that's who you brought in. Katriona didn't say specifically."

"We're dating."

"Well," Julienne said, not exactly sure how to respond to this revelation. He seemed to be expecting some sort of reaction and she suddenly doubted whether the good wishes she'd had planned would be what he was looking for. "I don't really know her. She just joined the faculty last spring, but on the few occasions we've met, she seemed very nice."

"She is. *Very* nice."

His thick black lashes fell over his eyes, a sultry heavy-lidded look that alluded to sex. At one time, Julienne knew she would have found that look sexy. Right now she just wasn't sure what to say. She didn't want Ethan to launch into details about his *very* nice new girlfriend with Nick outside the door.

Fortunately, Ethan seemed to recognize that, because he pushed away from his desk and stood. Reaching for her hands, he sandwiched them between his own, before she could gracefully avoid their capture. "Julienne, I want you to know that I'll always be here for you."

"That's…nice of you, Ethan."

"Roger always asks me when we're getting back together. You promised him a dance at our wedding."

Julienne forced a smile, purposely overlooking his reference to reuniting and focusing instead on Roger, the president of the university and a close friend of Ethan's. "I'll make it a point to pop in and say hello soon."

"You do know I'll always be here for you, don't you, Julienne? Other people don't matter to me as much as you do. Not even people we may be dating. They're not important. We were together a long time. That's important."

Julienne wondered how the *very* nice Honoria Bainbridge would have felt being considered unimportant. She knew Nick wouldn't like it a bit and forced herself not to glance at the door, though she half expected him to come strolling in.

She didn't have any intention of relegating Nick to the "unimportant" category. Not now. Not even after their steamy affair ended and he moved on to his next naughty girl. But she knew Ethan meant what he said and all she could say was, "I know. I won't forget."

She didn't feel anything for him, except a fondness for the good times they'd shared and perhaps some relief that they'd never gotten around to the wedding.

*This relationship was meant to be relegated to past history status, girl!*

Julienne agreed because if it hadn't, she'd have never known the abandon, the breathtaking excitement of loving Nick. And not even this mess she'd created and the imminent heartache of losing him could make her regret one second of their time together.

Judging by Ethan's disappointed expression, she knew

her best wishes for a bright future with Honoria wouldn't go over well, so she gave his hands a squeeze and changed tack. "I need your advice on this whole *Hush-Hush Honeys* thing. Two of my students are producing the show and they're so caught up with it, I'm not sure if I should worry about their mental health. What do you think?"

Asking for Ethan's advice certainly switched the balance of power and perked him up. Letting her hands slip away, he sat back in his chair, steepled his fingers before him in what she recognized as his professional mien. "I wouldn't worry too much about them. Not at this stage of the game." His brow furrowed. "The whole thing is ridiculous, I agree, but it's understandable. People are always grasping at things to make them feel good. That impacts our students particularly, because they're so focused on what's ahead of them. The future can seem uncertain. If this ridiculous radio show calms their fears, then I say let them have at it."

"Whew," she said, propelling herself away from the desk and glancing down at her watch. "I feel so much better hearing you say that, but I've got to run. My class starts soon. Thanks."

"My pleasure." He stood and caught her hand before she got away. She bumped against the door, closing it, hoping that Nick had the presence of mind to take off down the hallway. He kissed her cheek. "Anytime, Julienne. I'm here for you. Remember that."

She smiled up at him, a fond smile for all the memories they'd made together. "I will."

Ethan was a good man, just not the man for her. Then she turned and left, silently wishing him and Honoria well and saying goodbye to her past.

She caught up with her present on the stairs. Nick crowded her against the wall, apparently unconcerned that anyone could appear in the stairwell and catch them, and engaged her in a steamy kiss. Their kiss didn't last long, but by the time he broke away, her breath came in a gulp because she'd forgotten to breathe.

"What…was that…for?" She gasped out the words.

"To remind you I'm more important than ex-Ethan."

Julienne already knew that and might have reassured him if a student hadn't chosen that moment to bound down the stairs, causing her and Nick to launch into motion again. As it was, she just savored the glow inside at Nick's male reaction to Ethan's comments. She shouldn't be so happy to hear him admit he cared.

*Give it up, girl. No matter how hard you try to convince yourself to break off with Nick, you want the man and you know it.*

"And for being so brilliant," he added, holding the door as she swept outside into the crisp autumn day. "You think quick on your feet."

"Glad you approve."

"I do. Do you have a few minutes to grab a cup of coffee?"

She glanced at her watch. "If we get a cup from the faculty lounge and drink it in my office."

"Let's go."

They walked briskly back to the science building, grabbed coffee from the lounge that was three doors away from her office. Nick had no sooner closed her door behind them when he asked. "Tell me about your breakup with Ethan."

"Why?"

"I'm curious to know why the pompous Dr. Whiteside is so stymied that his intelligent, independent and extremely beautiful former fiancée hasn't gone running back to him yet."

She stalled by taking a gulp of coffee. "I can't answer that. What makes you think he thought I would?"

Nick shook his head and stared hard at her. "Did you and I just overhear the same conversation?"

"I didn't overhear anything," she informed him curtly. "I actually participated in the conversation, which means I saw Ethan and there was nothing in his manner that would lead me to believe he expected me to run back to him."

"The guy practically came right out and said he'd drop his new girlfriend in a heartbeat if you went back to him."

"But he *didn't* come right out and say it, did he?"

Nick scowled so hard Julienne thought he might crack his jaw. "That would mean admitting he'd been an idiot to let you go. I don't think he's up to that, do you?"

"Um, no." Naughty may mean keeping secrets, but it didn't justify lying. "Ethan was never very good at admitting he was wrong."

"No small wonder with that ego." Nick sucked down another steaming gulp and avoided her gaze. "I thought mine was big."

"It is." She shrugged innocently when he shot her a sidelong glance. "What are you thinking, Nick? That Ethan wrote the *Hush-Hush Honeys* to make me run back to him."

"Is it so far-fetched?"

She gave a snort, a sound so unladylike Uncle Thad would have cringed. "I'm telling you, I saw him. He's not our 'interested party.' He thought the whole thing was ridiculous."

"You and Ethan broke up what, six months ago?"

"Seven and a half now."

"Okay, seven and a half months ago. Beautiful, didn't it ever occur to you he'd want you to come running back to him and he'd get mad when you didn't?"

"No."

Plucking the cup from her hand, Nick set it on the desk

and looped his arms around her waist, not letting her get away.

"Do you think it could be a possibility?"

"Now that you mention it, I can see how Ethan might have expected that of me. But not enough to pull something like the *Hush-Hush Honeys*."

"If he was expecting you to run back to him, wouldn't me showing up in your office with a gift come as a rude shock?"

She nodded, following his logic, although she didn't agree.

"Maybe even make him get another girlfriend, so it looks like he's moving on with his life, too. Or to make you jealous."

"The scenario doesn't sound so far-fetched when you explain it like that." In her head things had been over with Ethan since she'd given him back his ring. But if Nick was right, Ethan had been lying in wait for her to come to her senses.

"What I don't get is why?" Nick said, tugging her a little closer until she was forced to press her thighs to his just to keep her balance. "Why would he think you'd go back? You don't strike me as a woman who has trouble making up her mind."

That's because Nick knew the new improved version of Julienne Blake, a woman called Jules who hypnotized herself into believing she was bold enough to take what she wanted. The woman Ethan had known just breezed through life, letting him call all the shots.

"Why would he think that, beautiful?"

She met Nick's gaze, recognized he wasn't a man who would judge her, even if what she revealed did dent her naughty image. For one moment she thought about avoiding his question, leaving his memories of the bold woman he'd known as Jules intact. Neither Jules nor Julienne was a coward and she owed Nick the truth.

"I wasn't so sure of myself or the decisions I made when I was with Ethan. That's predominately the reason why he credits himself for my professional success."

"We've already covered that ground and decided he credits himself too much. So why weren't you so sure of yourself when you were with him?"

"I've spent a lot of time trying to figure that out," she admitted honestly. "As near as I can guess I was just young and inexperienced and too worried about making the right choices."

Nick considered her thoughtfully. "Let's talk about being young and inexperienced. For you to have become a full professor when your uncle retired, you'd have had to earn your doctorate by what...twenty-five?"

She nodded.

"Now this is just a guess, so hear me out." A smile played at the corners of his mouth, but he managed to subdue it with effort. "I'm thinking that a girl who spent most of her life in the field with her much older uncle probably didn't have too much time for normal school things like dances, sororities and say...dating. Am I right?"

Julienne tried to break his grip, but he held her tight. She scowled, knowing he was dragging out this melodrama, and gave a curt nod.

"A girl who'd earned her doctorate by twenty-five probably didn't spend much time socializing outside of school, either?"

*Uh-oh, busted.*

"Which would mean you probably hadn't had much time to play the field before you started dating ex-Ethan. You would have been rather...inexperienced, which would make me—"

"The second man I've ever slept with."

Nick's eyes gleamed and the grin that had been playing around his mouth widened into a full-fledged, very satisfied smile. "Yet you presented yourself to me as much more experienced than you were because…"

"I didn't think a diehard playboy would be interested in a woman who'd only had one lover in her whole life. Happy now?"

"Except for the diehard playboy part, I've very happy." He dropped a kiss onto her lips. "I think you're charming."

She wondered how charming he'd think her if he knew she'd been hypnotizing herself to shed her inhibitions to sleep with him. Julienne might not be a coward, but she wasn't stupid, either. Nick was passion incarnate. How would he understand a woman who needed self-hypnosis to be passionate?

He wouldn't and that was the price she'd pay for presenting herself as someone she wasn't. Nick had wanted to postpone conversations about their relationship until the weekend, when they were alone, but as long as he'd brought the subject up, she might as well use the opportunity to prepare him so her confession didn't come out of the blue.

Taking a deep breath, Julienne steeled her resolve, but before she'd even opened her mouth, a raised voice right outside her door, yelled, "It's going to be on the local news." The voice grew louder as its owner presumably sped down the hall. "Turn on the television in the lounge. The *Hush-Hush Honeys* is on the local news."

She stared up at Nick, and the arrested look on his face made her heart sink.

# 15

*HAVING YOU SO CLOSE today made me want to touch you every time I walked by.*

The soundbite rang through the faculty lounge. Nick identified the voice as Brit's, obviously playing the part of Darling again, but he recognized the words from his first telephone sex encounter with Jules. Judging by the way Jules's face had drained of all color she recognized it, too.

"Who are the *Hush-Hush Honeys?*" the announcer asked from the television screen. "The University of Savannah wants to know. The *Hush-Hush Honeys* is a serial broadcast that airs on Rebel Radio, the University of Savannah's AM-radio station. It's a story about a couple forced to conduct a secret love affair. The entire campus wants to know if this couple is fictional or real and no one at Rebel Radio will tell." The announcer smiled into the camera. "One thing is real, though, this campus broadcast is creating a sensation reminiscent of the Mercury Theater and the *War of the Worlds.*"

Inclining his head, Nick motioned Jules to follow him and they slipped from the faculty lounge unnoticed by the crowd who'd gathered for the news.

"It's the telephone, Jules. Yours or mine."

She only nodded, looking so vulnerable with her too-wide eyes and trembling lips. He wanted to kiss her, chaffed at his damned disreputable past and her damned need for secrecy. This depriving himself of touching her when he wanted to was getting old fast.

"Whoever's tapping the line probably culled all those details about our trips from our conversations."

"Just the thought of someone listening—" she broke off, if possible her cheeks paled another shade.

He grabbed her arm, thinking she looked unsteady, but she shook him off, waving her hands frantically and walking right past her office toward the hallway with the classrooms.

"I can't think about this. I've got to get to class."

"Are you going to be okay?"

She nodded, but he recognized the glint of tears in her eyes, saw her distress. "I'll stay. In fact, why don't you give me a chance to tell the class about how the theater renovations are coming along? What are you lecturing on today?"

"Preservation philosophy."

"I can handle it."

Jules only nodded and as he accompanied her to the classroom, that angry helplessness that had been gnawing at him ever since her frenzied call last night started in on him again full force.

Nick was out of his element here. He'd never been involved with a woman long enough to face a crisis and the last time he'd been the recipient of unwanted media attention, he'd just curtailed his activities until the interest had passed.

He didn't want to curtail his activities with Jules and resented being pressured to. He wasn't ready to let her go. Simple. He didn't have the time or the energy to dwell on how to prove himself to her or her uncle, or anyone else right now. Right now he had to focus on helping Jules get through her class. He didn't have time to dwell on why the thought of suddenly being without her made him feel so angry, and empty.

*Later that night*

BY THE TIME Nick followed Jules from the electronics store where they'd purchased new telephones for both their homes, night had long since fallen. He followed the gleam of her red taillights through the quiet streets of her neighborhood, pulled into her driveway behind her. He held the bag of equipment as Jules unlocked the door, then waited as she entered the dark hallway.

"Where's your uncle?"

"He'll be upstairs asleep," she whispered. "I didn't see the light in his office when I pulled in."

"Are you sure you don't want me to install these phones now?"

She didn't flip on a light, but cast a glance up the stairs. "No thanks. Uncle Thad's a light sleeper and I don't want to disturb him."

"Will you have a problem getting him to the site tomorrow, so I can send Chuck over to check out the phone lines?"

"There's nothing wrong with the phone lines," a familiar voice cut through the gloomy quiet.

"Uncle Thad." Jules spun toward the sound, which had emanated from the dark living room, and her slim body went ramrod straight. "I didn't realize you were awake."

"Obviously. Why don't you come in, Nick?"

Nick met Julienne's gaze, knew by her stricken expression that she didn't want to contend with this situation in addition to their other troubles tonight. Unfortunately, she didn't have a choice. If her uncle already suspected they were involved, Nick would address his concerns face-to-face.

"Good evening, Dr. Blake," he said.

"Nick."

The exchange gave Jules just enough time to recover. She flipped on the hall light, motioned him to set the bag on the floor beside the coatrack and strode into the living room.

"I think there is something wrong with the phones, Uncle Thad. The recorder hasn't been recording. Several people have mentioned it. Nick helped me shop for replacements."

Clearly she hoped to avoid questions about what they were doing together. Following her into the living room, Nick found Dr. Blake sitting in a recliner and knew the instant he saw the man's grim expression that Jules wasn't going to get her wish.

"The recorder has been picking up," Dr. Blake said matter-of-factly. "First ring, every time. I've turned the sound of the message off."

Experiencing a prickle of foreboding, Nick took a step toward Jules, who gave a nervous laugh and asked, "But why?"

Her uncle leveled a steely gaze at Nick. "So the machine recorded all our incoming phone calls."

Jules stared, clearly struggling to reason through the implications, but Nick understood.

"I believe I was wrong about Ethan," he said quietly. "I think we've found our interested party right here."

"You have." Dr. Blake frowned, a somber expression that stabbed Nick with the full effect of his disapproval. "I'm responsible for the *Hush-Hush Honeys*."

Jules blanched. Steering her toward a nearby ottoman, Nick forced her to sit. "You've been recording incoming calls to catch our conversations on tape. Why, sir?"

"To try and understand why you're both sneaking around like you're doing something wrong."

"How did you know?" Jules asked.

Dr. Blake's gaze trailed to Jules. "Coincidence, actually. The night Ramón called to tell you about Nick's flowers you picked up the phone but never turned off the recorder. I listened to your conversation when I played back the messages the next morning. I admit to being very curious about what kind of man could make you so leery of becoming involved again. When I realized you'd met Nick at the Risqué, I understood why you were afraid."

"I wasn't afraid."

Even though Jules denied her uncle's charge in no uncertain terms, Nick didn't believe her. What had he ever done to make her think she was any different from the other women he'd dated?

"You listened to our phone conversations, Uncle Thad?" she asked. "All of them?"

Nick heard her panic and tightened his grip on her shoulder.

"Only parts of them, my dear. I'd shut off the recorder as soon as steam started pouring out of my ears."

Jules shivered, a full-bodied shudder that vibrated beneath Nick's fingers. With a groan of pure mortification, she dropped her face into her hands and didn't glance up.

Nick, though, met Dr. Blake's gaze squarely. He couldn't dwell on the fact that this man he admired knew he'd not only been having sex with his niece, but had turned the house phone into 1-900-babe. He couldn't think about that with Jules down for the count. One of them had to be thinking straight. He'd have to wait his turn to have a meltdown.

"Did you really think Ethan had written the *Hush-Hush Honeys* scripts?" Dr. Blake asked.

Nick nodded but he supposed the serial's title had been

a clue to the real perpetrator. *Hush-Hush Honeys* ranked right up there with Frank Sinatra swing and *Captain Midnight*.

"Forgive me, Julienne, but the man doesn't have the creativity to come up with an idea even half as imaginative. Or clever, if I say so myself. Trust me, Nick, I've read several of his treatises. He writes inflated narratives that take three pages to make a point."

"What was the point, sir? I'm sure you don't want to see Julienne professionally discredited."

He stroked his white beard and looked thoughtful. "No, of course I don't. Or you, either, for that matter. Though I don't imagine anything I've written compares to the reality of your past antics with the ladies."

Nick cringed at the man's tone, but before he had a chance to reply, Jules glanced up at him.

"Ohmigosh, Nick, I never realized…" Something in his gaze must have given him away, because she frowned hard. "You knew all along if you were connected to the *Hush-Hush Honeys* the tabloids could pick the story up, but you never said anything. That's why you wanted to talk with your attorneys."

"The possibility was remote at best. My fifteen minutes of fame are over. But, on the off chance my name did come up, I wanted my lawyers ready to suppress. I didn't want you dealing with that type of press. It can be trying, trust me."

"So you can act like a proper gentleman when you choose, Nick," Dr. Blake said. "I'm pleased to hear it."

Jules looked shocked and Nick addressed the issue head-on. "You have a problem with me dating Julienne, sir."

"Yes, I do." Dr. Blake rose to his feet, commanded their attention in that same quiet, yet authoritative manner Nick remembered so well from that lecture back at Berkeley. "I don't think you have my niece's best interests at heart."

"Uncle Thad, please. No matter what you think of me dating Nick, we didn't deserve to be tossed to the wolves," she said hoarsely. "Did you know the *Hush-Hush Honeys* made the local news?"

"I'm the one who called them. I asked Brit and Wendy to call, too."

"They were in on this?"

Dr. Blake nodded. "Actually, they gave me the idea the night we had dinner at the Olde River House. Your interns were trying to figure out a way to play matchmaker for you two. They think you and Nick make the perfect couple."

Jules massaged her temples as though her head were about to explode, but Nick remained silent as Dr. Blake turned on a lamp, chasing the shadows from the room.

"I didn't write the serial to throw you to the wolves. I wrote it because I couldn't see another way of getting you both to wise up. You seemed quite content to treat your relationship with very little respect, like you were conducting some sort of sordid affair. I hoped if other people viewed it with an equal lack of respect you might just come to your senses."

Jules's mouth had popped open and Nick was too busy following the logic to react.

"I'm sure your steamy romance was all very exciting." Dr. Blake clasped his hands behind his back and rocked on his heels. "But the truth is I don't credit either of you with enough intelligence to realize how much more you could have together."

Breaking away from Nick's grasp, Julienne launched to her feet and began pacing in front of the window.

"Now don't go getting all offended, my dear."

Nick wondered what Dr. Blake saw in his niece's rigid

stance that led him to believe he'd offended her. She just looked mortified to him.

"You're a lovely woman, Julienne, but you can be very single-minded when you choose to be. You've chosen to live your life following along in my footsteps and while I'm immensely flattered, I believe your sense of obligation to me is holding you back."

"What?" she asked, a strangled sound.

"Ever since we settled in Savannah, all you've talked about is going back into the field but when the time came, you gave up your dream to intern with me."

"That was my choice."

Dr. Blake's white brows dipped in a frown.

"Okay," Julienne said with a huff. "I factored Ethan into my decision, too. He didn't want me to travel. You know how difficult it is to have a relationship when you're traveling all the time. We lived that life."

"Yes, dear, we did."

Nick thought he heard a hint of regret in Dr. Blake's admission and suddenly understood. Dr. Blake knew all about the sacrifices working in the field required. He empathized with the decision Julienne had been forced to make.

"But Ethan's feelings weren't the only ones you factored into that decision were they?"

Jules frowned beneath her uncle's assessing blue gaze and a long searching moment passed between them. She shook her head.

"Baby-sitting me in my dotage isn't what I want for you, Julienne. I don't expect you to live your life for me just because you're grateful I took you in after your parents died. You've been my greatest gift. I want to watch you fly. That'll give me more pleasure than you can possibly imagine."

His admission filled the ensuing silence with such richness of emotion that Nick had never before seen the like. Jules seemed to melt before his very eyes, her gaze suddenly bright with tears. She lifted trembling fingers to her mouth and blew her uncle a kiss. With a wink, he pretended to catch it in some private game. A charming little girl and her devoted uncle.

Some of Nick's tension eased. Dr. Blake obviously knew the way to his niece's heart and as long as his dating Julienne hadn't harmed her relationship with her uncle, Nick could address his own interest....

"Which leads me to my next point, dear. You've found something special with Nick and I respect that. I've been watching you closely and you're happy for the first time in a very long time."

He frowned, glancing askance at Nick. "But you've given your heart to a man who doesn't make commitments. I'm not sure where you think you're going with this relationship but I don't want to see you hurt. You came out of your breakup with Ethan remarkably unscathed and I'm worried for you."

Nick dragged his fingers through his hair, blasted from all directions with emotions and realizations, and the first explosion had to do with...Jules had given her heart?

They'd never once spoken about love or how they'd felt about each other. They'd operated in fling-mode—the only way Nick had ever operated. He, who prided himself on paying close attention to a woman's feelings, had been struggling so much with his own he hadn't even considered Jules's.

Or had he deliberately ignored them?

He'd never had a problem recognizing when a woman began getting too attached to him. That was his clue to move on. Had he purposely ignored the signs of Jules's affection because he hadn't wanted to give her up?

Out of his league, Dale had said, and he'd been right.

Careful to school his expression, Nick watched Jules's reaction to her uncle's concerns, knew when he saw her smile melt away as quickly as it had appeared that her uncle had seen what Nick had missed. Jules did care for him. A lot more than as a bedroom buddy.

Nick opened his mouth to explain that while he couldn't argue his previous avoidance of commitment, his feelings for Jules had prompted him to take a long hard look at the way he lived his life. He needed her to know he wasn't entirely the self-serving bastard her uncle had nailed him for.

Dr. Blake cut him off. "Nick, no offense, but your relationship history speaks for itself. You're still carousing like a man half your age and I'm not happy about you carousing with my niece."

"Ouch."

"Ouch, indeed. I didn't believe you'd recognize the gem you have in her."

Nick met Dr. Blake's gaze evenly. He couldn't deny the charges leveled at him, swallowed another bitter gulp of living with the consequences of his choices. "I recognize her, sir."

"If that's the case, what are your intentions?"

"Uncle Thad, please," Julienne cried. "No more. I understand what you're trying to do. I know you mean well, but this is a mess. We have to fix this."

"There's only one way to fix this, my dear. That was the whole point."

Clapping her hands over her heart as if trying to keep it in her chest, Jules stared at her uncle in bemused horror.

"Each of you will have to make a decision. Nick will

have to decide whether or not he's capable and desirous of having a real relationship. And you'll have to decide if you're willing to give him that kind of chance.''

Jules blanched, wouldn't meet Nick's gaze. "Uncle Thad."

"Now, Julienne, Nick, what's the problem with a relationship that might lead to—brace yourselves because I'm going to say it—*marriage?*"

"You don't understand." Jules's clear eyes were wide, her face devoid of all color. "It's not like that between us."

Dr. Blake's expression softened for the first time since this conversation began. "I do understand, Julienne. You seem to forget I lived an entire lifetime before you were born. Just because I've chosen to devote the past twenty-five years to rearing you doesn't negate the fact that I lived the first fifty-five years of my life as a single man."

"Which gives you a unique perspective on the way I've chosen to live my life, sir?" Nick asked, following up on a suspicion he suddenly had.

"As a matter of fact it does." Dr. Blake's gaze pierced the distance between them and Nick recognized regret in the man's eyes. And maybe a glimmer of respect, too, that Nick had understood the connection between them. "I know where you're coming from, Nick. I was never successful at finding a balance between my work and making a life with the people I loved. By the time I woke up, I'd hurt too many people who cared about me and found myself quite alone. I got a second chance when Julienne came to live with me and I took that chance. I learned how to make my life work for us and I succeeded. I've been grateful for every second we've had together."

"Oh, Uncle Thad." Jules paused by the window, tears sparkling on her lashes.

"I appreciate your honesty, sir."

"Then take my advice, Nick. You won't be sorry."

"You can't bully Nick into wanting a relationship," Jules said softly.

Nick frowned. Damn, but he hated the way that sounded, so shallow, so…*empty*. She made it sound as though he *couldn't* have relationships, not that he'd *chosen* not to. Big difference. He didn't like the fact she didn't believe him capable of making their relationship more than just a torrid fling.

True, he hadn't actually figured out how yet, but he damned well could if he chose.

"He'll take my advice if he's as smart as I think he is." Dr. Blake waved a hand as though her comment was of only minor concern. He smiled. "I trust you'll both figure out what you want and rise to the occasion. You should marry Julienne, Nick. She'll make you a fine wife."

Jules cast a wild-eyed glance between him and her uncle. "I can't talk about this anymore."

She fled from the room and Nick stared after her, listened to her feet flying lightly up the stairs, not stopping until she'd slammed some door on the second floor. The glass panes in an antique hutch rattled ominously.

Nick forced himself to meet Dr. Blake's gaze. "Marriage, sir?"

"You'd be a fool to settle for anything less, and I don't think you're a fool."

Small comfort. But Nick had learned a great deal from Thaddeus Blake throughout his career and it looked like his inestimable hero was about to teach him something about life this time around.

JULIENNE HAD NEVER been more mortified in her life. Throwing herself face-first down on her bed, she shoved *The Naughty Handbook* out from beneath her pillows and sent it sailing over the edge of the mattress, where it landed with a resounding thud on the floor.

What a mess. All because she'd wanted to prove she could experience passion. No more tepid emotions ever again, isn't that what she'd said? She'd given them up right along with tepid sex.

Well, there was nothing tepid about the humiliation she felt right now. She couldn't strike the image from her memory of Nick's face when Uncle Thad had mentioned marriage. She squeezed her eyes shut. No help. His face in all its stunned glory was burned onto the backs of her lids.

*You're in love with the scrumptious Nick Fairfax, so don't deny that the thought of marriage hasn't crossed your mind.*

Okay, so it had crossed her mind, but only in her very weakest moments, when she could actually convince herself that she didn't need self-hypnosis to keep up her naughty girl act. Rare moments indeed.

She'd also managed to convince herself that Uncle Thad had seen Nick out and she wouldn't have to face any more of this madness tonight, when a knock echoed on her door.

Julienne couldn't decide which was worse—facing Uncle Thad, who'd been listening in on all the sexy details of her steamy affair, or facing Nick who was being bullied into marrying her.

"Go away." She pulled a pillow over her head.

Unfortunately, the goose feathers didn't muffle the click of the opening door.

"Hello, beautiful."

Nick plucked the pillow off her head, chuckling when she resisted. But his strength won out and she was suddenly turning to stare up into his somber expression.

"You okay?" he asked, then as casually as if the last half hour's insanity hadn't transpired, he sat on the edge of her bed. "Your uncle said to tell you he needed to go across the street to visit Mr. Patrick."

"At ten-thirty at night?"

Nick just shrugged.

Taking a deep breath, Julienne sat up and tucked her legs beneath her. "Oh, Nick, I'm so sorry. I had no idea."

"I know. And there's nothing to be sorry for. Your uncle promised me he'd finish out the series by writing the *Hush Hush Honeys* onto a whole new adventure that won't remotely resemble us. There, all fixed."

"Is that before or after we walk down the aisle?"

"Before, I think. He seems to feel he's made his point."

"Thank goodness." She laughed, a feeble sound. "Part of me wishes I could blame this on senility—that being eighty has finally caught up with him, but that's not the case."

"No, it's not. Your uncle seems quite clear about what he wants and very determined to get it." Nick hooked a knee up on the bed as she tried desperately to remember how good his legs had felt twined with hers under the covers, in the steamy hot shower, in the ice-cold ocean, *anything* but on how utterly gentle he sounded right now. "You have to give the man credit for knowing how to make a point. He has a good one. I knew I wasn't ready for our relationship to be over, but I wasn't giving much thought to the future, either. Too comfortable living in the moment I think. What about you?"

"Yeah."

*Liar, liar pants on fire!*

Julienne drowned out that naggy little voice with a heavy sigh and Nick responded by reaching out to stroke her cheek. She leaned into his touch, helpless with need to feel his warm fingers against her skin, greedy to savor just one more touch before she'd miss out forever.

"When I think about how ready I was to blame your ex for trying to break us up, I've got to wonder where my head is. I was jealous."

"Of Ethan?"

Nick nodded. "Of everything you'd shared with him. Of course, this all just occurred to me as I walked up the stairs, so I haven't had a chance to mull it over yet. But it makes sense, don't you think?"

Julienne stared at him. Maybe she'd already had too many rude shocks for one day, but she couldn't believe what she was hearing. "Oh, Nick. Tell me you're not buying into this."

That black gaze stared right back and she realized he was serious. "I'd be lying if I said the thought of marriage had ever crossed my mind, but I haven't been content seeing you at work and on weekends. I don't want to drive across town to be with you in the middle of a crisis. I want more, Jules. I think your uncle has a point, we should give some thought to where we want our relationship to go."

"Where can it go? We're having a steamy affair."

"I thought we were having a torrid fling."

She ignored his smile. "We moved past torrid fling when we went and got our hair cut together."

"So you have been thinking about our future." His expression softened, a mixture of pleasure and surprise and amusement, but Julienne wasn't amused. Not a bit.

"Nick, listen to me, I knew the limitations when I got involved with you. I went into this looking to prove that I could get a playboy to notice me. You did. And then some. I don't expect anything else from you."

"I know." He shrugged, his gaze sliding past her. When his smile widened, she turned around to find him staring at the crazy balls that dangled from the side of a jewelry box where she'd hung them, as though they were no more than a bright blue ornament. "I do know one thing for sure, Jules, I'm not ready to give you up. So what comes after a steamy affair?"

Julienne watched him slide his gaze from the crazy balls over bottles of perfume and lotion that sat neatly arranged in front of the mirror. Her heart just broke. Here was the man she loved, miraculously willing to consider what might come next in their relationship, and *she* was the one who couldn't take the next step.

This was it, the moment of truth. The moment when she confessed to Nick she wasn't half the woman he thought she was.

Sliding off the bed, she suddenly found herself unable to sit still, unable to bear being close to him. "I appreciate what you're doing, but there's really no place to go. I'm…I'm not who you think I am."

Something in her voice must have clued him in on how serious she was, because when he turned back around to face her, all traces of amusement were gone.

"You're not?"

"No."

"So who are you, beautiful?"

The concern she saw deep in his gaze dislodged another few pieces of her heart. She shrugged, willing that thoughtful expression off his face, willing her tears back. "I'm Julienne Blake, professor of historic preservation at the University of Savannah. I spend most of my time working and have a history of exactly one *very* tepid relationship."

"I've met Dr. Blake. She also goes by the nickname Jules. A very beautiful, very passionate woman, whom I happen to be crazy about."

"She's not me." Her tears flowing freely now, she whipped out Ethan's latest treatise on hypnotherapy techniques from inside the drawer of her night table and retrieved *The Naughty Handbook* from the floor. She handed them to him.

"I'm not bold, Nick. I spent years trying to live up to Ethan's expectations and trying to fulfill his goals instead of my own, all because I wanted to do the right thing, marry the right sort of man, live up to my uncle's expectations. I didn't like what that said about me, so I've been reading books and practicing suggestibility techniques to help me shed my inhibitions and become a woman who takes what she wants from life. But I can't keep up self-hypnosis forever."

Nick stared between her and the books he held and she saw surprise flash in his eyes.

"Uncle Thad's right about me. I haven't wanted to leave him. I think I've been preoccupied with doing everything right to make sure he never regretted all he's done for me."

"You've been hypnotizing yourself to sleep with me?"

She could only nod.

"Well, that's a first," he said lightly. "I don't think I've ever had a woman do that before."

He was trying to ease the tension and she felt terrible, *terrible* for putting him in this situation. This was a steamy affair, no realities, no baggage. Not hers. Not her uncle's.

"Look at this mess I've created. My uncle trying to bully you into marrying me. And the joke is that without self-hypnosis, I'll go right back to being plain old *un*exciting, eager-to-please, *good girl* Julienne."

Nick set the books back on her night table and came to stand before her. With his thumbs he swiped the tears from her cheeks. "I like Julienne."

"You don't know Julienne. Trust me, Nick, she doesn't know the first thing about rolling on a condom with her mouth."

He shook his head as though to clear it and she realized

he didn't understand her reference. She was too entrenched in the moment to explain.

"You're a wonderful man, a passionate man. You need a woman who'll keep your interest. None have so far and I'm probably the worst possible candidate." She waved at the books he held. "I'm all smoke and mirrors."

"No passion, hmm? So you were faking those orgasms?"

For a second she could only stare. "Of course not."

He smiled and she realized he already knew she hadn't been faking. "Then I'd say you're a very passionate woman."

"But it's not me, Nick. It's the hypnosis helping me shed my inhibitions."

Nick frowned, clearly at a loss for a rational argument, because there wasn't one. Nothing she'd done was rational.

"So where do we go from here?"

She couldn't meet his gaze, couldn't let him even suspect how her heart was breaking. "I don't see where we can go."

"Are you telling me you don't want to see me anymore?" He didn't look nearly so surprised as he did puzzled and hurt. "You're willing to let us go?"

"We both knew our affair was going to end anyway, so why don't we just make a clean break now before we spoil our good memories? Then we can keep working together without bad feelings."

With a gentle grip on her chin, he forced her to face him, and his gaze bored into her, made her feel trembly and wretched. She hurt, and now she'd hurt him, too.

"I'm not willing to accept that." He used the heel of his palm to wipe away another fresh burst of tears. "And I'm at a disadvantage here because I hadn't thought about the future."

"I can't talk about this anymore." She couldn't absorb

anything else tonight, not with her head pounding and her nose running and her heart broken. "Not tonight." She broke away. "Please go, Nick."

He stared at her, his hurt so unbearably obvious. Finally he said, "I'll agree to table the discussion for now. We both need time to calm down and think. But we've got some decisions to make. This isn't over. I'm not leaving unless you agree."

She nodded, if only to get him to go, because she couldn't face him for another minute, not when she felt so terrible for hurting him, not when she knew how horribly empty her future would be without him.

NICK GOT INTO his SUV, pulled the door shut and glanced up at the second story of Jules's house. The light in her bedroom still shone through the sheer curtains.

"Sleep well, beautiful. We'll sort this all out tomorrow." Self-hypnosis. Who'd have guessed?

Shaking his head, he jammed the key into the ignition. The irony didn't escape him. He'd dated more women than he could remember and had let each and every one go without a thought. Figured that the first one he wanted to keep around didn't want to be kept.

Nick wasn't sure how he felt about the day's revelations or what he wanted for tomorrow, let alone the future, but he did know he wouldn't let Jules go. That was a place to start.

He'd meant what he'd said. He didn't like being so out of touch with himself that he'd blame Ethan for the whole *Hush-Hush Honeys* business, despite Julienne's belief that her ex hadn't been a viable candidate. Nick had been jealous, even threatened by the history they'd shared. But none of that had even occurred to him until after the fact.

Turning over the engine, he threw the gear shift into Re-

verse, forced his foot to the gas and backed out of the driveway, when he wanted to be in that house climbing into bed
with a woman who claimed to be a stranger.

He steered toward town instead, knowing he had work to
do. He had to figure out how to play this commitment game.
Not only was he a novice, but he had to somehow help Jules
believe she was the very passionate woman he knew her to
be—the right woman for him.

# *16*

---

*Saturday night*

JULIENNE'S HEART leapt when the telephone rang, a pathetic reaction to a heartfelt wish that Nick would call. Setting the stack of her interns' reports on the end table, she slipped out of the recliner and managed to wrestle the thought under control as she went to retrieve the phone.

She hadn't heard from Nick all day and assumed, given last night's debacle, that he'd canceled their plans to visit Stone Mountain. So Julienne had spent her day taking her own words of the previous night to heart, steeling her spine to relegate their affair into a naughty-encounter-to-remember, when she so badly wanted to be the woman to help Nick explore commitment.

But she knew what she had to do. She'd tried to shed her inhibitions and buck her very nature with self-hypnosis and she'd hurt the people she loved the most in the process. Not again, thank you. She would do the right thing, no matter how much it hurt. And the right thing meant giving Nick the time he needed to make whatever decision was right for him.

She wouldn't tell him how much she loved him, wouldn't pressure him in any way. If he wanted to walk away, she'd wave goodbye with a smile. If he wanted to explore commitment, they could…well, talk. She didn't think he needed a woman with emotional baggage. He deserved a woman who could roll a condom on with her mouth without chanting key phrases.

She reached for the receiver. "Hello."

"I happen to have it on good authority that this will be your first Saturday night alone since Dr. Divine came to town," Ramón said. "So put on that gorgeous red leather and let's party or else Kat and I will show up on your doorstep and put it on for you."

Her heart constricted painfully, a pang that drove her to close her eyes. "Where'd you hear that?"

"Dr. Divine himself, sweetheart. He said you'd need a pick-me-up tonight."

"I won't let you in." False bravado. Nick had cared enough to send in a support team and just knowing that lifted her spirits. She was truly hopeless.

"Uncle Thad will. He likes me."

"Ramón. I appreciate what you're trying to do, but honestly, I've got a ton of work. I'll be okay."

"Not if Kat has to tighten your corset. She's into pain."

All right, that made her smile. "Really, Ramón. What's going on tonight that could possibly be worthy of the red leather?"

"Opening night of a brand new show. I told you most of the actors in town are my clients and their company has been rehearsing an interim show so the erotic theater goers don't find another hobby to entertain them."

"Where are they performing?"

Ramón snorted. "No place exciting, trust me. Just a strip plaza, but it'll do until the Risqué's up and running again."

"Ramón, the only reason I ever went to the Risqué was to see the building. A strip plaza doesn't hold the same appeal."

The absolute last thing she needed to see tonight was a

hair-curling performance that would make her remember all the hair-curling sex she'd had with Nick.

"Sweetheart, I promised Dr. Divine I wouldn't leave you home all alone tonight. Don't make a liar out of me or else I won't guarantee your next cut. You might catch me on a bad hair day."

"Ramón." She didn't really believe he'd give her a lousy haircut just because she wouldn't go out tonight, but his threat did remind her about the appointment she'd scheduled with Nick's. She'd have to call the salon and cancel.

*Naughty girls know when it's time to move on.*

Even though she'd officially sworn off key phrases, the thought sprang to mind unbidden, a habit by now she supposed, and one that made her already aching heart ache even more.

"Please," Ramón wheedled.

"No."

"Damn it, Jules. You're going to spoil the surprise."

"What surprise?"

"Dr. Divine asked me to get you in your red dress and bring you to him tonight. There, are you happy now? I've just betrayed my client's confidence and I pride myself on keeping secrets."

"Nick wants you to bring me to him? Where?"

"The Risqué. I don't know what he's got planned, but something's up. He made me swear I'd have you there by eight."

"Oh."

Julienne knew what this was all about—Nick recreating the night they'd met. The idea was really very sweet. Perhaps he wanted to bring their relationship around full circle.

However, the last time she'd gone to the Risqué in her red leather dress, she'd wound up having sex with a stranger and falling head over heels in love. Did she trust herself to resist Nick if he wanted to make love again tonight?

She'd have to. Their relationship deserved no less. She'd go to the Risqué prepared to face anything. She'd hold her head high, face Nick with a smile and never let him know that she'd fallen madly in love with him. If necessary, she'd let him go with an I-wish-you-well that left all their incredible memories intact. If she had to say no, she'd say it. *No.* The word came so easily when she spoke to the refrigerator. She only hoped she found it as easy when staring into his potent black gaze.

Nick had been right last night. She felt much clearer now that she'd had a chance to calm down and think. They had to talk and now was as good a time as any. The hours ahead stretched too long and lonely to bear with things still unsettled between them. And if Uncle Thad suspected she was pining away, he'd put that scientific mind of his to work and want to discuss how to fix the problem. He'd whip out the Halloween candy and insist she sit at the kitchen table where they could talk....

"All right," she said.

"Now you're talking. Kat and I will pick you up at eight. Get pretty, sweetheart."

"I can meet—"

"Eight."

The line disconnected. Julienne heaved a sigh, wondered how she would put on her dress without dissolving into a miserable mess. Blinking furiously, she refused to give in to tears.

*Naughty girls don't lose their cool.*

Not a key phrase but a reminder. Donning red leather should be just like riding a bicycle. Better to hop back on quickly before fear set in. The thought fueled her resolve and she was ready and waiting when Ramón and Katriona arrived at eight, her beautiful red leather dress and the glitter dust she'd sprinkled in her hair effectively shielding her broken heart.

"Oh-la-la, sister," Katriona said from her seat in the front of Ramón's inferno-red PT Cruiser. "That dress wasn't meant to sit in a closet. You're going to kill tonight."

Julienne slipped into the back seat, settled in as Ramón shut the door behind her. "I suppose that's better than killing myself trying to walk in these heels."

Katriona glanced over her shoulder, the dramatic spangles adorning her eyelids flashing as the interior light flipped on when Ramón opened the driver's door. "That's why the seam is split so high up the side to give you room to maneuver."

"Oh, and I thought it was just to show my leg."

"Thigh, Jules." Ramón informed her as he cranked the car. "With a slit that high you're showing thigh, and then some."

"Right." Julienne peered through the window as they drove out of her neighborhood, searching for something to distract her from this ache inside her chest.

Being with Ramón and Katriona usually proved a distraction in itself, but she still had to question her intelligence at heading back to the Risqué in this dress. Wouldn't a rational discussion be much easier on neutral turf?

Fortunately, Julienne didn't have much time to dwell on her intelligence, or lack thereof, because Ramón and Katriona proved as distracting as ever when they dragged her into an argument.

"Get over it, girlfriend," Ramón told Katriona. "You're not getting highlights."

Katriona just lifted a dragon lady hand to her mouth and

yawned. "You're tedious. I'll have someone else do them, if you won't give me what I want."

"I'll fire anyone on my staff who touches bleach to that fire-engine red hair. You'll scare my clients right out the door if they see you looking like a Day-Glo rooster. God forbid anyone should think *I* did it. Tell her, Jules."

But Julienne couldn't tell anyone anything because they approached the Risqué and she saw Nick's SUV parked beneath a streetlamp in the empty parking lot. Her heart took up such a breakneck beat she thought she might just have a heart attack on the spot. It would serve her right for causing all this trouble.

Ramón pulled around to the back entrance and brought the car to a stop. "Go have fun with Dr. Divine, sweetheart."

Fun, right. Julienne slipped from the car, smoothed the red leather over her hips with a growing sense of trepidation.

"You'll need an invitation," Ramón called through the open window. She saw him hand Katriona an envelope. "Give her this."

Katriona stuffed the envelope down her ample bosom, shooting Julienne a wicked grin. "I'm not doing anything for you, if I don't get blond streaks."

"Don't make me go in there after it."

"Like you could, skinny man." Katriona laughed. "Put your hands anywhere near my breasts and I'll break all your fingers. You won't be able to cut hair until the splints come off."

Ramón snorted.

"Do I get streaks?"

"Oh, hell. Only if I tone down the red so you don't wind up looking like a neon sign."

"Deal." After retrieving the envelope from the swell of

her bosom, Katriona hung her head out the window and winked. "Here you go, sister, you've got a date tonight."

Julienne accepted the envelope, noticed her name in an elegant computer-generated calligraphy.

"We're jealous, sweetheart," Ramón said, before speeding off, laughing maniacally and squealing his tires.

Not until his red taillights disappeared did Julienne open the envelope to find a notecard and a key.

*Nicholas Fairfax requests the pleasure of your company for his debut performance at the Risqué Theatre on Saturday, October 26th at nine o'clock.*

Debut performance of what? She couldn't think of many things that topped sex in a love swing on an empty stage. Gritting her teeth, she tried to stem an outrageous swell of excitement, told herself she had no business feeling this way.

Unlocking the back door, she slipped inside. At first the theater seemed quiet, but after a moment, she heard the faint strains of Frank Sinatra penetrating the dimly lit corridor that led to the auditorium. She couldn't help but smile.

Following the music, she entered the auditorium through an entrance near the orchestra pit and noticed the single folding chair propped in the middle of the dismantled seating section. Her seat. Just far enough from the stage to allow a good view of the man up there.

Nick. He sat in the love swing, which had apparently been retrieved from storage and rehung since she'd left the site yesterday. Rocking back and forth with an idle motion, he looked so dashing in his black tux that Julienne's breath caught audibly, a sound that carried over the strains of Sinatra's sultry voice.

"You came," he said, and even from this distance she could feel his gaze sweep over her.

"Not much of a choice. My ride dumped me on the sidewalk and took off."

He chuckled. The sound echoed in the empty theater, resounded through her, leaving no doubt in Julienne's mind that she wasn't going to be getting over this man any time soon.

"It wouldn't have been much of a show without you, so as long as you're here, why don't you have a seat."

Slinging her purse over the back of the chair, Julienne sat. "This is your debut performance of what?"

"You'll see. But first…atmosphere." He lifted what appeared to be a remote and with one click, wispy clouds trailed toward the stage from the wings. "What do you think?"

"You got the old cloud machine working. I'm impressed."

"Yeah, well, Chuck and Roy helped. The sucker's old. It was originally installed in 1926…but you knew that already, didn't you?"

"Yes."

He smiled, a bit sheepishly, or nervously perhaps, Julienne thought, if he felt anything like she did at the moment.

"Well, then, these are my props." He swung over to a small table she'd only now noticed. Clicking off the cloud machine, he swapped the remote for what appeared to be a book. She didn't miss the bottle of champagne chilling on ice or the two fluted glasses, either. Looked like he'd recreated closing night perfectly.

"No," she mouthed as practice.

*Maybe he wants to toast your future together,* that little voice said.

Julienne squelched the thought immediately.

"Ready for the show to start?" Nick asked.

"Lights, camera, action."

"I don't have any acting ability and I won't hum unless you dance for me. So I'll be delivering a monologue."

He was nervous. She could tell by his goofy half grin, could sense it by the way he rocked the swing excitedly, and in response, she found herself barely able to catch her breath.

"Tonight marks my debut into the world of commitment and love," he began in a husky voice. "I've finally met a woman who makes me think about what I want for the future, a woman who excites me in a way I've never been excited before."

He held up one of his props, a book, and she recognized a copy of *The Naughty Handbook,* not hers, but his, a sweet gesture that struck another blow to her composure.

"I enjoyed being your one-night stand, Julienne. I enjoyed our torrid fling and our steamy affair, but I don't want to become a naughty encounter-to-remember.

"The night you called me about the *Hush-Hush Honeys* all I could think about was getting over to your house, being able to hold you and deal with the problem together. I may not have a lot of experience with relationships, okay..." he grinned. "*Any* experience with relationships. And even though it took your uncle to point out the obvious, I know I felt that way because I want to share my life with you. Not just the fun and the passion, but the difficulties, too. I'm a fast study. I'll learn to do commitment if you'll give me a chance."

The tears had started again, stupid little prickles at the backs of her lids. She blinked furiously, hoping he couldn't see her, as she'd likely have a mess on her hands with all this mascara. She wanted to run up to the stage and wrap her arms around him, tell him she'd give him any chances he wanted... But she'd promised herself not to influence him either way. "Nick, please don't let my uncle bully you into thinking—"

"Do you honestly think anyone could bully me into doing something I don't want to do?" His gaze pierced the distance between them, his voice as hard as the floor beneath her feet. "I don't have trouble making decisions and I'm entirely too selfish to put others' needs above my own. I knew I wanted you the minute I laid eyes on you. Do you doubt that?"

How could she? Julienne thought wildly. He'd seduced her—a total stranger—on an empty stage.

"It's not about giving you a chance." Her voice betrayed her by sounding waterlogged and trembly. "I'd give you anything if I thought for one minute plain old Julienne could satisfy you. But I've given up self-hypnosis."

"Let's talk about that, plain old Julienne, because I've thought a lot about your arguments. I don't know much about hypnosis, so in the interest of time, I went to talk with Ethan about those hypnotherapy techniques you've been using—"

"You talked to Ethan?"

Even from this distance, she could see his eyes twinkle. "I didn't tell him I was asking about you specifically, but he was very helpful anyway. Apparently he enjoys hearing himself talk about his work. No wonder you know so much about hypnosis. I could probably write a treatise on the subject myself now."

Julienne swiped away tears and gave a soggy laugh.

"Ethan assured me that hypnosis—self or otherwise—can only help someone accomplish what she *wants* to accomplish. Hypnosis can't make you do anything against your nature. That means you're one very passionate lady and your argument doesn't hold water."

"Ethan said all that?"

"He did, and he's the authority."

She forced a laugh. "No doubt there. But how do we know it'll be enough?"

"We don't know anything for certain. Just like opening up an old building. We haven't a clue what we're going to find. We just deal with it."

*Listen to him, girl. He's making sense.*

"Here's what I think we should do," Nick said. "We've both got new ground to cover. I want to cover it together. You help me tackle commitment and I'll help you keep up passion without hypnosis. I'm definitely getting the better end of the deal here."

"But what if I'm not the right woman for you. What if—"

"Let me be the judge of what's right for me." Nick cut her off. "I want a woman who loves me and excites me and makes me think about waking up with her every day. You're that woman." He paused, his earnest expression driving home just how much he believed what he was saying. "You're my naughty girl. The *right* naughty girl."

With a huge swell of emotion rising up and choking her, Julienne sat forward in her chair, her hands clasped uncertainly in her lap and said, "You think I'm in love with you?"

His black gaze pierced the distance between them. "I'd bet money on it. Am I right?"

She only nodded, her tears flowing freely now.

"Good, because I'm not happy without you. I love you and I want to be with you. It's that simple. I'm going to prove it."

He loved her. She let her eyes flutter shut for the briefest of moments, just long enough to block out all stimuli and savor the sound of those words.

The stupid tears squeezed past her lids anyway. "You're going to prove it. How?"

"You've officially given up hypnosis, right?"

"Yes."

"Then, I'm going to excite you. I figure if you can't resist me, then you must be passionate. Sound about right?"

"That's crazy." She tried to keep her voice calm, to sound rational when her emotions were going wild inside, when she'd begun to hope that she might not have to say no, after all.

"Not crazy at all, Dr. Blake. It's science. We've got to test our theories. I say you're passionate without the hypnosis and you say you're not. There's only one way to find out and we need to know now because there's something else I have to ask you."

Before she'd thought of a reasonable argument or even to guess what else he might want to ask her, Nick had maneuvered himself out of the swing and leaned toward the table. Reaching for something—the remote, she thought, though she could barely see through her tears—he took aim at some unseen equipment offstage and suddenly Frank Sinatra's voice soared to the rafters in a smooth swell of sound that made her adrenaline rush apace.

Another click of the remote and smoke pumped in from the wings, wispy threads that clouded the air and blurred the black of his tux. And then he strode toward her, all devastatingly handsome smiles and masculine grace—the man she loved with all her heart.

He tugged the neckband at his collar. With a few sharp motions, he released his neck from confinement and sent his bowtie sailing toward her. It landed a few feet away.

Julienne shifted her gaze from the bowtie to him shrugging his jacket off his shoulders, slowly, deliberately as though his every action was designed to draw her attention. For her pleasure.

A striptease?

*A striptease!*

"Oh, my," she said, sinking back in her chair to enjoy the show. Her voice must have carried over the music because he shot her a slightly embarrassed grin while he worked the jacket down his arms.

Where had her arrogant playboy gone and who was this devilishly handsome man willing to dive into the uncertain waters of a relationship?

Julienne didn't know. She only knew that she had this man's heart...and his jacket. It snagged on a trench in the concrete beside her, another tangible reminder that he intended to give himself to her piece by piece.

He loved her.

Nick didn't dance like she had on that infamous night, but did a slow striptease instead, one that kept her gaze following his long fingers as they worked the buttons down the front of his shirt, unfastened his cufflinks....

There was something so intimate and unabashedly male about him half-dressed in slacks and a white undershirt, something that screamed potential sex and started that lusty little ache between her legs—the ache he'd promised wasn't a result of self-hypnosis.

Julienne suspected he might very well be right, because she wanted him so much, she couldn't resist him. She didn't have to.

He wanted a future with her.

He wanted *her*.

Unable to sit still any longer, she launched to her feet and went to the stage just in time to get a bird's eye view of tanned muscles rippling along his back as he whipped the undershirt over his head. Anchoring her elbows on the edge, she stared up at him.

"Am I wearing you down yet?"

"I'm aching." Her admission came more easily than she'd have ever imagined, but she suspected that had everything to do with the sharp flare of pleasure in his dark, dark eyes.

"So my theory's washing?"

"Yes."

He nodded with obvious approval, smiling a satisfied smile as he released his waistband with a quick flick of his wrist. He let his pants part just enough to reveal his impressive erection straining against the white cotton briefs below. By the time he toed off a dress shoe and then the other, Julienne's breath came in short bursts and she was no longer content to just watch.

He loved her.

Hiking up handfuls of red leather, she followed the edge of the stage until reaching the stairway that circled the orchestra pit. She raced up, heels tapping on the wooden steps, the staccato beat echoing her impatient heartbeats, her eagerness to show Nick how willing she was to test the unknown with him by her side.

She reached him just as he shoved his pants down his hips. She placed her hands on his and stayed his motion.

"May I?"

The passion in his dark eyes flared and Julienne knew she'd never loved him more than in that instant when his smoky expression revealed that she had carte blanche to take any privileges she desired.

"I'm all yours, beautiful. For as long as you'll have me."

Such a simple, heartfelt admission that made Julienne blink back her tears, made her reach for this man and this moment with a self-assurance she'd never known before.

In a move so reminiscent of their night on Tybee Island, when the wind had whipped around them and the ocean stretched before them so moonlit and vast, Julienne sank to her knees. She drew his slacks and his briefs down his legs, experienced a thrill when his erection sprang proudly free.

Tonight the moisture that burst in a silky sheen on her skin wasn't from a cool ocean breeze, but a cloud machine, and Nick wanted more than a steamy affair.

Tugging his slacks away and then his socks, Julienne left him standing above her breathtakingly naked and the sight aroused her more than ever before. There was just something about having a future spread unexplored before them that was so liberating...she pressed a kiss to the sleek skin of his erection. Just a peck really, a promise.

His low growl rumbled from deep in his chest and suddenly his hands were on her, dragging her up against him. His mouth descended onto hers and she felt another rumble vibrate against her lips, his kiss so demanding, so utterly possessive, she felt devoured by the strength of his need.

He loved her.

Almost before she realized what was happening, Nick had the red leather unzipped and was sliding the jacket over her shoulders. His mouth never left hers as he freed her arms from the leather, let the jacket fall to the floor, shoved the dress down, down, until it collapsed into a pile at her feet.

Like she had *that* night, Julienne stood before him, wearing her red corset and garters...only tonight Nick wanted her even more.

"I love you," he whispered against her lips.

Tonight he was naked rather than fully dressed, utterly and desirably without apparel. And he loved her.

"Ah, Jules." He rode his hand along the silk-covered curve of her tummy, down between her thighs as though he had every right in the world to touch her so intimately, so possessively. He curled his fingers along her moist folds and found her ready for him.

Because she loved him.

With another growl, he backed away and hoisted her into his arms before she had a chance to recognize his intent. She gasped, flinging her arms around his neck to steady herself, then laughed with an abandon that echoed through the theater, through her body, straight to her heart. Nick loved her. They would take on the future together. No matter where their relationship went, no matter how long it lasted or whether commitment led to deeper commitment, Julienne knew that each step of the way and every moment with this man would be one to remember.

"Hang on," he said, "You got to be on top the last time we used this thing. It's my turn tonight."

"That's only fair." She helped him maneuver her into the padded seat, watched with growing excitement as he tugged her heels off and guided her feet into the stirrups. She lay spread before him in the love swing, a position primed and ready for sex and though she could sense his urgency, his expression softened as he raked his gaze over her.

"I love you, Jules."

"I love you, Nick."

"Which makes me the luckiest bastard on the planet." He flashed that charming smile and made her heart race. "Except that…"

His brow furrowed and Julienne, practically breathless with desire and expectation, didn't want to deal with any more obstacles before she could pull him into her arms and satisfy this need inside. This need had nothing to do with hypnosis and everything to do with wanting this man more than she'd ever wanted any man before.

Passion. She'd found her personal supply in Nick's arms.

"What's wrong now?" she forced the words through lips that would rather be kissing his.

He slid a fingertip along the inside of her thigh, made her shiver, then he slipped his finger into the crotch of her silk thong. "Forgot to take this off. Guess we won't be able to make love after all."

Julienne sat here with her legs spread wide in a love swing, wearing red lace and thigh-high hose, and they weren't going to make love?

"Nick!"

He snapped the soft fabric against her sensitive skin and stood upright. "Can't resist me, can you?"

"Never could."

Her answer seemed to satisfy him, because he strode away to retrieve his slacks, an impressive display of shifting muscle and tanned skin. Instead of pulling a condom from his pocket though, he held up a...

*Swiss Army Knife?*

"Naughty girls are always prepared," she whispered, and the memory of the last time she'd uttered those words made her smile. "Naughty boys, too, it seems."

"My personal motto, when I'm with you."

Julienne held her breath as he used the scissors to snip the fabric and suddenly his fingers were glancing across her sensitive skin to brush the fabric away.

"That's better."

"Much."

The knife clattered to the stage and Nick sheathed himself with a condom and then wedged between her thighs.

Suddenly, he was touching her, his hot flesh at her moist entrance, pushing into her heat, the driving shock of him stretching her, her body tightening as she greedily tried to hold him inside.

"This is right, Jules." He groaned before leaning forward to catch her mouth in a kiss and plunge his tongue deep.

Julienne believed him with every shred of her reason and surrendered herself to the urgency of the moment, to the power of his touch and his need. She slipped her hands over his shoulders and locked her legs around his waist, the stirrups levering her against him. The swing owned all of her weight, leaving Nick free to anchor her against him, to thrust deep and then retreat with only the slightest effort.

Then urgency claimed the moment, fueling their motions as his mouth slid from hers, raking along her bared throat, nipping her skin around his slow-building groan that filled her ears. She thrust her fingers into his hair and tried to hang on as her blood rushed and her muscles gathered to meet him in a climax that left no room for denying what they'd found with each other was unique and special and right.

Julienne gasped for air and found his mouth instead, his kiss demanding, his tongue thrusting in time with his body that pulsed in decreasing increments.

And then he broke their kiss to whisper raggedly against her lips, "I'm looking forward to our future. How about you?"

She tilted her head back to look at him, found him looking as devastated and overwhelmed as she felt.

"If it means you might strip for me onstage again then I wouldn't miss it."

*You go, girl!*

Nick sucked in a deep breath and laughed appreciatively. "Glad it worked for you. The very beautiful, very passionate woman who last danced on this stage was a tough act to follow. I had to make sure you couldn't resist me."

"I can't, Nick. I never could."

"Then marry me, beautiful. I don't need to explore our

relationship anymore to figure out what I want. I've explored enough to know that I hate waking up without you beside me. What more do I need to know? We'll handle whatever comes up.''

If Julienne could have moved, she might have jumped up, but impaled as she was on Nick's still impressive erection, with her feet caught in stirrups and his weight pinning her to the swing, all she could do was ask, ''Marry you? But that's...crazy. The logistics don't even work. Even if we were nuts enough to jump into such a big commitment, you're in the field and I'm here.''

He nibbled her earlobe and traced the shell of her ear with his tongue. ''That's a problem, I agree. As much as I enjoy our sexy phone conversations, I want to be with you, which is why I spent the afternoon talking to your uncle about a solution.''

Unsure whether to smile or cringe when she imagined Nick and Uncle Thad with their heads together over a drafting table, Julienne braced herself for the worst. ''What did you cook up?''

''The Thaddeus Blake Historic Preservation Internship Program.''

''And what's that exactly?''

''ADF's brand new program. My design team will sponsor interns from universities all over the country, just like we're hosting your interns now. I figure with your uncle's name and endorsement, I'll be able to convince the President to nationally recognize the program. Now all I need is a professor on my team to coordinate and instruct these interns...''

He smiled, one of those charming smiles that made her heart skip a beat and her eyes grow misty again. ''You wouldn't happen to know anyone who might be interested in the job, would you? It'll mean travel, and working for me, which isn't a selling point because my team tells me I'm a tyrant.''

''It's a selling point.''

He must have heard the tears in her voice because he reared up and stared into her face. ''Is that a yes?''

''Yes.''

''Yes to the job or yes to the marriage proposal?''

Before she could answer, he lifted her hand to his lips and pressed a soft kiss to her skin, his eyes shuttering for the briefest of instants. Then he lifted his gaze and the love she saw in his face told her that no matter what the future held it would be bright because they'd face it together.

''I'll spend the rest of my life proving to you that you're naughty enough to keep me interested,'' he promised.

''Then yes, to both.'' She brought Nick's hand to her lips, sealed the deal with a kiss, because...

*Naughty girls know a good thing when they see it.*

The Trueblood, Texas
tradition continues in...

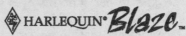

## TRULY, MADLY, DEEPLY
### by Vicki Lewis Thompson
### August 2002

Ten years ago, Dustin Ramsey and Erica Mann shared their first
sexual experience. It was a disaster. Now Dustin's determined to
find—and seduce—Erica again, to prove to her, and himself, that
he can do better. Much, *much* better. Only, little does he guess
that Erica's got the same agenda....

*Don't miss Blaze's next two sizzling Trueblood tales:*

*EVERY MOVE YOU MAKE by Tori Carrington*
*September 2002*
*&*
*LOVE ON THE ROCKS by Debbi Rawlins*
*October 2002*

*Available wherever Harlequin books are sold.*

**TRUEBLOOD,
TEXAS**

HARLEQUIN®
*Makes any time special*®

If you enjoyed what you just read,
then we've got an offer you can't resist!

# Take 2 bestselling love stories FREE!

# Plus get a FREE surprise gift!

**Clip this page and mail it to Harlequin Reader Service®**

| IN U.S.A. | IN CANADA |
|---|---|
| 3010 Walden Ave. | P.O. Box 609 |
| P.O. Box 1867 | Fort Erie, Ontario |
| Buffalo, N.Y. 14240-1867 | L2A 5X3 |

**YES!** Please send me 2 free Blaze™ novels and my free surprise gift. After receiving them, if I don't wish to receive anymore, I can return the shipping statement marked cancel. If I don't cancel, I will receive 4 brand-new novels each month, before they're available in stores! In the U.S.A., bill me at the bargain price of $3.80 plus 25¢ shipping and handling per book and applicable sales tax, if any*. In Canada, bill me at the bargain price of $4.21 plus 25¢ shipping and handling per book and applicable taxes**. That's the complete price and a savings of at least 10% off the cover prices—what a great deal! I understand that accepting the 2 free books and gift places me under no obligation ever to buy any books. I can always return a shipment and cancel at any time. Even if I never buy another book from Harlequin, the 2 free books and gift are mine to keep forever.

150 HDN DNWD
350 HDN DNWE

| Name | (PLEASE PRINT) | |
|---|---|---|
| Address | Apt.# | |
| City | State/Prov. | Zip/Postal Code |

* Terms and prices subject to change without notice. Sales tax applicable in N.Y.
** Canadian residents will be charged applicable provincial taxes and GST.
    All orders subject to approval. Offer limited to one per household and not valid to current Blaze™ subscribers.
® are registered trademarks of Harlequin Enterprises Limited.

BLZ02-R

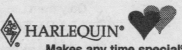